FOUR DAYS' WAR

Borgo Press Books by S. Fowler Wright

Arresting Delia: An Inspector Cleveland Classic Crime Novel
The Attic Murder: An Inspector Combridge & Mr. Jellipot Classic Crime Novel
The Bell Street Murders: An Inspector Combridge & Mr. Jellipot Classic Crime Novel
Beyond the Rim: A Lost Race Fantasy
Black Widow: A Classic Crime Novel
The British Colonies: No Surrender to Nazi Germany!
The Capone Caper: Mr. Jellipot vs. the King of Crime: A Classic Crime Novel
Crime & Co.: An Inspector Cleveland Classic Crime Novel
Dawn: A Novel of Global Warming
Dead by Saturday: An Inspector Cleveland Classic Crime Novel
Dream; or, The Simian Maid: A Fantasy of Prehistory (Marguerite Cranleigh #1)
Elfwin: An Historical Novel of Anglo-Saxon Times
The End of the Mildew Gang: An Inspector Cauldron Classic Crime Novel (Mildew Gang #3)
Four Callers in Razor Street: An Inspector Combridge & Mr. Jellipot Classic Crime Novel
Four Days' War: The Alternate World War II, Book Two
The Hanging of Constance Hillier: An Inspector Cleveland Classic Crime Novel
The Hidden Tribe: A Lost Race Fantasy
The Jordans Murder: An Inspector Combridge & Mr. Jellipot Classic Crime Novel
The King Against Anne Bickerton: A Classic Crime Novel
Megiddo's Ridge: The Alternate World War II, Book Three
The Mildew Gang: An Inspector Cauldron Classic Crime Novel (Mildew Gang #1)
Murder in Bethnal Square: An Inspector Combridge & Mr. Jellipot Classic Crime Novel
The Police and the Public: Some Thoughts on the British System of Justice
Post-Mortem Evidence: An Inspector Combridge & Mr. Jellipot Classic Crime Novel
Prelude in Prague: The Alternate World War II, Book One
The Return of the Mildew Gang: An Inspector Cauldron Classic Crime Novel (Mildew Gang #2)
The Rissole Mystery: An Inspector Combridge & Mr. Jellipot Classic Crime Novel
The Screaming Lake: A Lost Race Fantasy
The Secret of the Screen: An Inspector Combridge & Mr. Jellipot Classic Crime Novel
The Song of Songs and Other Poems
Spiders' War: A Novel of the Far Future (Marguerite Cranleigh #3)
Three Witnesses: A Classic Crime Novel
Too Much for Mr. Jellipot: An Inspector Combridge & Mr. Jellipot Classic Crime Novel
The Vengeance of Gwa: A Fantasy of Prehistory (Marguerite Cranleigh #2)
Was Murder Done? A Classic Crime Novel
Who Murdered Reynard? A Classic Crime Novel
The Wills of Jane Kanwhistle: An Inspector Combridge & Mr. Jellipot Classic Crime Novel
With Cause Enough?: An Inspector Combridge & Mr. Jellipot Classic Crime Novel

FOUR DAYS' WAR

THE ALTERNATE WORLD WAR II

Book Two

by

S. FOWLER WRIGHT

THE BORGO PRESS

An Imprint of Wildside Press LLC

MMIX

BOOK ONE

CHAPTER I.

IT was Saturday, February 5th, 1938. The time was 4:57 P.M.—the afternoon following the night on which Germany had stunned the world by the destruction of Prague, and the announcement that Czechoslovakia must be spoken of in the past tense.

The British cabinet was in session. Fifteen minutes before, Mr. Ganston, the Secretary for Foreign Affairs, had entered the room bringing an ultimatum from the German Ambassador.

He had said that Germany did not desire war, that she did not ask that England should take her side if she should be attacked by any combination of foreign powers, as a result of the act of aggression which she had committed in the darkness of the previous night and consummated during the day. All she asked was an immediate assurance that England would remain neutral in such event. As guarantee, she had required that the fortress of Gibraltar and the control of the Suez Canal should be surrendered to Germany until the crisis should be averted or overcome. As a reward, he had offered assurance that a victorious Germany would not require return of the colonies which had once been hers, and were now under British control.

A refusal of these conditions, to which an explicit answer was required not later than 5:00 P.M., would be the signal for instant war—and the German air-fleets had shown during the previous night how numerous they had become, how swiftly they could attack, and how terrible was their destructive power.

In delivering this ultimatum, Baron Kronin had pointed out that the fact of its presentation should be sufficient evidence of the reality of the friendship which it professed, for did not Germany forego thereby the opportunity of surprise attack? Had it not been equally in her power to have struck without warning during the coming night, and perhaps to have completed the work of death before morning came? As it was, Mr. Ganston could observe, without calculation from him, that there would be an interval of about two hours, should England be stubborn to meet her fate, before the battle-fleets of her foe would darken the moonlit skies.

As to the guarantees which were required, Baron Kronin expressed surprise that Mr. Ganston should be moved to protest or indignation, for had not the day gone by when they had been of importance to an Empire which was now breaking apart? What were they now but the reminders of ended power, the keys of an empty chest, the right-of-way to properties which were falling to other heirs? Mr. Ganston, after losing some time in argument and expostulation, had realized the finality of the ultimatum which he had received, and hurried to the cabinet meeting which was then sitting, with little more than a quarter of an hour remaining for a decision on which millions of human lives, born and unborn, the future of the British race, and perhaps even the civilization to which it belonged, must ultimately depend.

For the past ten minutes, Mr. Marmaduke Bewdley, the British Premier, had sat silent while the contentious voices around him were no more than the sound of a distant sea. For he saw that there would be no unanimity to be reached by the divided cabinet of which he was in little more than a nominal control, no wisdom or inspiration to come from them. Almost to a man, he could have guessed correctly what the decision or indecision of each would be, and there was no gain in listening to their clamour of anger or doubt, of courage or prudence now. At the last, the decision must be his, and he was too honest in the process of his mind to attempt to confuse the fact by appealing to those who would support him from either side.

It must be his word which, for the coming hours, must continue peace or loose the horrors of war on the unconscious city and the wider country beyond. And he knew that it was Mr. Ganston's belief, which had been largely supported by the annihilation of Prague, that the secret air-fleets of Germany could attack in instant, overwhelming strength the slender barriers of plane and battery which the pacific temper of the English people and the exigencies of internal politics had provided for their defence.

It was too late to regret that now, futile to ponder whether it had been under his premiership that history would record the ruin of the British Empire—or else its shame. There was this decision to be made, and, though it would be in the nation's name, it must, in reality, be resolved in his single mind, as he regarded the price of peace: by himself alone, as courage or caution ruled, by his fortitude or his fear.

Through the din of voices there came the sound of a striking clock. A voice said: "That's three minutes fast. There's time yet."

So it was. There were three minutes yet. There was still time. Time for honour or shame: for prudence or many deaths.

Mr. Bewdley rose. He said: "I will see Kronin myself. I must suppose he will wait for that."

Mr. Lloyd-Davids said sharply: "But you must tell us what you intend."

Mr. Bewdley was impatient in his reply: "How can I say that? I must be guided by what I hear. But I shall not give Germany what she demands."

A voice asked: "Even though it mean war?"

"Even though we may be subject to unprovoked attack, such as I suppose will stir the world to become aware of the common peril of all."

He looked round the confused, excited groups of ministers among whom little of calmness or self-control had survived the sudden news of this monstrous threat.

He said: "Gentlemen, I shall seek peace if by any means it may yet be found; but you have heard that we are menaced with instant war, and the seconds count. There is no use in remaining here. But, till you hear more from me, there must be no mention of this."

He looked at the Foreign Minister as he passed him, feeling that there was one at least whom the moment would not confound. He asked: "You will inform France?"

"It will be done as the hour strikes. I gave instructions before I came."

As he spoke, the voice of Mr. Denver, the Minister for Transport, rose in irritable impatience, his usual truculence subdued to a nervous note: "I don't see what he means. We can't do anything till we know. There'd be a panic at once."

Mr. Bewdley heard, and turned back to reply: "Isn't it Saturday? London will have been emptying itself about as fast as it can. *Don't let anyone come in.* That alone may be the saving of thousands of lives. But panic? Don't you know your own countrymen better than that? Aren't you prepared for this hour?" He turned his glance from Mr. Denver, as he went on: "It will be well to stop all the broadcasting programmes, and warn everyone to leave their receivers on, and to await news of urgent national importance. No one will be surprised at that, after what's happened in Central Europe today."

In the outer room, he paused to speak to his secretary: "Telephone Baron Kronin that I will be with him in four minutes. Say that I ask him to conclude nothing till I arrive."

He went out to the street, facing the little crowd that was round the door, and looked about for the quickest vehicle he could find. Its horn screaming for other traffic to stand aside, an ambulance shot down the street. Mr. Bewdley spoke to a uniformed constable on the pavement: "Stop me that."

The man knew him, and obeyed the urgency of his command. He stepped into the street, standing with lifted arms in the way of the approaching vehicle.

The driver braked sharply, and stopped no more than two feet from the obstructing constable.

"Don't stop us, officer," a young man who sat at the driver's side, and had the aspect of a medical student, protested earnestly, "There's a woman inside who's near bleeding to death now."

Mr. Bewdley, showing no sign that he heeded or even heard, clambered up to the driver's seat, making a third on the narrow front of the vehicle.

"The German Embassy," he said. "Stop for nothing. Make the best speed you can."

The driver looked a bewildered hesitation. His companion protested again. "But you cannot. It is a matter of life and—"

"It is a matter of peace or war," Mr. Bewdley answered sharply. "Of peace or war, and the seconds count. I suppose you know who I am?"

It was the first time in his life that he had evoked the authority of his position as giving him precedence over the movements of lesser men. An hour before he would have said that it was an impossible thing for him to do.

He was not sure whether the medical student knew him. Perhaps he guessed, but was less than sure. But the plea prevailed. The young man was no fool. He recognized the significance of the fact that it had been a policeman who had assisted Mr. Bewdley into that crowded seat. He said: "Well, sir, I suppose you know. Go ahead, Bill."

The ambulance had not halted for more than fifteen seconds before it shot forward again, and its horn screamed to the crowded evening traffic to give way. Mr. Bewdley had a moment for thought. He was still unsure what he would say, but he realized that it might be well to have some record beyond the memory of the spoken word. He drew out a pocket memorandum book interleaved with carbon sheets in which he was accustomed to write memoranda for his secretary or others, copies of which he wished to retain for his own reference. He wrote with such steadiness as the moving vehicle allowed.

"We have no intention of war. Any attack made upon us will be an act of unprovoked aggression."

CHAPTER II.

BARON KRONIN received Mr. Bewdley without delay, and with the courtesy due to the high position he held. That this courtesy was of more than a formal kind, that it had any real cordiality, would have been as difficult to decide as to demonstrate any evidence of antipathy to the English Premier.

The Baron was not typical, either in appearance or manner, of the race to which he belonged. He was small, spare, bald-headed, coldly suave in speech, and very sparing of words.

He had been in diplomatic service at the time when Hitler had come to power, and he had accepted the position without protest, or, indeed, any avoidable expression of opinion of any kind, and having continued in service abroad, he had not been associated with the periodic measures by which the Führer intimidated his foes and rid himself of lukewarm or potentially dangerous friends, which negative advantages may have assisted his reputation for discretion and some other qualities that the office required.

He rose as Mr. Bewdley entered the room, and advanced with an outstretched hand.

"You have come," he asked, "that we may discuss the details of our accord?"

"I have come in friendship, and to make accord if I can. I have come to tell you that, even after what has happened in Prague, you can rely upon our influence in the councils of Europe to find some way to a common peace."

"Do you wish me to understand that you reject to offer which we have made, for which, indeed, the hour is already gone?"

"As it came to me, it appeared to be of an almost incredible kind, such as no government could propose to a friendly power, unless it were resolved to provoke war, which, if I may say it without offence, it would be foolish to do. It is an hour when Germany should seek friends, and the aid of those who desire peace."

Baron Kronin was not direct in his reply, and, for the first time in his diplomatic career, something of the usual suavity left his voice, for he felt that its need was gone.

"We are resolved," he said, "that our race shall take its rightful place in the world, but there will be no more war than this end requires; and, I suppose, it will not be much."

"You will have such a war as will shake the world and in which your own land will be most certain to fall."

"Do you think that? Well, I must say you are wrong. You have witnessed the fate of Prague. Do you call it war? We have done no more than impose our will."

As he thought of the power of his own land, it seemed to him, for the moment, as it had been regarded by his Government in Berlin, a folly too great for a responsible statesman, and one of Mr Bewdley's moderation to choose, that he should reject the terms which had been proposed.

At a cooler moment, he had been of a different opinion, but now he remembered that his instructions had been to persuade the English Government to yield, if it were any way possible, though he was not to abate his terms. He had done what he could to this end with Mr. Ganston an hour before. Now he went on: "I can understand that you may be reluctant to grant our terms, but there are some facts that you should not miss. We offer peace, which your nation values— perhaps too much. We offer security, under the shadow of German power. We do not even require that you shall draw the sword at our side. There may be shedding of German blood, while your own people shall sleep in safety and undisturbed."

Mr. Bewdley was blunt: "We should be as safe as a sheep in a butcher's field."

Baron Kronin thought: "Even so, does a sheep challenge the butcher to prove his power, while he would be engaged in another way?" But he replied in more courteous words, though their meaning was no less plain.

"Yet I still say that you must face facts, be they pleasant or not. We are a nation that has been long arming for war. For the past four years we have worked for no other end, while you have gone by another road. It is too late for regret."

"We have striven," Mr. Bewdley replied, "to make friendship with you, without falsehood to those who were our allies at a former time."

"And you have counted on that! Had we any quarrel with Belgium twenty-four years ago?"

"You had none, as we know. But is not the unprovoked invasion of that country already condemned by the verdict of history? Is it not recognized as the fatal error which roused the indignation of many lands, which ranged this country among your foes, and was no less than the blunder by which you fell?"

"There may be those by whom that is said, but our own writers, whom you may have no leisure to read, give us a different blame, and have an opposite cause for our non-success at that time. They say that our respect for the neutrality of Holland was the error by which we fell. Had we been—"

Baron Kronin was not unaware that he was speaking with an unusual freedom, the excitement of the hour, even to one of his own severe mental discipline, having an effect of fatigue, loosening control, and rendering him more voluble to the impulse of thought than it was his habit to be. But there was calculation also in his freedom of words, for if he failed (as he saw he did) in persuading Mr. Bewdley to yield, then there was gain in every second that he could be delayed, while the German air-fleets were rising into the skies.

But Mr. Bewdley, having seen that he came on a useless quest, was as alert to this point as he. He interrupted now with a brusqueness which he would not have used at a quieter time.

"If you say that, we are wasting words. With such code, your country could be no more than a trustless friend, and a less peril to those who call her an open foe. But we have made no quarrel with you, and so that there may be no doubt on that point, I will give you this, which I have worded with care."

As he spoke, he handed Baron Kronin the written slip which he had prepared.

The Baron read it and smiled. What use was there, he wondered, in writing such words as that? He had heard it said that the pen was mightier than the sword, which he would have agreed to be true while the sword is sheathed, but no longer than that. He thought that all chatter was futile now.

He dropped the slip on to the table beside which they stood, and the slight movement of his hand was as contemptuous as though it had been thrown to the lighted grate.

"Well," he said, "if you can find comfort in that...!

"But you have proved me right. It is what I told Berlin that you would, on which, as I had some reason to judge, they had thought me wrong. But it may be best, even for you. You have had your day, and the next is ours. You have chosen to come to ground with the harder bump, but your doubt will be sooner done. You will let me have my papers that I may leave, which I would prefer to do in the next hour?"

"It is late tonight. Tomorrow morning, I have no doubt—"

"I would prefer to take earlier leave."

Mr. Bewdley was ironic in his reply: "Those who make unprovoked attacks— We must hope that, for so short a time, our airfleets will be sufficient for your defence."

Baron Kronin said: "It is a poor hope," but he made no further protest at that delay, the refusal to give him instant permission to leave by the usual channels actually suiting his plans, which his request had been intended to blind. For his orders were to remain in England, making his way to a secret German resort in Wiltshire during the night. There would be much occupation in England for such as he when they should take control on the next day, as it was intended that they should do.

Mr. Bewdley said: "Well, I may see you again, but I think not." They shook hands with formality, and a consciousness that they played their parts in a drama that dwarfed themselves.

Mr. Bewdley went out at a sharp pace, and took a taxi to Downing Street, telling the driver to lose no time, but having no thought after that for the pace at which he might drive, whether fast or slow, his mind being busy with many thoughts.

Now that his decision was made, he had lost consciousness of himself, or of the years by which, at times, his shoulders were somewhat bowed.

He knew now that he had given the only possible answer to the insolent ultimatum that would have made his country the vassal of German power, and that his decision would still be right, even though it should lead to no better end than that England should be destroyed in a night of blood—would still be right, even though (which he did not think) English people should curse his name for the words he had spoken then. For he saw that, for the race as for the single man, there is a small question of death, but a great one of how they die.

He turned his mind to wonder at the arrogance of this sudden assertion of German power, which seemed willing to flout the world in the confidence of its single strength. And yet—sudden? Had not all its energies been openly spent in the world's sight, during the last four years, to prepare it for such a day?

Even so, he wondered. With Southern Europe to face, with England upon its right, and Russia upon its left—it had made a mistake once, underrating its foes. But would it do so a second time? What diabolic, unimagined engines of war might it not have contrived with which to enslave the world? Well, he might know before the next dawn should come.

But fundamentally, and with a profundity of relief, under all these thoughts there was the consciousness that his part was done. He had loosed forces which, within the next hour, would pass beyond his restraint, and which he would have little power to control.

CHAPTER III.

M. Bonnier considered the position of France, which he did not like; he considered his own, with which he was no better pleased.

He had been in office for seven months, which is a long time for a French Government to endure. He was menaced by the Agrarian party on one side, and on the other by the Royalists of the Right, who had become formidable in their own guise since Fascism had ceased to be a name by which enthusiasm could be aroused. The troubles in Syria and Algeria did not lessen, and now there was this crisis in Europe which appeared to give him the sour choice of disastrous war, or accepting the domination of Germany in Central Europe to a degree which must be inimical to his country's honour, and to her safety in later days. And the latter course must mean, when it should become known, that his Government would fall in an hour.

Even those who might approve the prudence of what he did would observe the expediency of his disappearance from power, as though its shame could be lifted thus from the shoulders of France to fall wholly upon his own.

Yet to resist? It was a question which—unless in the negative— France could not answer alone. What, he asked himself, would Russia—would England—say?

A secretary entered his room. "Sir Charles Duffield," he said, "is on the telephone. He says it is a matter of extreme urgency. He would speak to you only."

M. Bonnier became alert at the call to action, which he did not doubt it to be. England, he thought, must have obtained some new information concerning German intentions, or have proposals to make, and she therefore approached her ally to confide, or as one seeking advice. Subconsciously, he was somewhat heartened by this evidence that England stood at his side at the critical hour. He did not suppose that Germany would make advances to England of first importance before approaching himself; for the problem, as he saw it, was one of Central Europe, military in character, and which primarily concerned his own country, and Russia, with which France was allied.

Yet it was possible that Germany was using London to discover whether, or at what price, she would be left to the peaceful digestion of the prey she had so suddenly seized. He said: "Have him put through at once."

He heard the British Ambassador's statement of the ultimatum which his Government had received with a moment of consternation, until the assurance followed that Germany would not obtain the guarantees for which she had asked; and then with a very natural weakness of human relief as he realized that the first fury of German attack would not be directed towards the frontiers of France; and that England, or what of England would remain when the night had passed, would be at war with those who were the foes of his own land. It may have been a natural though a baser thought that found a moment of satisfaction in the fact that the German and English air-fleets would be the first to meet in a mutually destructive encounter, while that of France might remain entire to a later hour.

He rallied his mind to reply. "You can tell your Government that France will be speedy to act, for it is plain that the hour is come." He was too rational to suppose that his country could stand aside, unless it would be destroyed on a later day, and it may have been without meaning more or less than his words implied that he added: "But it is a matter on which, as you will comprehend, my colleagues must be informed. Fortunately, they are not distant to call. In half an hour I will give you a more formal reply."

Sir Charles Duffield accepted this assurance, being very much what he had expected to hear, and did not delay M. Bonnier with further words.

He knew that France was unwilling to face a war which came, for her, at a most inopportune time, when she had armies abroad, with some hundreds of the best of her battle-planes; but he did not doubt, and M. Bonnier's own words had confirmed, that she would recognize that it was to be thrust upon her, unless she would bend her neck to the Führer's foot. If England had been asked to stand aside, it could only be that Germany wished for a clear field in which France might be trodden flat. If England, having refused that ignominious neutrality, was to be attacked in the night, then it was vital for France to strike also with no avoidable second's delay, either to give relief to an ally who might yet be potent for her own aid, or to wound her foe at a time when the larger portion of her own air-fleets would be absent from German skies.

Sir Charles reflected, with satisfaction, that the air-fleets of France must be already alert, for the destruction which had fallen upon Prague was a warning that her Air Minister would not ignore, however willing she might be to delay the issue of war. And when he considered the strength of France, and the number of bombing-planes, after deducting those that were absent in her colonial wars, that she could still send out for the destruction of German towns, he had the same wonder that had passed through Mr. Bewdley's mind that Germany should have been so rash in unprovoked attack on the British Isles. He saw that it was no more than assumption that such attack would be made in immediate force. A threat might have been made in anticipation that England would yield, and in excess of any hostile movement which would occur. Yet that was not a probable supposition, for if there could be any military excuse for provoking Britain to war, it could only be on the calculation that she could be destroyed before her allies could become active either in assistance or counter-attack.

Well, these were doubts that would be resolved before morning should come! He lost no time in telephoning to London that the French cabinet had been convened, and that its meeting would be a matter of minutes rather than hours, for it had been a day during which the governments of Europe had been in almost continual session, and he added a confident word as to what her action would be. M. Bonnier, he said, had spoken as one who saw the crisis for what it was, and would face it in a resolute way.

But when, having waited for nearly an hour for a message which did not come, he had called up M. Bonnier again, and heard his voice after some prolonged, and, it had seemed to him, evasive delay, the reply was less satisfactory than he had been expecting to hear.

M. Bonnier did not endeavour to discount the urgency of the position, nor did he suggest any doubt of the ultimate purpose of France. But a question had arisen as to the construction of a clause in the Russian treaty, concerning which it was of vital importance that no error of procedure should occur.

The position was that, in the event of either France or Russia being attacked, her ally was bound to take arms in her support. But if a war of aggression should be commenced, this obligation would not apply. The fact that Germany had threatened war upon England could not, in itself, be regarded as an attack upon France, particularly as England had declined to become a party to the Franco-Russian alliance, as, Sir Charles Duffield would recall, she had been invited to do.

M. Bonnier had discussed the position with the Russian Ambassador, who had expressed his personal conviction that the Soviet Republics would recognize the attack upon England, following the seizure of Czechoslovakia, as evidence that Germany had resolved to dominate Europe, which must either submit to be subdued in detail, or unite in resistance now. Faced with such alternatives, there could be little doubt of what their answer would be. But, he had urged, it would be, at the best, imprudent, at the worst disastrous, for France to interpose in a quarrel which was at present confined to England and Germany, without preconsultation with her ally. And what difference could it make? It was no more than a matter of a few hours, and most probably less than that. He would get into communication with Moscow immediately, and there was no reason to doubt that she would accept the occasion for common action in the spirit of a treaty the letter of which France would have been scrupulous to observe. And meanwhile, would the time be lost? Could it not be used—would it actually be more than was required—for the dispositions which caution and good generalship would require before the frontiers of Germany could wisely be crossed?

So M. Bonnier reported the Soviet Ambassador's words; and so, in fact, he had said.

That he had gone somewhat further was more than it had seemed necessary to repeat. For he had not scrupled to throw out a quite different suggestion—that it might not, even yet, be too late to avert the horrors of continental war, for which France was, at the moment, so ill-prepared. The British Empire was large and rich. Suppose that Germany could satisfy herself from that dish, even to the point of repletion, and of throwing some unpicked bones to those who should not disturb her meal?

M. Bonnier did not entertain that suggestion. Judgement and inclination combined in its rejection, for which he gave the Russian Ambassador good reasons enough, and such as appeared to bring conviction to that gentleman's mind. But he was not surprised that it should have been made, knowing that there was no cordiality between the English people and the tyranny which had Russia so surely beneath its heel; and while he put the suggestion aside, he saw in it an additional reason for having the position of Moscow clearly defined before he should cast the fortunes of France to the hazard of a war from which her ally might make excuse to stand aside. If Russia desired to put a limit to German power (as he did not doubt), then she must take her place in the field, as she would be no less likely to do if she found that France would not hazard a separate war.

So he thought, and so he found the feeling of his colleagues to be. That which he told Sir Charles Duffield was the truth, though not all. It was true that France was arming in haste; that she was ready, even eager, to spring at the throat of her ancient foe while it was engaged in attacking the British Isles; that she both desired and anticipated that Russia would support her in that policy.

In evidence of the friendship of France, M. Bonnier added information that had just come to his hands. The neutrality of Holland had already been violated, with her own consent, if such it could be called, where she had no reasonable alternative but to submit.

Germany had notified the Dutch Government, less than an hour ago, that she intended to cross Holland with air-fleets which she had herself put at a strength of four thousand planes. They would drop no bombs, would do no damage to the cities of Holland, if they were allowed unobstructed course. Resistance would mean that the fate of Czechoslovakia yesterday would be that of Holland today. What could she do but submit? Even now, M. Bonnier said, his information was that these air-fleets were passing over the Dutch coast in a formation having a front three or four miles in width, and taking a direction from which it appeared that their objective must be considerably north of the Thames estuary.

Sir Charles thanked him for information which showed on which side his sympathies lay, though he did not suppose that London would be less accurately informed. He said that he would pass the information on without any delay.

"So you may," the French Premier replied, "for the telephone service will be cleared for your use, and you may also wire if you will. Our communications with London should not be easy to interrupt. But most of the services with Northern and Eastern Europe have been out of action for the last hour, and there is confusion upon the air."

CHAPTER IV.

EUSTACE ASHFIELD glanced at the clock and rose hastily. It was 4:55 p.m. and if he left with no further minutes' delay he could reach New Street station in time to catch the 5:15 for Bromsgrove, which he was determined to do though the heavens fell—or should he say, though the Germans came? Certainly a more possible though still widely improbable thing.

It had been an exciting, eventful day. He had waked with the pleasant anticipation of how its later hours were to be spent, which, of itself, would have been enough to engage his mind; but after that there had been the news of the destruction of Prague, and the stark horror of that event had been the inescapable topic in all men's mouths, with wonder, or indignation, or pity, or perhaps fear, as their natures were; and everywhere through the Midland Metropolis there had been speculation or apprehension of what the next day would bring. It was plain to see that Europe lay under the shadow of war. The question was: would France fight, being so ill-situated as she now was? Or would she protest and yield, as she had done when Austria had fallen into the arms of the Third Reich? And if she made this a cause of war, would England be able to stand aside? Opinions had differed about that. Some said that it would be foolish for her to intrude into problems of Central Europe, with which she had no concern. Why should she interfere with Czech and German and Frank and Slav? Let them make Europe a slaughterhouse if they would. England had preached peace for the last twenty years, and if she practised it, who could blame her for that? And the Germans were a virile race who could not be kept down. The more the strength of German armaments, secret and open, were disclosed or guessed, the more obvious it became that England would be wise to avoid the storm. And Germany had shown, more than once in the last four years, that that was all she desired. Let the brutes in the bear pit fight, if they could be content in no other way, and let England look over the edge, and perhaps bring them to reason at last, when they had shed as much blood as they were willing to lose!

There were others who saw facts in a clearer light, and even some who were not greatly averse from war, which, they had little doubt, would bring fortune to them. There was a tale going about of a manufacturer in the last war who had papered his dining-room walls completely with one-pound notes, in the exuberance of wealth which was thrust upon him at a bewildering and ever-increasing rate. There was a bootblack who recalled having been paid six pounds ten a week for nearly two years for the simple labour of binding hay.

Eustace had heard such talk, and its excitement had warred with that of his more personal concerns; and then at midday he had had a new subject for thought when he had opened a War Office telegram which read: *Commence manufacture gas-masks to your utmost capacity report maximum output tonights post acknowledge this by wire our confirmation following.*

Well, be it peace or war, there was financial security for himself; there was the prosperity which would mean so much, and had seemed so doubtful, twenty-four hours before.

He had not neglected what was required. He had stopped all other work, putting every machine that he had on the gas-mask parts He had reported the maximum that he could do, by the aid of a night shift, with his present plant, and the increased deliveries he could make by the purchase of some extra lathes. He had applied to the Labour Exchange for the additional hands he would require for the night shift. He had neglected nothing, and on Monday he would put in any hours that the work required—but tonight he was catching the 5:15, though the heavens fell.

It was only three months before that Eustace Ashfield, then in his third year at Oxford, had found his studies suddenly interrupted by his uncle's death, and then that they were not destined to be resumed.

His uncle had supported him while he lived, and dying, had left him all that he had. Unfortunately, it was not much; and it was in the form of a business from which, in his uncle's hands, a small, diminishing income had been derived. Interviews with lawyers and accountants had made it clear that, if the business were closed, capital and income would both be gone. The business was like a horse, skinny and tough, which might yet be useful to drive or ride, but, if it were knocked on the head, there would be little flesh to be scraped from its ancient bones.

He had had the choice of letting it go, and pocketing any surplus it might provide, or taking his uncle's place; and he had chosen the bolder course, the wisdom of which had not been beyond doubt, as the turnover had shown a tendency to decline, and the expenses to rise, under his sanguine but inexperienced management.

Among the more doubtful assets of the business had been a patent for improvements in gas-mask construction taken out more than two years before, and concerning which there was a long correspondence with a War Office department, and evidence of several journeys to London on his uncle's part, all of which appeared to have been of an exasperatingly inconclusive character.

The department had hesitated, criticized, tested, required alterations of pattern, invited quotations for very large quantities—but it had not bought.

Now it seemed that fortune had come through the bombs that had ruined Prague. And it could not have come at a more opportune time. Eustace Ashfield was not indifferent to the sufferings of others, nor oblivious of the shadow that fell darkly across the face of the world, but his heart was light as he slammed his desk, and ran down the narrow winding stair that led to the street door.

For nearly two months now, since three weeks before Christmas, when he had seen her first (he had, of course, heard of her some months earlier, and seen her pictured in the daily press), the thought of Imogen Lister had disturbed his sleep, and dominated his business hours. But to meet her socially, in the absence of mutual acquaintances, and at a time when she was not seeking friends, but had come to visit her aunt's Bromsgrove home to avoid an unwelcome publicity, had proved difficult, even to the persistent purpose of his infatuation; and it was only a week before that he had achieved it in what he foolishly supposed to have been a natural and casual manner. Using his opportunity with commendable adroitness, he had mentioned a near performance of *Journey's End* by the local dramatic society, and on her saying that she had not seen that once-popular play, he had replied, in advance of fact, that he had two tickets, and would she care to do so?

"Which day is it?" she had asked, and then: "Saturday? Oh, yes, I could manage that."

So, in a moment, it had been concluded. And after that, in view of the fact that her aunt's house was near the hall where the play was to be performed, and that he lived nearly two miles away from the railway station in the opposite direction, it had been almost inevitable that he should be expected to call for her.

"You will come for tea?" she had asked "It won't matter it being late if you're kept in town. I shall be going in myself in the afternoon."

Imogen Lister was one of whom few had heard six months before, but whose name had now become one of those of which the whole world talks for a time, after which it is forgotten by most with an equal ease. She had won a notoriety less pleasant in experience than imagination when she had made a solitary non-stop flight which had crossed the Antarctic from Tasmania to the Falkland Islands—the most spectacular crossing of lonely seas and forbidding land which had not been already attempted and overcome.

CHAPTER V.

THE train which Eustace Ashfield caught was one which would be filled during the week with the more prosperous of Birmingham business and professional men—those who could afford to leave their offices at a comparatively early hour, and to reside some considerable distance from the city on its more expensive residential side—but would be comparatively empty on Saturday. The men among whom he sat, most of whom had been detained, like himself, by the unusual circumstances of the day, were more or less known to each other, and there was a feeling of excitement among them, of the imminence of momentous event, of apprehension which was less than a painful dread, and yet enough to make them abnormally conscious of their surroundings and of themselves, sufficient to somewhat diminish the reticence of speech and emotion which is characteristic of the Midland English.

This feeling was not decreased when the door of the compartment was pulled open, as the train was already moving at some speed round the curving platform, and a young stockbroker tumbled in.

"There'll be a war before morning," he said, without waiting to gain his breath. He stood by the door, for the seats were already occupied beyond further crowding. He addressed no one in particular, for, when he had leisure to choose, he was accustomed to the comparative emptiness of the first-class carriages, and these men were strangers to him; but he was answered by: "A good many are saying that." "And a good thing, too, so long as we've got the sense to keep out." "Yes, it's bound to come now, and the sooner it's over, the better." "Between France and Germany, I suppose?" "It isn't hard to guess that." "What's the news now?"

The stockbroker, having recovered breath, answered the last question: "There isn't any news yet. But they've stopped everything on the radio, and told everyone to keep tuned in and wait for something that's coming through. I wouldn't have missed it, only I'd promised to be home tonight on this train."

A voice discounted the importance of this information: "Well, I don't know that there's much in that. There's nothing much on the radio at this time of day. There'd be next to nobody listening in."

"I wouldn't say that," another voice answered from the far corner, that of a quiet, elderly man, with a tired, lined face, "I believe it's the Children's Hour."

So it was agreed that it was. If there were few others, there would be many children waiting for their accustomed programme who would hear unexpected words. Would hear what? Something that, if they should live, they would always remember as the beginning of great events? Of a sudden horror disturbing the security of a million homes? *If they should live.*

To the man in the corner the remembrance had brought a sharp fear and a sudden shame. He was past any thought of military service himself. But he had children at home. He had a young son who might be called up. He had a brother in the Naval Reserve who certainly would. And his own feelings during the day had been little else than a great relief. Relief since the moratorium had been hurriedly declared, as the news of the bombing of Prague had threatened financial chaos throughout the world, and had come to him, with a miraculous suddenness, to suspend the incessant struggle by which he had maintained the outward solvency of a business of meagre capital and obsolescent plant, since it had been crippled by the delusive prosperity, the impossible taxation of unreal profits, and the following depression that had been the nightmare experiences of the last war.

Well, he would be wiser if another had come. He would fake his profits this time, as his neighbours had done then. But he did not like the word that had come to his mind. For one who had maintained a difficult probity for thirty-six years of business life, who had always made straightforward taxation returns—now he was not one who would fake accounts. Camouflage was a better word. But even if there were an outbreak of war, England might not be involved. She had stood out, solitary in her efforts for peace, avoiding entangling alliances, niggardly only in her reluctant expenditure on defensive armaments under the darkening skies of the last three years. At least, he told himself, he did not desire war, which was so far true that, if the power of decision had been in his own hand, he would have resolved on peace without a moment's debate, even though he had known that his own financial ruin would be entailed. It would have been a decision monstrous to doubt! But that did not change the feeling of relief which the moratorium brought, the pleasant consciousness of prolonged anxiety lifted and perhaps permanently removed.

He woke from the oblivion of a moment's thought to become aware that the conversation around him was on kindred topics of a man who had plunged in leather on the eve of the last war and during its opening week, thereby making a fortune which had grown since, until he was now one of the richest men in the Midland capital of a large Birmingham business which had suffered an experience not unlike his own, having sunk its wartime profits in machinery bought at fantastic prices, and new buildings erected in the same financial delirium, which had become useless or empty as the war-orders ceased, leaving only a similarly fantastic claim for eighty per-cent of these unreal profits to be paid in cash at the tax-gatherer's demand.

"They skinned them out for the next few years, and then the slump came, and they had to write most of it off."

"We shan't be such mugs, if we're going to have it over again."

"They weren't all such mugs then."

"You won't get the chance again," the young stockbroker said, with the assurance of youth. "You'll all be controlled more likely than not."

"Well, it might be better than E.P.D."

The statement was received without enthusiasm or pronounced dissent. The imposition of Excess Profits Duty, with its crude inequities, its pledge of brevity cynically broken by a Government which yet expected its victims to observe the standard of honour which it contemned, its offer of fortune to those of sufficient wit and latitude of conduct to evade its provisions with easy minds, its impossibly oppressive demands upon more scrupulous men, the maddening anomalies of its "pre-war standards"—it had been a method of taxation which only a low standard of commercial probity could endure, and only ignorance could defend. But the idea of control was not congenial to those who were masters of their own factories, however insignificant they might be, in an area in which the independence of the individual manufacturer had been more stubbornly and success-fully maintained than either in Lancashire or the farther North. They felt that, even at the call of patriotism, even under the extreme ordeal of war, the interference of controlling officialdom would not be lightly endured.

Eustace Ashfield listened without intruding his own opinions. He was too young to have any business memories of the last war, and the mystic letters E.P.D. had little meaning for him. But he disliked the thought that the War Office might claim the right to interfere with the work of his own factory; perhaps, he vaguely imagined, to send someone to superintend the manufacture of the patented gas-masks that they required. And then he was relieved by a dim memory of having read the awards of a committee which had been set up after the last war to provide compensation for patentees and others whose brains or properties had been seized or exploited in the hour of crisis without their leave, or without a legal bargain being made at the time. He had an idea that some of these had been granted enormous sums.

Of course, if the gas-mask were as good as his uncle had claimed, it might be required in quantities far beyond the possibilities of his small factory, or his limited capital; and, of course, at an urgent national need, it must be made as it could best be, without waiting for him. But he would be recompensed in the end. And all this was conjecture only. There might be no war, or one from which England would stand aside. The sure facts were that he had an open order to manufacture all that he could at his own price—and that he was going out with Imogen Lister tonight. He could not feel that overmuch was wrong with the world, though there might be rumours of coming war, and the ashes of Prague still smoked to a frosty sky.

The train pulled up at the Barnt Green station, where about half its passengers would alight to cross the platform for the branch line to Redditch. The platform was already occupied by an excited crowd who had been induced by a cry of "All change here!" to leave a train which had come up from Redditch, and would normally have taken them on to Birmingham, and who had then been told that they could not complete the journey unless they could show urgent private or business reasons for entering the city that night. A few only were anxious, or even willing to proceed after the significance of the order had reached their astonished minds. The doors of the train, which had been locked as they left it, were opened to let them in, and it was hurried off, its ordinary schedule abandoned, on a non-stop return to the city, in accordance with an instruction which had been broadcast ten minutes before, that all centres of population be evacuated for the night, as far as means of transit allowed.

From the babel of voices upon the platform, disputing among themselves, or giving information to those who had alighted from the Birmingham train, Eustace heard enough to leave no doubt that the shadow of war, long feared and yet only half believed, as though it could be no more than a dreadful, incredible dream, had fallen upon the land.

"You say Germany's declared war? War with England *alone*?" "You must have made some mistake." "Well, that's what the radio said." "Why should she do that? I tell you it isn't sane. We've done nothing to her." "Unless she's gone utterly mad." "She couldn't pull that off if she tried." "You'll never make me believe that." "There'll be all the world in it by this time tomorrow." "Well, we've been expecting it long enough." "But there's lots of places more likely than this." "They said we were to give up the Suez Canal, or they'd attack us in half an hour."

The voices died as the train moved forward again to run rapidly down the steep Bromsgrove gradient. The occupants of the compartment, who had become less numerous, so that the stockbroker found a seat, might have discussed a certainty where they had had no more than a doubt before. But they said little, being occupied with their own thoughts.

They thought first of themselves and of those dependent upon them, as was natural and perhaps right for them to do. And for the most part they still thought of the coming war as a matter of future days, rather than as that which might be at their own doors in the next hour. They thought first of their own affairs, of a score of doubts which rose as they strove to adjust their minds to this sudden, overwhelming event. Of the order which had been placed, at what had seemed a stiff price, for five tons of copper this morning. Would it stand now? There might be a difference on Monday of twenty-five pounds a ton! Of the flotation which had been underwritten, and the advertisements already placed—who would be responsible, what would happen about it now? Well, if there should be a food shortage, there would be the two pigs to kill. That was the best of living a few miles out. You had some garden and stock. Perhaps it would be better to kill them at once. The live animals would be more likely than sides of bacon to be commandeered. And it might be difficult to get any more sharps. It was to be hoped Beryl wouldn't take it the wrong way! She might say she didn't believe a word, or she might be frantic with silly fears.

So their thoughts went, but under all there was an exhilaration of consciousness that they were no longer alone in the civil war, social or economic, which had been the routine of their lives till an hour ago. They had become comrades in common danger and common cause.

CHAPTER VI.

EUSTACE alighted on the Bromsgrove platform, and, as he did so, the lesser thought of a war with Germany left his mind, for Imogen Lister was also leaving the train, scarcely five yards away. Hadn't she said she would be going into the city this afternoon? What an incredible fool he had been not to think of that! But he had no time to reproach himself, for she looked round, and met his eyes as someone she had expected to see. It seemed that she also was oblivious of this talk of war as she shook hands, and said: "I hope you won't mind walking. It's such a short way that I didn't think it worthwhile to have the car brought down."

No, he said, with sincerity, he didn't mind that. It was what he would much prefer.

They went out through an excited, hurrying crowd, above the murmur of which a woman's voice rose hysterically: "But I tell you I've got to go. Both my children are there!" And then again, in response to the station-master's soothing inaudible words: "But that's no good to me! They'll be frightened to death if there's any noise in the night. They'll think it's a storm."

They went out, walking quickly through the cold February evening on a road lit by infrequent lamps and a rising moon, and sparkling with a thin sprinkle of frozen snow. They were more aware of each other than of the calamity which was commencing to shake the world, but it was already too imminent in its effects to be excluded from whatever conversation they might commence.

"I only just managed to catch the train," he said, leading towards the promise of business prosperity that the day had brought.

"Yes, I saw that. You passed my carriage just as the guard's whistle blew."

"I didn't see you, or—"

"No, you couldn't. Anyway, we were full up, and a bit more."

"It wasn't easy to get off. I had a big order from the War Office in today. It's for a new gas-mask which we've had patented for the last two years, but they've only just decided to take it up. They've ordered as many as I can turn out."

She did not congratulate him, as he may have hoped that she would, nor appear interested in the event as affecting his own fortune. She took the news in a less personal way.

"I'm not sure that gas-masks are any good. Captain Malins says that it's wicked to teach people to trust them. They're no good against breathing some of the worst gases; and, besides that, people may be frozen, or burnt with acids all over the body, just the same whether they've got them on or not. And when you think of that, and of how ugly they are to wear! Captain Malins says they won't be a bit of good for the next—I suppose I should say for this war, if it's really come."

"I don't know that you're quite right about that," he answered, striving with some success to keep the annoyance he felt out of his voice, and to discuss the matter in the same abstract manner. "In some ways, this is the best mask that has been invented yet. That isn't only my own opinion. The War Office evidently agrees."

He would have liked to say: "And they may be better judges than this Captain Malins, whoever he is," but he ended with more discretion: "The order shows they must have been preparing for war earlier in the day."

"Yes, I suppose it does. They'd have been silly if they hadn't begun to look round after what happened to Prague during the night. Captain Malins said it was certain to come, and will be over within a week. He doubts whether he'll be in it at all."

"I suppose Captain Malins is R.A.F.?"

"No. Or he wouldn't have said that. He thinks they'll have all the show. He's something to do with tanks. He thinks there'll be no fighting at all, except in the air, and when our air-fleet gets smashed, there'll be no more to be done. The other side will go on dropping bombs till we say that we've had enough, and just lie flat to be kicked."

"I don't suppose," he answered, "it will be quite as simple as that." He was less interested in the military problem than in the fact that what he heard had the sound of quotation rather than original expression. Evidently Captain Malins was one whose words were treasured. He was aware that if the Captain of Tanks had been quoted as asserting that the world was round, he would have been disposed to examine the proposition with a hostile scepticism. But he must not allow an absurd jealousy to make him talk like a fool! Nor to waste the moments that now were his. What was it she had just said? "Isn't it rather proved by what happened in Prague last night?"

"Yes," he answered, "it does rather look that way."

But his mind returned, in the half-minute's silence that followed, to a stubborn argument that it couldn't be as simple as that. Not, for instance, with a large country. Not with a Great Power. Not with England, for instance. Few things are as simple and as one-sided as that. Even the proposition that the earth is round. Isn't it said to be flattened at the ends? The thought of those frozen ends naturally brought his companion's flight to his mind.

"It must have been a terribly lonely time," he said, thinking aloud; and then: "I suppose you're about sick of talking about it now?"

Sick of talking about it? Yes, she was. Sick beyond words. It was to avoid that talk that she had left London and come here, telling Aunt Bella, more in earnest than jest, that she would walk out the first time she heard mention of anything within a thousand miles of the southern seas.

But there had been an imaginative sympathy in his voice, and in the word he had used. Loneliness. That was what it had been. Unimaginable and incommunicable to other minds. He had not fatuously praised her courage, as such countless men and women had done before. However dimly, he had imagined what it had been.

She answered readily: "Well, it did get a bit boring, till I came here. Perhaps monotonous is a better word. Everyone meant to be kind, but they all said the same thing, and had to be answered in the same way. But you're right as to what it was. It was just loneliness above all. Of course, it wouldn't have been possible even two or three years ago; but the machine was quite safe.... It was a silly thing to do, all the same. I shan't try anything like it ever again."

"Oh," he said, "I expect you'll feel differently after a time."

But she made no answer to that, for her mind had gone back, and she heard again the unceasing purr of the engines that never failed, and saw the unsetting sun, and looked down—far down—upon jagged mountains and black ravines that had lain desolate and alone for a million years, alone with the snow and the iron cold, until her plane had appeared, a speck of invading life in the empty sky.

Flying high, she had gone to sleep at last, as she had been trying to do in vain for so many hours. She had slept secure in the knowledge that at any dangerous difference of altitude, any atmospheric disturbance, she would be waked at once by the warning bell; but she had opened her eyes again to become aware that the plane still flew steadily, swiftly, on wasp-like wings, and to look down on the glacial heights, and the black ravines, and the plains of frozen, unending snow.

But she had been glad of that sleep when she had been struck by the blizzard against which she had fought, with little progress, for seven hours, for it had been a gale of such fury as seldom comes in the world of men. She had not known whether she were over ocean or land, for the frozen sleet drove too thickly for anything to be seen a yard ahead or below, and after the first moments of peril were passed, when she had been saved by the great height at which she had been flying before, she had thought only to soar—to beat upward as long, as much, as the growing weight of ice on the wings allowed.

It was a danger from which she had supposed that she would be free, for her machine was fitted with a device by which the ice could be scraped away with a movement like that of a fly cleaning its wings, and this had worked with the mechanical perfection which the makers had guaranteed; but the sleet against which she drove had settled so thickly, had caked so fast, that the plane had been forced far down before the interval passed after which its wings and back would be cleaned anew. So, for seven hours, she had struggled on, through a blizzard to which, it seemed, there could be no end. To be alone, where no life has been from the dawn of time. So many thousand miles from a human voice. Alone in the empty sky, above the death-cold wastes of the frozen snow. No, she would never do it again. She had only done it because she had rashly said that she would, and been annoyed when she had been ridiculed by someone whose contempt would have been unpleasant to have. There was no courage in that.

What she wanted now was a normal life. To meet people to whom she was neither more nor less than a normal girl. A girl of twenty-two, with a good figure; and with good brows, and a dimpled chin that it should be easy to praise. Not merely an airwoman, with those little wrinkles about the eyes which would never go…

"We go in here," she said. And then, with a laugh: "I was almost passing the gate."

CHAPTER VII.

"I SHALL be down in five minutes," Imogen said. "Clara, show Mr. Ashfield where the cloakroom is. You'll come into the lounge when you're ready? It's the first door on this side."

Eustace found his way to the lounge, which was empty, though he could hear voices talking, with a high pitch of excitement, in a room not far away.

There was a wireless set which must have been turned on, for he heard the concluding words of a sentence as he entered:

"… will be met with quietness and courage, and in confidence that the right will triumph."

But after that, which had been the end of a short appeal that the Prime Minister had made to the spirit of a nation not without stubbornness to endure, there was a long minute of silence, and then another voice said sharply:

> "Attention, all listeners! The blackout of east coastal districts is to be extended to Northern and Midland areas, from Newcastle and Carlisle in the North to Northampton and Coventry in the South. This operation is to be carried out with the utmost promptitude in the districts mentioned, and within fifteen minutes later in Lancashire and generally in the counties west of the Pennine range"

There was another short pause, during which Imogen entered the room, her step quick, and her eyes bright with excitement, as she said: "We missed hearing a lot while we were in the train. There's a war on with Germany, and they're said to be on the way to attack us now. They—"

She stopped as another voice came from the radio, this time that of one of the regular announcers, who spoke in his usual pleasantly inflected voice, as though deliberately intending to give assurance to those who heard, that it was no more than ordinary news of the day:

> "This is the British Broadcasting Company speaking. This is the first news, copyright reser..."— (he checked himself, and went on)—"which may be freely used by the press, and by all listeners. A large German air-feet, believed to consist of between three and four thousand fighting and bombing-planes, has violated Dutch neutrality, and, having now passed across Holland, is heading west over the North Sea, its apparent objective being the industrial areas in the North and Midlands. This unprovoked attack, which may be compared to the invasion of Belgium twenty-four years ago, follows a demand from the German Government that England should surrender to them both Gibraltar and the control of the Suez Canal, as guarantees of neutrality in the event of a European war resulting from the seizure of Czechoslovakia earlier today. This demand was made less than two hours ago, and it is evident that preparations for the attack which is now launched must have been already

completed in anticipation of its rejection. Suitable military and other dispositions are being made to deal with the emergency. All loyal and patriotic citizens are earnestly requested to obey the instructions of local authorities, to evacuate urban areas so far as circumstances and means of transport allow, and in particular to avoid the showing of lights, which may be a danger to others, as well as to themselves. Night attack from the air, whatever means may be employed, can never be a serious menace to a civilian population which is sufficiently scattered."

"I wanted you to meet my brother-in-law, Captain Malins," Imogen said, as the radio became silent again, "but he's had to go. There was an announcement calling on all officers who were on leave to rejoin at once." She added, with a smile: "I suppose he'll find out whether he was right about the tanks now."

"I didn't know that you had a sister," Eustace said. (Indeed, how should he? He knew nothing about her, except what had appeared in the public press.) He took courage in the thought that he had no rival to fear, which changed to a measure of doubt again as she answered gravely: "I haven't now. Ethel died about two years ago."

She moved to the window as she spoke, drawing heavy curtains across the dropped blinds. "I shouldn't think any light would get through that. I suppose *Journey's End* will be off now? Or will they still try carrying on? I should like to go, if they do. But anyway, there's no reason why we shouldn't have tea. And I want you to meet my aunt."

She spoke, he thought, with some effort to be casual, to carry on quietly, as English people under such circumstances may be expected to do. But the thought of the three or four thousand planes that might be overhead in the next hour, dropping their cargoes of death, and of what had happened in Prague last night, were not easy to put aside.

His own thoughts were on herself, to the obstruction of other considerations. But her words caused a doubt as to what, in these unforeseen circumstances, he would be expected to do.

If the performance should be cancelled, which there was small reason to doubt, he might be said to have little excuse for remaining there at such a time, it was not everyone who would wish to have strangers (and he was no more than that) invading their privacy, watching, actions and words. Should he offer to go? Or should he take advantage of the event to propose to stay for a time in a house in which, he supposed, only women were?

"If," he began, "there is anything I can do to help—"

"Help?" she said, in a puzzled voice. "You might go round after tea to see that there aren't any lights showing. But I expect Clara'll do that better. She wouldn't stumble over anything in the dark. You can help eat the scones before they get cold. I don't see that you can do anything more important now."

He saw, and was pleased to see, that she was resolved to treat the event without any display of emotion, such as most Englishmen dislike more than the calamities by which it may be provoked, but as they moved to the door, and he opened it for her, the radio spoke again:

> "Attention, all listeners, please. All airmen or airwomen having 'A' Flying Certificates are required to report forthwith to the nearest aerodrome, and to hold themselves at the disposal of the Royal Air Force Command as their services may be required. Report should be made by telephone if possible in the first instance, when further instructions will be received."

She laughed slightly, as she heard this unexpected call, but there was a nervous tone in the light words: "Well, that's come to the right address. It seems that the scones are to get cold after all. The telephone's in the next room. You can come with me, if you like; or perhaps you'd better go into the dining-room and begin tea."

"I'll come with you, if I may."

He heard her give her name, and ask to be put through to the nearest aerodrome, with which it seemed that she was connected without delay. He heard her repeat her name, and then after a moment's interval, reply with emphasis: "Good gracious, no! I shouldn't know what to do. I've never seen one in my life. Not to look twice." And then, after another pause: "Oh, yes. I could do that. Yes, I suppose I could." And after a short interval: "Yes, I can be there. Yes, there'll be no doubt about that."

She put back the receiver, saying only: "It hasn't taken as long as I thought it might. They shouldn't be cold after all," and led the way to the dining-room, where she said nothing more of the undertaking he had heard her give, till he had been introduced to her aunt, Mrs. Rowntree, an old lady of genial manners, and an infirmity of deafness which she would not willingly admit, and the tea had been poured, and he had sat down to a more substantial meal than afternoon tea is usually expected to be, doubtless in consideration of the fact that he had returned from a day's work, and that the next meal would be far ahead, if they should fulfil the programme for which he came.

Then she said, in a slightly raised voice, clearly worded for Mrs. Rowntree to hear: "I've got to go to the Northfield Aerodrome tonight. They want me to fly one of their old machines. I don't suppose I shall be back before morning."

Mrs. Rowntree said: "Yes, my dear. They're sure to want the best help they can get."

If she felt surprise, or any other emotion, she did not allow it to appear. Her tone was kind, but as casual as though she had heard that her niece would spend the night at a friend's house.

"I should have thought," Eustace said, in a voice of protest, "that they'd have had enough men for that. On the first night!" He knew that the call had been general, and not only to an airwoman of special skill.

Imogen answered: "Yes, it does seem a bit startling. But they've been building machines rather rapidly in the last three months, and now they must be getting out all the old ones as well. They asked me," she added, in a lower tone, which she knew that her aunt would not readily admit that she did not hear, "whether I had had any machine-gun practice, and I told them I never had—it wasn't a very likely thing—and then"—slightly raising her voice again—"they asked me if I could pilot one of the old biplanes, and I said I thought I could manage that."

"I thought," Eustace said, still vainly resenting a fact which he could not change, "that the biplane was out of date as a fighting machine."

"It's not quite obsolete," she answered. "I believe one or two patterns most recently built are very good fighting machines. But what I'm asked to pilot is one of the old 'dustbin' pattern of night-bombers, that was reckoned a good machine of that class two or three years ago."

"They must want it," he said stubbornly, "either to fight or for dropping bombs, which is the same thing. It isn't a girl's work, and they ought to have managed better than to be calling you up the first minute a war begins."

But," she said reasonably, "they haven't asked me to fight or to drop bombs. There'll be someone else to do that. They want me to fly the plane, which I'm able to do. I suppose they've got men enough, but they're short of fully trained pilots, with all the new machines they've had built, and now sending up the old ones as well. A pilot can't be fully trained as quickly as they can build a machine. I needn't have rung them up if I hadn't wished." She added, after a moment's pause, in which he did not reply: "They didn't seem to be in any muddle. They gave me the number of my machine, and told me where and when to report without any delay, as though they'd been expecting me to ring up, but I suppose they felt certain that someone would. I'm not wanted till half-past ten. I suppose they can't have the machine ready before then. It's probably not been out of the hangar for months."

"Well," he said, "I think it's a rotten shame that you've got to go." And after that he fell silent, having thoughts that were best not spoken aloud. For how could he attempt to dissuade her, even if he had been less sure than he was that it was a waste of breath? Hadn't it been said for the last three years that the next war would be one in which women and children must be exposed to the same risks as the men? If there were death in the air, could it be said that there would be safety for any upon the ground? And it was easy to guess that England would have need of all who were skilled in flight before morning should dawn again. Doubtless the R.A.F. had been preparing every airworthy machine they had, since the news of the destruction of Prague had shocked the world twelve hours before.

It was easy also to guess that the old lumbering bombers, which could do little more than a hundred miles an hour with a full load in the upper air, would be more vulnerable than the newer planes, and that few would return in safety if they should be dispatched (and of what other use could they be?) to drop bombs in the enemy's country. They were too clumsy to fight, and too sluggish to flee. But what use was there in saying this? Probably she knew it as well as he.

"I suppose," she asked her aunt, "Harry hasn't gone in the car? No, I didn't suppose he would." She turned to Eustace in explanation: "There's no one here except myself who can drive, if Harry— Captain Malins—is away. Auntie's given it up. I wonder whether you'd mind driving me to Northfield and bringing the car back, if it isn't asking too much? That is, if you're used to driving, of course."

"Yes," he said, glad to be asked, but controlling an unreasonable annoyance that she should not have assumed his ability as well as his willingness. "I shall be very glad to do that."

"Thanks," she said, and their eyes met in an intimacy of understanding, such as could not have been so quickly reached at a quieter time. "I shall be grateful for that. It won't be like going alone, and I couldn't take auntie's car without knowing that it would be got back safely."

"I suppose," he said doubtfully, "it's certain that they won't have the play now? And you wouldn't want to go if they do? Though there'd be about time if I were to drive you straight on from there."

She hesitated in reply. It might be a relief to watch. Better than sitting there for the next three hours, talking to hinder thought, for she was fighting down a fear—almost a belief—that she would not live till the light returned. She could judge the risk for which she had volunteered better than Eustace Ashfield could do, and fuller knowledge did not make it a less desperate chance.

"If they're having it," she said, "it would be rather rotten to let them play to the empty seats. We could telephone and find out. And there's that wireless been talking away for the last ten minutes with no one to hear, unless cook's gone in to listen. We don't know what news we've missed."

"We'd better go in there," Mrs. Rowntree said, "if you've both finished," but the telephone rang urgently as she spoke.

CHAPTER VIII.

"THIS," Imogen heard, "is the Bromsgrove Police Station. You are advised, for your own security, to evacuate your house in the next ten minutes, and sooner if possible, and you are requested to leave all lights burning."

"Burning? I suppose you mean out?"

"No, burning. You are in an area which will be camouflaged to draw the German attack. You had better switch on every light that you have."

"Where do you expect us to go?"

"You've got a car, haven't you?"

"Yes."

"Will it hold all who are in the house?"

"Yes, it will do that."

"Then you can't do better than stay in it during the night. Don't block up the road. Get into the open country and turn into a field. That'll be the most sensible thing. But don't lose any time now."

The voice ceased abruptly, doubtless having many similar admonitions to give, and Imogen repeated the message to her two companions.

Mrs. Rowntree took it with equanimity. "Well," she said cheerfully, "I suppose they won't mind if we lock the doors when we go. I expect the Germans will hit something else if they aim here. I suppose I shall get an allowance for what light I waste from the next quarter's account. Imogen, you might tell cook and Clara to wrap up well, and be as quick as they can. No, I can look after myself. Perhaps Mr. Ashfield won't mind helping you to get out the car. I'll see to the lights while you're doing that."

The old lady bustled around the house, switching on the lights and withdrawing curtains and blinds. When she entered the room where the radio had been giving momentous news to unheeding walls, she bent to it for a moment to listen, as she would not have cared to do had she not been alone. She heard:

> "...the Southern division of which approached the Norfolk coast flying high and changing formation as it neared the land, so that it was massed with a narrow front. It has been met by the East Anglian patrol air-fleet under Air-Commodore Lubbock, reinforced by Southern and Midland squadrons, and heavy fighting is now proceeding."

The voice paused a moment, and resumed:

> "A German submarine attack is reported upon naval units stationed in the Firth of Forth, in which H.M. battleship *Beatty* has been slightly damaged, and the Swedish freighter *Tronheim* has been sunk, apparently by a torpedo that missed the mark at which it was aimed. It is reported that the submarine, which must have entered the harbour before war was declared, is already netted, so that it cannot escape."

Well, she mustn't lose time listening to that! She thought, with a vividness of imagination that would have surprised those to whom she was only outwardly known (for she had spoken intimately to none since her husband died in the Jutland battle twenty-two years before), of that deadly strife in the darkness and bitter winds of the night, the battle that must be raging still in the heights of air over the bleak flat land and the winter sea. She saw the high wastes of air loud with the noise of quick-firing guns, and black with great clouds of smoke that the fleets spread for their own defence or to mask attack. From these clouds the swift warplanes swooped and swerved. Their gun flashes stabbed redly into the night. She saw them collide and fall headlong with shattered wings, or interlocked to an equal death, as Dante's demons grappled and fell above the sea of the boiling pitch. She prayed that this battle over the Norfolk coast might exhaust the invading foe, so that there would be the less danger to face when Imogen should ascend at a later hour. But she prayed with a poor hope, for she knew that the air fleets of England had not been designed to resist such an invasion as had now swept in sudden tempest upon her coasts.

At the worst, they were to have had the support of more powerful friends, for England (such had the argument been), seeking only peace, need have no fear that she would rouse the wrath of a stronger foe. Should she fight at all (and many held that she should not do so for any stake, and would talk as though the decision must rest entirely with her), it would be at the side of puissant allies, in a war in which all the forces of world justice would unite to chastise an aggressive foe. And none had known, and few guessed, the strength of the secret forces which had been built and trained to enslave the world.

If the air force of England could, by heroic sacrifice, and at the cost of its own destruction, hold back the attacking fleets from working such ruin as Prague had felt, until they should be compelled to withdraw to defend their frontiers from other foes, it would be the most that could be hoped, and more than could be expected that they would do.

But this idea of disguising the dark landscape of night with deliberate lighting of places of small account might not be vain, if it were done on a large scale, and had been designed with sufficient skill. Mrs. Rowntree switched on the last light, wrapped herself in her warmest coat, ascertained that the cook was not neglecting to bring a thermos flask and ample food for the night, and went out very cheerfully to the waiting car.

CHAPTER IX.

"Do you want me to come?" Eustace asked, as he threw open the garage doors, and the car lights shone on to the drive. There was room for five in the car—just. There would be more comfort for four. The very strength of his desire to remain with her during the short hours that remained made him more sensitive to the ambiguity of his position in that household which he had only entered an hour before.

Could he leave four women at such a time of threatening danger and death? Obviously not. Having no responsibilities of his own for the night, his duty was to stand by them and be of what service he could.

Could he assume that his company would be desired by people who were almost entire strangers to him, and who showed no sign of inability to handle their own affairs? The answer seemed equally clear. Yet he did not think that she would wish him to leave. He had little doubt of that, or anticipation of what the answer would be.

"I don't want you to come. I want you to go, if it isn't asking too much. Unless you've got anything else on that you ought to be doing now. Perhaps it's more than I ought to ask, but—"

"Of course, I'll do what you wish. My time's free enough. But I'm not sure that I understand. If you'd rather I didn't stay now—"

"I suppose I wasn't quite clear. You'd better get in, and I'll take it round. I'm used to backing it at the bend. I meant that I've got to be at Northfield in three hours' time, and the car ought to be going the other way. I believe Northfield's about six miles from here on the Birmingham road, which is about the last that you ought to take. I wondered whether you'd think I'm asking too much if I ask you to drive my aunt and the maids somewhere where they'll be out of the way of any trouble that's likely to come?"

"You mean that you're not proposing to come yourself?"

"How can I? I've got time for getting to Northfield now, even if I find that I've got to walk, but I don't want to get farther away."

He saw the difficulty more clearly than he would admit in his blank distaste for the part he was asked to take, and his reluctance to part so quickly, or to leave her to face alone the dangers of an area which was being lighted to attract the bombs of the German fleet.

"I don't see why we shouldn't drive you there first. It's the only sensible thing to do."

"And when we know that the Germans may be here any moment now?"

"It won't take long if it's only six miles."

"No? Have you thought what the road's likely to be? It's the main road out of Birmingham for everyone going to Bristol or Worcester, and all the places between and beyond them. What will it be like for a car trying to get the opposite way?"

They were round at the front of the house as she said this, and she assumed his assent as she turned to Mrs. Rowntree to explain: "Mr. Ashfield's kindly undertaken to drive you. I suppose it doesn't much matter where, so long as it's somewhere dark, and sufficiently out of the way."

Mrs. Rowntree appeared not to hear or to understand. She said, as Imogen would have guided her to the front seat: "No, my dear. If Mr. Ashfield's to drive, you'd better be in front. You'll be able to tell him the way to go." She added with the candour which emergency brings: "I shouldn't hear what he said, more likely than not."

"But I'm not coming, Aunt Bella. I'm going the other way."

"Nonsense, Imogen, don't be absurd. We shall drive you to Northfield first."

"No, you couldn't do that. I've explained to Mr. Ashfield. Besides, I'm not ready. I've got to change. You don't think I could fly like this?"

"Then you'd better change quickly, my dear, unless you want us to be here when the Germans come, if they ever do."

She looked up to a sky which was bright with frost and unclouded stars, though it was now obscured by the lighted houses around. She could hear or see nothing of present menace, not observing a low mutter of distant sound—was it of guns or of bursting bombs?—which came to the ears of her younger companions.

"I think everything's in now, madam." It was the cook's voice that interrupted, reminding them that there were others for whose safety they were responsible.

But Mrs. Rowntree was one who knew her own mind and was accustomed to have her way. "It's no use, my dear," she said; "the longer you argue, the longer you'll keep us here."

Imogen saw that she could not solve the problem simply by walking off into the night, for it was true that she must change into garments more fit for flight in the freezing heights of the air. She ran back quickly into the house and the car stood at the lighted door, while the mutter of distant sound grew louder, nearer, out of the east. And then for a few minutes, it died away.

Mrs. Rowntree, crowding into the back of the car with the two maids, remarked cheerfully that the letters of the Bible are said to be less numerous than the Yorkshire acres, and that, if the Germans thought they were going to bomb them all, they would find that it would take them some time to do; and in what seemed an incredibly short time, even to those who sat waiting thus, Imogen came running, out, looking shorter, broader in the loose-fitting, fur lined leather garments and hood in which she had faced the Antarctic cold a few months before.

"You'd better turn left at the gate," she said, as she scrambled quickly into the car. "The radio is still chattering away, but I couldn't stop to hear what it said. It was something about feeding each other if difficulties of transit arose, as I ran up, and 'a form of refuge which cannot be recommended in congested areas,' as I came down. We shall have to manage without its wisdom as best we can. Pity we haven't brought the portable in the car."

She was of better courage than in the earlier evening. The excitement of action had come, and the speed with which she had changed had stirred her blood. Perhaps, more subtly, she felt the difference of the garb she wore.

Two hundred yards away a house burned, lighting the frosty road. They drove towards it, as they must, and the wind swept the hot smoke upon them, so that they must slacken speed on a road that they could not see. They questioned whether it were an accident of the night, or had been deliberately fired, and decided that the camouflage was being very thoroughly done.

Clear of the smoke, and with the light of the burning house at their backs, they ran rapidly along a side road that was now empty of life, for they had been among the last to be warned, and there were few who had not been quicker to flee.

They could only vaguely guess what the scheme of illusion might be, but they saw that the district was not widely lighted in a crude general way, but in patches only, and, as they left Finstall Park on their right, and came to a narrow hilly lane, their purpose being to avoid the main roads, and approach Northfield from the south, they became aware that the sky above had become black, and that a widespread smoke-screen was overhead.

Overhead too was the noise of airplane engines, but whether of friends or foes it was vain to guess. There was no dropping of bombs or sound of conflict above, though the night was disturbed by a low confused thunder of distant sound, telling of that terror out of the east that the darkness bred.

CHAPTER X.

THEY were near the new bypass road when they came clear of the pall of smoke, and as they slackened speed, facing the problem of a stream of traffic that ran without lights in one direction across the whole breadth of the road, and which they must ask themselves how they could hope to cross, or whether they could make progress against it when they had gained what should have been their own side of the road, the airplanes that they had heard before became visible in the sky. There were seven planes that flew in the shape of an arrow's head. And then seven again. And a third seven behind them. They came from the east, not flying low, but sufficiently so to be under the thin stretches of almost transparent cloud that drifted across the moonlit sky.

"They are German planes," Imogen said. "I wonder what they're meaning to do."

"You are sure they're German?"

"They're not English, I'm sure of that. I know all the patterns."

The planes were nearly overhead now. Two or three fields away, a bomb burst. The next moment they were surrounded with light and with dreadful sound. The bombs fell round them on every side. The maid, Clara, screamed hysterically.

In ten seconds, it was over for them. Flying swiftly, the German squadrons passed on, scattering a continuous hail of bombs upon the smoke-blackened area from which they had come. The noise of their bursting was a deafening but rapidly receding thunder of sound.

Shouts and screams came from the road ahead, where a bomb had fallen with disastrous result. The car which had first been struck was buried beneath the piled wreckage of a dozen others that had run into it, or been run into by those that followed, before the stream of unlighted vehicles could be brought to halt.

Imogen's hand went to the door. "We'd better see what we can do to help "

"Sit still," Eustace said; "can't you see what's coming? I'm going to back, if I can."

She did not understand the significance of the "if," not being able to see the gaping side of the radiator, where their own car had been struck by a flying fragment of shell, but the reason for getting clear was easier to perceive.

The main road ahead was blocked beyond hope of passage. Into the side lane where they were, with scarcely room for two cars abreast, a large Bentley, indifferent to everything but the safety of its own occupants, its horn's blatant warning piercing a score of surrounding discords, was endeavouring to force a passage into the lane.

Where it came, the stream of smaller cars behind it would surely follow. As they stood, they blocked half the width by which this crowded traffic could find release; when it should bear down upon them, they would find it hopeless to attempt to turn, and might have no better hope of release than to back down the mile-long lane, with the impatient, congested traffic jostling by, unless they would stand there until morning came. Even without being aware of that gaping wound, it was easy to see the purpose of what he did.

"There's a gateway a short distance back," he said. "If I can get there before the lane fills, I might find space to turn."

But this proved to be beyond the capacity of the wounded car, and the help of others, anxious to clear the way, had to be obtained to push it back to the gate and into a field where it would cease to impede the road, their efforts dreadfully lit by the pile of wreckage which had now burst into a pillar of flame, making it useless to hope that any maimed or unconscious life could still be released.

"Well, that settles it," Imogen said. "I've got to walk the rest of the way. But it can't be far now. It shouldn't be hard to find."

"If you'll go with her, Mr. Ashfield," her aunt proposed, without suggesting that it was a favour for which she asked, for her eyes were still good, though her hearing failed, "we shall be quite comfortable here till we can get someone to mend the car."

Imogen said: "Of course he can't leave you like this. Do you suppose I shan't find my way? Suppose they come back dropping bombs again?"

"If they do, my dear, I don't see that Mr. Ashfield could save us from getting hit. But they won't do that again. England's rather too large for them to drop them twice on the same spot."

There might be some defect of logic in this reasoning, but the old lady had her way, as she most often would; and Eustace found that his own object was to be further advanced, at least for another hour, by this catastrophe which had fallen upon the world.

They made their way with some difficulty back to the main road, having nothing but a precarious narrowness of gutter in which to advance against the oncoming traffic; but when they gained it, there was a side-pavement by which they could make better progress on foot than had they been attempting to force a car against a current of flight.

There were no lamps lighting the road, but the night was not dark, the last clouds leaving the sky bare to the moon and the frost-bright stars, and the cold becoming more intense as the night advanced. They passed dark houses which might or might not be deserted, but in which it was certain that no man slept. They were lighted for half a mile by a little pinewood that blazed with a scatter of drifting sparks and a pleasant resinous scent. They could still hear the noise of explosions at times, and lights flickered along the sky. Once, when they were in a dip of the road, with a high wall at the side, giving little view except of the sky that was directly above their heads, they heard a burst of machine-gun fire that seemed to be but little distance above. It ceased for a moment and then broke out again farther away, a drama of flight and chase that they could not see.

But they noticed that the eastward sky was dark, or only lit at times with local gleams of some flickering light. Birmingham had shut off the wide glow by which it showed itself during the hours of night over an area of a thousand miles; and it was plain that the German attack had failed to find it now, by the darkness in which it lay.

It seemed a good omen to these two, and to give reason for hope, as they came to the aerodrome gates, and were sharply challenged by an officer who was with the sentries whose bayonets guarded the entrance. But his voice changed as he saw that Imogen was clothed for the air, and heard her name, which he clearly knew.

"Oh, Miss Lister?" he said. "You're before time, but you're none too soon. You're wanted at once, if you'll come with me. You'd better keep to this side."

He led her away abruptly, giving Eustace no more than a hurried glance, which passed him as though he had no thought to spare at that hour for terrestrial men. She left in that haste with no parting word, and Eustace stood lingering for a moment at a gate that he might not pass.

In the shadow of the wall, where the officer had drawn Imogen to the other side, he saw something that lay like a large dog or a tumbled sack.

One of the sentries followed his glance, and could not resist speech on that which had been the excitement of ten minutes before.

"Shot him, the Captain did," he remarked, "shot him down like the dog he was."

He explained that the man who lay there, a heap that had ceased to twitch, had lived in one of the small houses outside the gate, and had been suspected for some time of spying and German blood, although suspicion had always been less than proof.

But tonight the sentries' vigilance had caught him climbing over the fence, with what object no one would ever know, and Captain Gibson's revolver had saved occasion for further words.

Eustace stood for some time in the frozen road, uncertain of what he should next do, his mind emotionally exhausted by the experiences of the day. He had waked with the one thought of the meeting the evening was expected to bring, and the fear that he might fail to use his opportunity to open the way to some further gain. Who could have thought that it would bring him, not only that which he had hoped, but a prosperity (as he supposed) which removed the most formidable obstacle from the goal he sought? Who could have thought that it would end in so strange, so momentous, so dreadful a way? He heard the roar of a rising plane. One by one, twenty-two great biplane night-bombers rose from the dark aerodrome grounds. After them, swifter and lighter far, a small scouting plane rose and circled round them as they formed into double line, and then shot forward to survey the dark path that they were to take. He did not doubt that one of those slow, cumbrous, obsolescent planes, which, if it were attacked by the battle-planes of the German fleet, would be too clumsy to fight or fly, was flown by the girl he loved.

Would he see her again? It might be held to be less than a likely guess. He did not even know that she would propose to come back to this Midland home, which had been no more than a place of visit to her.

But he saw that it was the one link that he had, and self-interest joined with nobler motives to return his steps to the field where he had left the three women to wait in the foundered car.

But as he walked back on the frosty, moonlit road, on which the traffic was becoming less now, but which was scattered with cars that had collided or broken down, or which had pulled aside as seeing no object in further flight, he saw the selfishness of the doubt that had troubled his mind. Did he think of himself alone, and nothing of her, that he should be most concerned of how they should meet again? Should not his first thought have been of her peril in distant and hostile skies? Would she return, would she be alive, when the morning came? He imagined the squadron pursued and surrounded by a fleet of swifter deadlier, more numerous foes. It became a centre of bursting shells: it was raked by machine-gun fire. He saw her plane fall earthward a flaming wreck. He saw her dead, or dragged out, mutilated but still alive, to be wounded prisoner in that foreign, now hateful land.

And he had been glad, a few hours before, that the coming war had promised fortune to him! God forgive! God understand and forgive! And what a poor part was to be his. Making gas-masks while others died! Gas-masks for profit, while others died! Gas-masks which Captain Malins (he still thought with a vague jealous resentment of the opinion of this man he had never met) had said would be of no use in the coming war. What was it likely that she, who had won previous fame, who was called to the place of danger at the hour of her country's need—the place which he would have been unfitted to take—what was it likely that she would think of him, if she thought at all in the future hours? But he would pray no less for her life and safety because he saw how vain were his own desires.

It was the next morning, while news was still being distributed from the Western station, that he listened to this announcement:

> "The Air Ministry issued this bulletin at 10:17 A.M. today:
>
> "'A squadron of twenty-two night-bombers under Squadron-Leader C. A. Withers, was dispatched from the Northfield Aerodrome yesterday at 10:28 P.M. with orders to destroy the naval stores and barracks at Cuxhaven, and the shipping in the harbour.
>
> "'This attack was carried out with success, and Cuxhaven was subjected to a heavy bombardment with incendiary bombs, as a result of which it is still in flames. The loss of shipping is also believed to have been serious.
>
> "'It is much regretted that the squadron when returning over the North Sea encountered a German air-fleet of overwhelming strength, and was shot down after a most gallant resistance, in the course of which important losses are reported to have been suffered by the attacking fleet, but exact details have not yet been received.'"

CHAPTER XI.

THERE is no reason to doubt that the German bid for the neutrality of the British Empire was genuine in its intention, and that it was regarded as a reasonable possibility that the stipulated conditions would be accepted.

The proof of this lies in the fact that it involved renunciation of the advantages of an absolutely unexpected attack, which it may be supposed that the German Government would not have scrupled to make in the entire absence of provocation, as they had invaded Belgium twenty-four years before, and in conformity with the standards of international conduct explicitly advocated by their military writers of later dates.

The possibility of such a surrender, however ignominious it might be, was based on the fact that England was inadequately armed to resist even the measure of German aerial strength which had been openly shown to the world, and still less to encounter that which had been indicated during the previous night; and it approached probability when consideration was taken of the pacific temper which had led to that inadequate and reluctant arming. Alone among the nations of Europe, England had shown that she dreaded war. She had argued, striven, intrigued for peace, amidst neighbours whose whole strength, under the urgency of hate or fear, had been organized for the ordeal of coming strife.

It is certain that the German High Command was anxious to avoid the error of 1914, and that considerations of both military and political strategy rendered it desirable to secure English neutrality while they proceeded to the conquest of continental Europe. It is even probable that they would have sought an active alliance, had not such a development been rendered impossible, not by any unfriendliness of the English for the German people, which did not exist, but by the policy of deliberate aggression, the crude atheism, and the tyrannic and bloody domestic methods of the German Government, which were antipathetic to English ideals of public and private life.

It is probable also, for reasons which will appear, that Germany had not desired or intended at this time to provoke a general war, for which she would have preferred to wait for another year.

Her first miscalculation had been the supposition that Prague would yield at a moment when she could have no encouragement from the preoccupations of France, and that a controlling German influence might have been established in Czechoslovakia without the necessity for military action. But, when that supposition had proved mistaken, she had struck at once, her plans for that and a score of other eventualities having been perfected in advance. And when she had concluded, in the following hours, that she had exposed her ultimate purpose too far to avoid the issue of wider war, she had then resolved, according to plans already matured, by one swift decisive act either of diplomatic or physical violence, to eliminate a potential enemy before her allies against that eventuality (if any such she had) could intervene for her relief.

The German strategy in the air attack which it had now made was sound, if not brilliant, in the broad outline of its conception, and of that character which is possible only to a High Command that has overwhelming superiority of numbers in its control. It left the suddenly improvised War Council of England waiting through the early hours of the night for an attack on London that did not come, as it waited also, with equal tensity, for news that the French air-fleets were moving to its support.

A German air-fleet had been assembled during the afternoon, consisting of 1,200 battle-planes and 3,000 night-bombers of the newest patterns, and this fleet had taken the air as the February darkness fell, and crossed the Netherlands in single formation, only dividing, as it left the coasts of that land, into two divisions, the smaller of which proceeded northward to attack the industrial and shipping area of the Tyne, while the main body advanced towards the Norfolk coast.

It was known that this coast, which was considered by the English military authorities to be most vulnerable both to attacks from the air and to the landing of a hostile army, was strongly protected by anti-aircraft batteries, and the orders the German Air-Admiral had received were that he should advance on a narrow front, and subject the country beneath him to a bombardment sufficiently intense to insure a lane of unmolested retreat for his night-bombers when they should be returning with their magazines emptied.

The fleet was about twenty miles from the Norfolk coast, and had slackened speed for the manoeuvres which the adoption of this formation required, when the British cruiser *Campaspe* opened fire upon it.

The *Campaspe* was one of the newest type of armoured cruiser, and had been primarily designed to resist attacks from the air. It had heavily armoured decks, and every gun which it bore could be thrown up at an angle sufficient to threaten some part of a fleet which was extended so far through the upper air.

It had been cruising without lights, and only revealed its presence as its gun-flashes struck upward into the night.

Never before had been, perhaps never again would such a target be offered to the guns of a British ship. With no more aim than a shotgun needs when a flight of wild fowl is overhead, the *Campaspe*'s guns flung upward their bursting shells. It was an audacious challenge against impossible odds; but it did not cease before it had demonstrated the difficulty of hitting a moving target from a great height in the air, and its end was so long delayed that a number of the German bombers were ordered at last to descend and destroy at close quarters a shattered wreck, with its decks awash, that was still serving a single gun. And by that time seventeen of the German planes had spun down in flames to the cooling sea.

The *Campaspe* sank, having done its part, leaving a raft afloat on which fourteen men were washed ashore during the night, and the German air-fleet passed on to its ultimate mission, which was to destroy whatever forces of the air might be mustered to bar its way, and then bombard the Midland industrial centres.

The German High Command had calculated that, up to this time, a considerable proportion of the British air-fleet would be held back for the protection of London, and that the forces which they would first have to meet would be consequently less; but it was not their expectation or wish that this position should remain. They had foreseen that, as the hours passed, and the news came to London that the German air-fleets were spreading destruction through the Midland area, while there was no sign of any threat to itself, the air-forces which had been stationed there would be sent northward to find their foes, and a fleet of 700 fighting planes was ordered to extend itself upon the left flank of the German position, both for its protection and to draw the attack of the British forces away from the London area. Its orders were explicit that it was not to advance southward itself, for the German strategy was to render London bare of defence, that it might be more absolutely destroyed before morning came, for which it expected to have new fleets released at a later hour.

But to explain clearly how even the secret air-fleets of Germany could be equal to such large demands, without exposing its own frontiers to the attack of its nearer foes, it is necessary to go back to a diplomatic event of the preceding August, and this may be conveniently done before considering the course which the war had taken during the night.

CHAPTER XII.

IT had been a hot afternoon in the last week of August 1937 when Dr. Schronberg, the German Foreign Minister, received Comrade Levinski, the Soviet Ambassador. The visit was one of formality, its occasion, which was openly known, being to convey the thanks of the Russian Government for an act of humanity and good seamanship by which a German destroyer had succoured a Russian ship in distress in the Baltic Sea. Those who hoped that the peace of Europe might be maintained observed it with satisfaction, as showing the brotherhood of mankind when faced by the hostile forces of Nature, which are their relentless and indifferent foes.

But the conversation which actually took place was on a more sinister and quite different subject, being no less matter than the terms of a secret treaty, by which the two governments that were so superficially opposite, so fundamentally alike in their ruthless suppression of individual liberties of thought or conduct, and in their conception of a community in which the single citizen exists for the state rather than the state for him, were to unite to enthral the world.

"If we were assured," Levinski said cautiously, "that what is spoken here will not be known in Paris in the next hour...."

"Information," Dr. Schronberg replied coldly, "does not leak out of Germany in these days. We have no jails for those who barter or blab. We use axe and cord, by which treason has become an unpopular crime."

"So I have observed," Levinski allowed, "or it is unlikely that we should make you the offer I now propose. I come to proffer you our alliance, which, at the right moment, will be the world to divide."

"But you are allied with France, who is no less than our bitter foe."

"So I suggest that we shall remain. It will make our compact with you of the greater worth, for we shall continue to hear the most secret counsels of France, and we can advise her in a false way. It will also make her more careless to keep her friends of another sort."

Dr. Schronberg recognized the good sense of this argument. France had not hesitated in previous years to alienate the sympathies of the United States by her unwillingness to reduce her debt, even when her vaults had been heavy with idle gold. Her press would abuse England at any hour beyond substance of fact, and on provocations that were not meant, nor always easy to see. She had acted thus in the assurance that Russia lay, a constant threat, on the flank of her major foe. So she must continue to dream.

Dr. Schronberg moved to a map of the two hemispheres of the globe which hung on the farther wall.

"Excellency, you talk of sharing the world." His eyes fell on the great expense of the two Americas, north and south, and Levinski, taking his meaning at once, made a confident reply.

"Will the New World face the Old when three continents own our power, and recruit our arms? Our fleets will be ten to one, both in air and sea. They would claim respect, were they now allied to our nearer foes; but they say it is nothing to them. They are too wise to be drawn again into Europe's wars! They will be there to take on the next day."

* * * * * * *

That conversation had been six months before, and now the hours passed until midnight was but a short distance ahead, and the French air-fleets were held in leash, waiting the word from Russia which did not come.

M. Bonnier sat in council with the three most trusted members of his cabinet, and with the leaders of the opposition parties of Left and Right, whom he had summoned to his support, that all should share the decision which might be no less than their country's fate.

"M. Smirnoff," he said, "is very firm on this point, that if we cross the German frontier with no further excuse than that England has been attacked, the Russian treaty will not apply, and his country will remain free to act as her interests may dictate without obligation to us."

"And for this doubt," M. Regnier, the one-time head of the *Croix de Feu*, protested with passionate impatience, "for this splitting of rotten straws, we are to delay our attack till the ruin of England is made complete, and the German air-fleets can be assembled upon our frontiers in all their strength! How shall you answer France in that hour for the chance you have thrown away?"

"If the Germans cross our frontier, though with no more than a single plane, if they drop but one bomb, Russia will be instant in our support, for to that her honour is pledged by a treaty which all men know. What do you say, M. Reval?"

He addressed the leader of the Radical Party, the one man who had not spoken till now. He had risen from a sickbed at this hour of his country's need, and listened in a sombre silence to the contentious voices around him.

"I am ill," he said, "and may be less fit to advise. But I do not understand why the answer of Moscow should be so greatly delayed."

"M. Smirnoff can only communicate with Moscow by wire, for Germany is troubling the air, and even by wire the direct lines are not prudent to use. But at any moment he is expecting reply."

"It may be that because I am ill I see with discoloured eyes; but to me, it has the look of a trap."

"I have thought of that," M. Bonnier replied, "but were it so, would not M. Smirnoff have encouraged us to attack, so that the obligation of Russia to us would be relieved, whereas he entreats us only to act in consultation with him?"

"But suppose—" M. Reval appeared to hesitate upon words that he would not speak. "No," he said, "I am ill. I do not ask that you shall listen to me." He sank back in his chair, in such evident physical distress that, for the next few minutes, the attention of his companions was directed to his relief, even to the exclusion of greater things. After which M. Bonnier said:

"Gentlemen, I propose this. We will wait until 2:00 A.M., and if no answer from Moscow has then arrived, we must conclude that it is someway blocked, so that it cannot come. By that patience our Russian friends will perceive that we have not acted in indifference to consultation with them, but at that hour we shall give control to our soldiers of land and air.

"We may equitably observe that, had we been selected for this German attack, England would have been under no treaty for our relief, and what she would then have done can be a guess and no more.

"We may also observe that we are, at the worst, at a less dangerous pass than had we been first attacked, for it is very sure that England, outnumbered in the air though she may be, will cause much loss to her foes, which must be the better for us at a later hour; and we may suppose, knowing how stubborn of temper she is of disposition to be against the jaws of a closing trap, that she will not he so cast down in a night that she will not bite on the crushing heel for a second day.

"But if we ask ourselves whether we should continue to stand aside so long as we are left to ourselves, Germany having made no hostile motion to us, we must consider what she would be likely to do if the fear of England had left her mind. I suppose that we must now fight for our land, whether Russia come to our side or remain still, lest Europe become no more than a German farm. And we must not overlook that while we wait for a Russian word, Russia may be also waiting for us. Or she may herself be attacked, and cut off in such a manner that she cannot reply."

There was a general murmur of assent to a decision which made some compromise of conflicting views, and still left two hours during which the reply from Russia would be likely to come.

Only M. Reval replied to M. Bonnier's last words with: "Would M. Smirnoff urge us to wait, if he were not well assured that Russia is not being attacked at this present hour?" And this argument, having a double edge, inclined those who heard to accept M. Bonnier's proposal with easier minds, for the thought that the German air-fleets might also be engaged on the Russian front, while France lost her chance from a foolish fear, had inclined more than one who heard to favour a more instant attack. And there was no other there who felt the doubt that had entered a sick man's mind.

So they sat on, waiting for a Russian word that would never come, the time passing quickly enough in debate of many matters affecting France and themselves, including the tentative construction of a war-cabinet which statesmen of all parties would be invited to join at this crisis of coming strife, as they could scarcely doubt it to be; and with news of moment coming in from all parts of the world, both of night and day.

It was 1:45 A.M. when M. Bonnier inquired finally of the Russian Ambassador, and received a reply that he was coming over to the Quai d'Orsay at once; but the minutes passed after that, and he did not arrive.

Instead of him, there was news of a battle in English skies, the stress of which was now spent, and become no more than guerrilla fighting among the clouds, for the British air-fleets which had been sent up to meet the German invasion, which were reported to consist of anything from five hundred to a thousand planes, but must have been much under the more sanguine figure, had attacked the invading fleets with the untried tactics of aerial strife, and had broken at last, after beating many times against the great host of their foes, as a wave breaks on the harder rock.

Until now the news had been that London lay quiet and distant from the more northern war, the noise of which could be heard at times by those who patrolled its outskirts above the clouds. And still, with the passing hours, its population poured outward on every side, until few were left in its silent streets, except those who were stout of heart to remain, or held by duties, or bonds of love. And its air-fleets, and even some of its mobile batteries, were ordered north at last, to meet the more urgent need. But now the tale was that a new German fleet, of unknown but enormous strength, was crossing the narrow seas, and that the batteries of the coasts of Kent, flinging fierce barrages to the skies, could be heard on the Flanders shore.

"*Mais, mon Dieu!*" M. Bonnier exclaimed. "If they have done that, they must have resolved that we are too frightened to make attack. They must have left the Rhine country bare. It is Heaven's chance that is ours tonight! Why does not M. Smirnoff come? He should have been here three...four minutes ago! Jules, you must call the Embassy up. Inquire if he have left as he said, and how long a time."

But the reply from the Embassy was not easy to understand. It came from a junior clerk, who said that he was the sole official now in charge for the night. The Ambassador and his principal secretaries had left more than ten minutes before. By the way they left, he did not think they were coming back.

There had been no time to discuss the meaning of this before there was the noise of shouts in the outer room, where an excited youth was insisting that he would see M. Bonnier himself, and that without an instant's delay.

"It is news I have," he could be heard to protest, "which will not wait for a second's time!"

M. Bonnier's secretary went to the door, and was pushed roughly aside by a breathless youth, who had come from the night-office of a famous international travel agency.

"M. Bonnier," he panted, "there was a Russian air-fleet flying west over the Bavarian mountains nearly an hour ago."

"You are sure of this? You dare not bring me an idle tale?" M. Bonnier spoke quietly, though his voice shook.

"Monsieur, it is surely true! It is our business to know. A Russian plane came down at Glocknei, having caught fire in the air."

"It fell fighting the German fleet?"

"No, monsieur. It was an accident of the air. There are German war-planes that guide them the way they come."

M. Reval's voice rose with a strength it had not shown until then. "And we have let the hours pass! We have ruined France! So I had seen it to be, and I thought it a fever's dream!"

He sank backward in his chair, but whether in faint or death there was none to heed. France must fight now at such odds as England faced a few hours before.

CHAPTER XIII.

THE England of 1938 was unready, alike in disposition and material resources, for the conflict which had been thrust upon her. Her armaments, though substantially strengthened during the three previous years, had been scaled upon the assumption that she would not be engaged in conflict with any major power, unless it were in conjunction with strong allies. Even on the sea, the element of her traditional supremacy, she had long abandoned the two-power standard, which supplied a bare minimum of security to her scattered Empire, and in recent years had allowed her navy to sink even below that of single equality.

In the air, she had followed with slow reluctance the programmes of other powers, who, urged by dreams of successful aggression, or under the impulsion of urgent fear, had strained their resources in open or secret building of air-fleets designed rather to destroy their neighbours' homes than to guard their own.

Her land army was negligible in numbers if not in quality, as she had continued in her traditional reliance upon the security which the water gave, although her fleet had ceased to be sufficient for its defence, and invasion had now become possible in another element. Unlike the great nations of Europe, her population was untrained for concerted military action.

This last difference might, in itself, be a disadvantage of less than decisive weight, in view of the fact that the land armies of future war were expected to prevail by mechanical rather than numerical strength, and it should, at least, have had the incidental effect of increasing the material prosperity of the nation which had not diverted its youthful manhood to the unproductive life of camp and barracks.

But this natural consequence had been obliterated by the insensate prodigality with which it had poured its wealth into the provision of instruments and channels of transit, as though motion were, of itself, of productive rather than destructive quality.

No waste of labour or of material resources, however fantastic, had been considered too high, no tribute of blood and tears from a million homes had been considered too great a price to pay for this boasted "progress" of continuous motion, which had not succeeded in enabling any person to be in two places at once, and which usually ended where it began.

For this national mania it had sacrificed its prosperity, its leisured amenities, its children's lives; and the size of its houses shrank as the breadth of its roads increased.

The utterances of its statesmen and economic professors showed that, if they spoke with sincerity, they had naively convinced themselves that the national prosperity was increased rather than drained away by the excessive production of mostly useless and always dangerous vehicles, and by the huge importations of fuel which they required. They observed with truth that a large part of the nation were employed, directly or indirectly, in rendering continual service to these vehicles, as though this were of itself a cause for satisfaction; and as though it would have been an inevitable alternative that they would not otherwise have been employed in more useful ways. Yet had it been proposed that the national prosperity should be further advanced by employing a similar number of men to stand on their heads for a daily period, they might have declined to discuss the proposition with the equal seriousness which it would have deserved.

It is difficult to find any explanation of the unchallenged dominance of this national nightmare which can be set down in sane and credible words, and to attempt to do so would require detailed analysis of a social order infested with accretion of laws which were not merely a dead weight of restrictions that would not lift, but which, like maggots in a sheep's back, bred fresh torments continually; and which was yet without any strength or vision of intelligent government.

The England of 1938 was governed by a complicated bureaucracy which had no reason to fear contending powers, except those of organized sectional interests, among which that of the motor industry was one of the bloodiest and most ruthless that has ever risen to scourge mankind.

Its numerical strength silenced the politician; its advertising expenditure stifled the press. Protests against its hundreds of thousands of ignoble casualties could become articulate, if at all, only on the assumption that relief must be by way of schemes of wilder and yet more fantastic expenditures, and no word of restricting the disease was even whispered aloud.

Meanwhile, the many industries of greater usefulness which must have flourished had the nation continued to breed and export a natural increase of population to occupy the waste lands that its fathers won, wilted and shrank, and even agriculture languished in this country of idle hands.

Even the experiences of the last war, with the additional sinister fact that English commerce now lacked the protection of an adequate fleet, had not induced successive governments to take effectual measures to secure that the land should be fully cultivated, and such disjointed efforts as they had made had resulted in little beyond raising prices to the consumer by the enrichment of middlemen, who, in some instances (as in the distribution of milk) were required, under heavy penalties, to take more profit to themselves than had been the entire retail price of competitive days. Certainly, much more could have been done for the cultivation of the land, for the prosperity which it must have brought, and for the security it must have given, by the simple taxation of imported foods, had such levies been equitably calculated upon the crushing totals of direct and indirect taxation imposed upon the home producer. But equity was not even a theoretic ideal in the imposition of British taxes, expediency (real or imagined) being the only recognized deity.

These adverse circumstances of national debility and neglect bad found open expression in confused preaching of a pacifism without clear foundation either of logic or principle, and which appealed less to Christ than Mammon for the arguments on which it relied. The fact, as it certainly was, that the nation had endured the four years of a previous war with a stubborn purpose, perhaps less wavering, though less bitter, than that which had sustained, and of the other nations of Europe who had been similarly engaged, may have been an indication of other and better qualities, which might rise in recovered vigour, as they had done in earlier centuries from such decadent periods.

But the strength of this hope was lessened by the fact that, great as the British effort in that conflict, and heavy as her losses had been, she had not been required to endure any extremity of privation; and to many thousands of those who had remained at home, and whose lives therefore endured, it had been an easier and more carefree existence than they had known either afterwards or before.

To observe this is not to deny the heights of individual valour and sacrifice, or the depths of personal agony, which had been the experiences of unnumbered and nameless lives. In such issues, it was neither greater nor less than had been a score of earlier wars. But the fiction that it had been a war of exceptional average hardship by which British civilian life had been profoundly changed, may be compared to that even more baseless legend that four years of warfare had, or could have, fundamentally altered the manners, habits, or beliefs of a civilization which had survived the event with its social and industrial organizations so slightly and superficially disturbed.

Indeed, so far had been the experiences of those wartime years from laying exceptional hardships upon the homes of British industrial workers that one of the few definite differences which could be observed in the post-war years was that it had become impracticable to thrust them back to the precarious privations that they had formerly experienced. For several years they had been without anxiety as to food or clothing, and that security of life could not be withdrawn if the system of capitalistic usury which was entangled, perhaps inextricably, with the fabric of European civilization were to endure.

It is true that the peoples of Russia and Germany had been subjected to harsher tyrannies, in which not freedom of action only, but of speech also had been repressed, but there were two differences. The two countries which had now become the declared enemies of their kind were in the hands of strong rulers who themselves supplied the individuality which they denied to others; and the laws which bound them, the ideals which their leaders taught, were not of softness and comfort, not the fancied security of sheep in the butcher's field, but such as would rouse them in spirit, and harden them in body, till they should be fit to subdue the earth.

It was on a country so ill-disciplined, so ill-prepared, so weakened by self-deception and self-indulgence, a country proud, stubborn, still professing devotion to the liberty which it was less than half aware that it had already lost, a country that, for nearly a thousand years, had not bent its neck to the heel of a foreign foe, that, in the hours of a single night, this storm of invasion came.

CHAPTER XIV.

WINDLESS and clear, the cold February dawn moved over the Northern world.

In Tokyo, where the sun rose while it was still night above the vast Siberian wastes and the smaller area of Western Europe, there was no more knowledge as yet, or at least no more that was publicly announced, than that the action of Germany on the previous day in seizing Czechoslovakia had made European war a probability of the next hours—and that Japan was already arming to take her part.

With the first news of the bombing of Prague, she had commenced to mobilize her military and naval forces, as though expectant of instant attack. Yet she did not suppose that there was any present menace to her, nor could she have said who would be her friends or foes of the next day.

Not that her own policy was in doubt. It had not weakened nor swerved in its patient hate since Russia had taken the fruits of victory from her grasp thirty years before. If Russia should be engaged in the coming strife, the Japanese wolf would take the chance to fix its fangs in her weaker side. It demonstrates the silent sagacity with which the statesmen of Tokyo had watched and judged the course of European intrigue, from which they hoped to take their profit at last, that, openly as the Franco-Russian alliance was known, and closely guarded as the secret of that of Germany and Russia had been, they were doubtful now on which side of the European conflict they would be the more likely to be.

In Moscow, a people hypnotized to a belief in their own freedom by one of the bloodiest and most brutal, but possibly the most intelligent of the countless tyrannies which have cursed mankind, stirred to delirium with the thought that the hour had come when they would impose their own servitudes upon a strangely reluctant world.

They gathered in the iron cold of the winter dawn to read the proclamations already placarded on a hundred walls:

> COMRADES! The hour has come! The air-fleets of the Soviet Republics are in the skies, to bear the Torch of Freedom throughout the World.
>
> Last night, our German allies invaded England, whose air-fleets were scattered and fled, as snow flies on the wind.
>
> Your own air-fleets have crossed Europe during the early hours of the night, and are now encountered with those of France, which they will as surely destroy.
>
> Awake Russia! Awake the World! Capitalism is doomed! The Proletariat triumphs! The Hour of Deliverance is at hand!

Negligible as always upon the sea, Russia was known to have taken more readily to the air, and, largely with German engineering assistance, to have built an air-fleet which was officially admitted to consist of 3,700 planes. But the vast extent of the country, its poverty of communications, and the rigorous police control which suppressed all unauthorized publicity, and restricted the movements not only of foreign visitors but of its own citizens, whose freedom was no more than that of prisoners in a roomy jail, had rendered it a simpler matter even than it had been in Germany to conceal the actual numbers which they possessed.

As General Goering had urged the German people in 1935 to go short of butter in the cheerful knowledge that all financial resources of the country were being expended upon such raw materials as could be converted into munitions of war, so the Soviet serfs had been persuaded to work hard for poor fare and a niggardly wage that they might not fail to defend the sacred soil of Russia from its ulterior foes. And yet it would have been hard to find, within the limits of human record, two nations with less cause to dread foreign aggression of any kind than Germany and Russia had been during the three years that their whole national resources had been concentrated upon preparations for ruthless war.

Now, while the drums of dawn commenced to beat, and the Russian armies to gather their sluggish, enormous strength, their battle-planes from a hundred aerodromes, secret or known, still rose and pursued the night.

Dawn rose on Berlin. It looked on crowded streets delirious with the news that a night had brought. The city had gone to rest half exultant with the knowledge that Czechoslovakia had been seized in a single day, half apprehensive of retribution which might descend as swiftly upon itself from an outraged world. Outside the inner, most secret Government circles, there were few who guessed that Russia was less than foe, or, at best, a most doubtful friend: few who would have been astonished to hear the falling of Russian, Polish, or Yugoslavian bombs upon their roofs before morning came.

They woke to the sight of flaming placards that told a most different tale. "GERMANY," said one, "UPON THE ROOF OF THE WORLD." "LONDON IN FLAMES" was another's boast. "GERMAN AIRPLANES CAPTURE ENGLAND," the even more startling claim of the news-sheet which, as having the reputation of being under direct Government control, spoke with the greatest authority of all. News of the night's events on the frontiers of France was given in less decided words, whether because they had so far been less conclusive in their results, or that they had commenced at a later hour, or merely because it was intended to direct the attention of the German public to the feats of their own arms, rather than to those of their unexpected allies.

But the High Command in Berlin, strained with excitement and lack of sleep, had neither leisure to talk and cheer nor did they regard the war as already won.

Time—time, they knew, was still the priceless factor of which so much was needed; so little theirs, if they were to overawe the world to submission before its scattered counsels could confer and a score of smaller states take courage to raise their heads. The mistake of the Marne must not be repeated in this battle along the skies which had swept out to a wider front.

The operations of the night had been carried out according to plan, and their success might be considered enough to stun the world with its morning news, as in fact it did.

The attack upon the English Midlands had drawn the defending fleets from the London area, as it had been intended to do, and the second German air-fleet had moved to the destruction of London at a late hour, as had been designed, so soon as the Russian approach rendered it safe for it to be withdrawn from the frontiers of France. So far, so good. And if the Russian fleets had not found it a simple matter, after their long flight, to overcome the air-fleets and mobile batteries which were the protection of Northern France—well, it had not been expected that they would find them an easy prey. They would have done their part if they had exhausted France's defence, so that triumph would be in sight when they should be reinforced during the day.

Yet there were two points on which the German strategists were not wholly pleased. The attack on the English Midlands had been a very partial success, with an enormous wastage of ammunition dropped on barren moors and deserted fields; and the losses of planes and pilots had been much heavier than they had calculated that the operations of the night would require.

The reasons for these qualifications of success lay both in the strategy and tactics of the English defence, which had been prepared by men who had faced the risk which the politicians would not admit, that they might have to encounter outnumbering foes.

The topography of the Midland counties, and, in particular, the absence of any river of conspicuous character or exceptional breadth, before the curve of the Severn and the great estuary of the Bristol Channel came into view, rendered it particularly difficult for airplanes operating at a high altitude to judge their positions with accuracy, and there had been some extraordinary discrepancies, twenty years before, between the areas on which raiding Zeppelins would report that they had dropped their bombs, and those on which they had actually fallen; although there had been, at that time, no attempt to mislead them, beyond darkening, as far as possible, the whole country over which they flew.

Now a fleet which was far better equipped with accurate instruments both to guide its course and to ascertain its position at any time, but flying far more rapidly and at higher altitudes than its predecessors had done, had found itself confused and baffled by elaborate simulation a partial blackenings; and the simple device of spreading elaborate smoke-screens over the four square miles of Packington Park in Warwickshire, and over Sutton Park somewhat farther north, with judicious hints of blanketed lights in the surrounding areas, had caused a concentration of bombs to be poured on these barren places, which had been continued at Packington with augmented zeal when its hundreds of ancient oaks burst into a sea of flame, which shone through the heavy smoke-screen that the explosions had already done much to break.

The inhabitants had, of course, been evacuated from areas which had been designed to attract the enemy's bombs, but in fact the events of the night had demonstrated how little reason there was, under any circumstances, to regard high-explosive bombing from high altitudes seriously as a menace to the existence of a civilian population sufficiently scattered, either by night or day.

Casualties there were, but their numbers, however distressing to those nearly concerned, were negligible in comparison with the number and capacity of the bombs which had descended during the night. The deadliness of the bombing-plane as a war weapon when using incendiary or high explosive bombs lay less in its menace to human life which should have sufficient warning to scatter about than in its capacity for destroying material of immovable kinds. The war factory, the railway junction, the munitions dump, the petrol reservoir, if they had escaped during the night, would be more vulnerable when the morning came.

Apart from the fact that the destruction wrought during the night in the Midland area had been inadequate for the huge expenditure of ammunition which it had required, the lesson of the night's fighting had been that the air is a scene of combat in which the losses both of men and material must be very high whenever two fleets should close in a stubborn strife.

This had not been apparent beyond previous anticipation in the clash which had taken place over the East Anglian country, and became known as the First Battle of Norwich, for here the outnumbered English fleet had been so manœuvred as to keep at some distance from, and retire before, the German advance, with particular caution that it should not be surrounded and subjected to annihilating attack. It had sought to inflict the maximum loss upon the crowding phalanxes of its foes, while retreating before them, and at last withdrawing as a defeated force, leading the German fleet in a direction that it was not unwilling for it to take. The whole action had been swift and short, as must ever be in the light clement of the air, but it had been relatively prolonged, as it had been indecisive in its result.

But in the fighting above the Thames which had taken place at a later hour, when the sole fleet remaining for the defence of the capital city consisted of between two and three hundred planes, and these, assisted by numerous anti-aircraft batteries, about fifty of the new untested robot planes, and a few guns from the shipping that lay in the estuary of the Thames, had had orders to resist to the last, although they had been finally overwhelmed by the severity of the attack which had been made upon them, and had fallen in fractured or flaming wreckage upon the roofs of the city they could not save; yet had done such damage before they fell, and so much more had been inflicted by the fire of the anti-aircraft guns, which had been more difficult to subdue, that as the depleted fleets of the German night-bombers returned to reload with fresh munitions of death, the High Command, becoming acquainted with the losses that had been sustained both of these and their fighting planes, must turn to calculations of how long such reductions could be endured, how many cities would be destroyed even by the battle-fleets, enormous and secret, that they controlled, before they would be exhausted by the costs of their own success. But London was destroyed—if the reports of these damaged fleets were no less than true and it should be a lesson to teach the world who its masters were. And if there were those in the world who were still of a stubborn mood—well, there were other modes of attack which were yet untried, but which it would become their plain duty to use, for there must be no scruple to hold them back from the destiny which was theirs that German culture should rule the world.

The light of dawn, the first faint light, moved on, and came to the narrow sea, and beyond was met by a redder and fiercer glare than that with which it chased the heels of the flying dark. For it was true that London burned in the night. Along the banks of the Lower

Thames, and widening, north and south, as the great city spread westward its hundred square miles of crowded buildings and teeming life, there was the glare of a conflagration such as the earth may not have known before, and a pillar of smoke rose, gigantic in the still air, and spread gently, slowly, southward, covering the Surrey hills and the fields of Kent with a smokescreen wider and denser far than any that could have been self-contrived for their own disguise.

The city burned. Sown with tens of thousands of incendiary bombs, its wharves and warehouses, piled and stuffed with merchandise of inflammable kinds, had been ignited beyond control. There were mile-wide areas within which the heat had become too great for a man to face it and live.

But farther west there were no more than sporadic patches of fire, around which men toiled in heroic effort to subdue that which had spawned too freely to be driven out by any effort of human hands.

But not all men were constant to fight the flames. Many of those who still lived, and who had not fled at an earlier hour, had no present thought except to escape with such property of their own, or such loot, as they were able to bear away.

A thousand streets were congested with the outflow of loaded lorry and cart and car, with here and there an empty one that, bent on some human or material rescue, strove vainly to make headway against the flood. The railway lines, so much and so far as they were still able to work within the furnace of heat and fire, and were still intact, strove in the same desperate, futile haste to save what could not be one ten-thousandth part of the wealth which had been there when the evening fell. St. Pancras, when morning came, was a ruin of blackened walls and glowing ashes that turned to grey, but at Euston there was still a platform that could be used, and a line of uninjured rails, and from Paddington the loaded freight trains were pulling out, while firemen fought to beat back the flames of the burning sheds.

War, the supreme test, the ultimate scales of God, brought out all that is heroic and all that is base in man, as it is ever potent to do. There were some who thought of no more than their own lives and their own loot; some who left the weak and wounded to die, though they were of their closest kin; and some who died as they fought to rescue the sick from their falling hospital walls.

There was a builder who stood on the crest of the Surrey hills, watching the dull-red smoke of the blazing city ascend and move towards him, an enormous covering cloud, and underneath the appalled horror that stunned his mind, a thought stirred, secret and small, like a tiny poisonous snake where the grass is deep, which gave him comfort in what he saw. He supposed there must be one certainty amid all the doubts of what would be in the coming days. The slump in building was over now. The slump which had followed the reckless insanity of overbuilding of 1935-36, and which had brought most of his fellow-speculators to ruin, and loaded him with a complication of loans and mortgages which had become every month more difficult to sustain—all that would be over now!

The shoddy bungalow with its low mean rooms, and its ampler temple to the Deity of the Day—the huge blocks of half-empty flats, built for a generation which had never learnt what a home should be, and which aped the congestion of city life without the excuse which compulsion gives—he supposed that he would be able to raise their rents, even beyond the peak of his early dreams, that he would be able to choose his tenants now from applicants ten times too numerous for all the buildings which covered the Surrey hills like an outbreak of spotted plague. He would no longer be obliged to accept with gratitude even families with numerous unsanitary children, as he had lately been reduced to do. He was subconscious that there would be for him (as he supposed) compensation for the catastrophe which had overwhelmed a city which had not fallen to foreign foes for nearly a thousand years—not since Duke William's horsemen had splashed through the Walling Ford, and swung round to interpose between London's weaker wall and any rescue that might have come from the sluggard North.

It was at about this time that a message was broadcast from the Western wireless station, which was still working, intermittently audible:

> "Attention, all listeners! The British Government which has removed from London to a place of greater security, announces to its own people, and all the world that this country, having been subjected to sudden and unprovoked attack, entailing a loss of life and property beyond present computation, is inflexibly resolved to resist to the last extremity, for the freedom of the British race and the future peace of the world.
>
> "In announcing this decision, your Government is confident that it speaks for all men of British blood, both here and beyond the seas. Attempts to confuse counsel and weaken resistance by enemy

propaganda will doubtless be made, and your King and Government are well assured that they will be treated as they deserve.

"From the time of the circulation of this announcement, all Britain is placed under martial law, and all citizens will obey all orders or requisitions of military or naval authorities which they may receive.

"All citizens of military age, and all others of whatever age or sex who may wear the sign of a white linen cross of not less than four inches breadth upon the upper right arm, are hereby enlisted in the military forces of the Crown, and are entitled thereby to the immunities and privileges which the usage of civilized warfare provides.

"All officers of His Majesty's forces of land, sea, or air, who, owing in the exigencies and extent of the war may be unable to establish contact with their superiors, will act on the general orders they hereby receive to inflict, at their own discretion, the utmost damage upon the invading enemy wherever he may be found.

"Private ownership in the necessities of life, or the munitions of war, is entirely suspended, and all patriotic citizens are required to produce and conserve them to the utmost of their capacity, and to apply or surrender them as they may be required for the general good, regarding themselves as one household to resist the attack of a common foe."

The proclamation was repeated more slowly, and in somewhat briefer wording, with a request that printers throughout the land would take it down, and publish it by placards that all could read.

CHAPTER XV.

THE winter dawn was still dim when Eustace Ashfield, having returned Mrs. Rowntree safely to her uninjured home and made his way to the works where his own duty lay, heard the proclamation of the English Government, and had occasion to wonder, as did many others in the Midland city, whether there would be much similarity between the financial experiences of the last war and that which had so abruptly broken upon the world. There was occasion to wonder also whether there would be any similarity between the course and duration of the wars themselves, the methods which they would pursue, or the decisive factors determining their results.

He might wonder also of what avail would be the belated activity which he was now organizing for the production of gas-masks which, if they were worth making at all, should have been prepared in advance and not in the midst of the attack they were meant to meet; might wonder from where his delivery instructions were likely to come, or whether any were now alive who would be aware that the order had been placed with him.

For he had learnt already from the *Birmingham Post*, the stolidity of which had refused to be stirred to excessive depth of headline, or other manifestation of journalistic hysteria, even by the events of the night, that London had. been largely destroyed, and that the saving of any part of it from the spreading flames was no more than a doubtful chance. The newspaper, the bulk of its material having been collected during the previous evening, and its production continued in a routine which had remained unshaken by surrounding circumstance, presented its ordinary appearance, indicating something of that stubborn, unimaginative quality in the composite British character which is so difficult to stampede, so obstinate to endure.

It was in the same spirit of stubborn refusal to be disturbed from that which he undertook that Eustace issued orders by which his machines started to life, and the halting, difficult processes of mass-production of an article for which the previous tool-making had been little more than experimental was commenced. But even those of fainter heart or more vivid fears might find some indication that the last chapter of the war was unwritten from a brief announcement in the *Post*'s stop-press column:

> At 11:15 P.M. (New York time) the United States Government issued mobilization orders.

It was profoundly significant of the moral aspects and of the probable consequences of the disturbance of Europe's peace, that few, if any, who read that news in any part of the world had a moment's doubt as to the side on which the great American republic would enter the war if the order which she had issued should prove to be of more than a precautionary character.

It was immediately after the General Proclamation of the British Government that the bulletin which has been already given was broadcast concerning the destruction of the squadron of bombing-planes which Imogen had been commissioned to join. To Eustace Ashfield it was news which, in one stunning instant, swept hope away with a finality that he could not doubt. He knew that war in the air is unlike any fighting upon the land, in which the wounded, the prisoners, and those who make good retreat, will almost always far outnumber the dead. And when planes join battle in darkness over the sea—

He knew also, though he was without specialized knowledge of aviation, that the squadron which she had joined consisted of obsolescent biplanes which might have a range of a thousand miles, as their makers had claimed, but with a speed of little more than a hundred an hour at a fair height, slow and cumbrous in manœuvre, and so crude in construction that pilot and gunner alike lacked even the protection of transparent hoods, and must fly and fight exposed to all the severities of the wintry air, clumsily goggled and wrapped and masked to endure its gales.

He knew that a fleet of Germany's fighting planes, three times as swift, better armoured and better armed, would chase them and shoot them down as easily as a machine-gun section would butcher a herd of cattle.

He went on with the work that he had to do in a dull way, but with the feeling that the war had ended for him as completely as for those bomb-shattered, flame-scarred bodies that littered the furnace of London streets.

The next announcement, which to most hearers was of a better kind (though it might be said that the last had been good enough for those who had none kindred or loved concerned), he heard with un-hearing ears, as he heard others, evil and good, that came through, as the hours passed; and the events of a crowded drama of air and land and sea, confusing, contradictory, or inexplicable as they often were, came to the knowledge of the broadcasting station, and were distributed as far as a watchful censorship might allow.

This incident which was next announced was one of those which are beyond forecast, and often emerge, to confuse the issues of ordered strategy from the cross-chances of war.

There was a mechanized territorial unit which, unlike most of its kind, had been fully equipped with all its technical requirements and with weapons of offence of the most modern descriptions. It had received these surprising favours from a War Office which appeared to consider the average Territorial sufficiently intelligent to learn all he needed to know from dummies and drawing-boards, and that the next war would commence (if ever) in a sufficiently leisurely manner to allow equipment to be afterwards distributed, even if its manufacture should not also be necessary; and these favours were understood to be in recognition of the exceptional keenness which the unit had displayed.

It included a mobile anti-aircraft section, which, under the revised 1937 organization, consisted of five rapid-firing guns and twelve of the new anti-aircraft rifles of the Lee-Enfield pattern, with seventeen-foot barrels, eight thirty-nine-oz. cartridges in their magazines, and a range of 20,000 feet.

This battery, which had been stationed in the neighbourhood of Kettering, under the command of Major A. G. Aitken, received orders to move southward to Dunstable, which were countermanded before its arrival by a later instruction to return northward upon the Coventry Road, and which was again reversed by an urgent call to the defence of London, so that it spent the night, like a cat chasing its tail, with no more than a single sight of the German air-fleets crossing the lower stars of the northern sky, and hearing no more than the distant horizon sound of their bursting bombs.

Finally, and at a time when it had appeared certain to Major Aitken that the utmost expedition that he could use would not enable him to reach the London area in time to intercept the return of the fast-flying German bombers, he had picked up a general order which gave all anti-aircraft arms a discretionary power to operate against the enemy wherever it should appear that most damage could be inflicted upon them.

Having this freedom of action, Major Aitken had decided that the farther east he should move before daylight came, the more probable it would be that he would be able to intercept some of the German bombers on their return, or, if he should meet with any which might be coming with further cargoes of death, the less opportunity of doing damage they would have had. He considered with equal soundness that they would be most likely to choose a line of return where they would least expect such a battery as his to be stationed, and these conclusions led him to turn almost directly eastward from the neighbourhood of Northampton where he then was, aiming to take cover in the fen district of Ely, or about Newmarket Heath, before morning should come.

As the first faint light of the winter dawn moved in the eastern sky he had come to a little hill about a mile from Balsham in Cambridgeshire having a rounded summit, crowned with a small wood of straight-standing pines, sufficient to provide the cover he sought, but which were not too closely grown to allow some freedom of sight to those who might lurk beneath them.

He had just stationed his artillery, and given orders for a good look-out to be kept on all sides while breakfast was served in such comfort as would be possible in the freezing dawn without the lighting of fires, which he would not allow, when there came the sound of the approach of a great fleet from the west which could be heard before it was visible in the twilight sky.

It came on a front of eight miles, or perhaps more, the last of the fleets of the night-bombers that had circled over the Midland counties during the night, and inflicted havoc enough, though far less than they had expected to do. They had suffered little, the losses of the night being mainly among the bombers that had first arrived, and the battle-planes that had preceded them and guarded their flanks.

Now they returned with some hundreds of battle-planes leading their way, and shepherding either side, as though a flight of wasps should array themselves to protect a swarm of more numerous bees, heavier, slower, but not themselves unable to use their stings.

Their holds were empty of bombs; their petrol-tanks had become light. They flew swiftly and at some height, but not so high as it would have been most prudent to do, for they thought the part of the country over which they passed to be bare of defence, and their first object was speed in their return to the depots where they would be loaded again.

Major Aitken watched them advance. Having ordered his men to their stations, he bid them reserve fire till there should be a signal shot from the rifle he himself controlled, and after that they were to fire at the best target they saw, so long as their lives endured, and any German plane remained within range.

They waited silently as the foreguard of fighting planes passed overhead, and longer yet till the height of sky from west to east was darkened as though a flight of wild fowl covered it beyond count in the growing light.

The *Campaspe*, going down to her cold grave in the winter sea, had no cause to complain of the target on which she had spent her shells, but she had fired from a swaying deck at far shadows that crossed the stars. The riflemen of Major Aitken's battery, lying at ease, each on his small platform, raised above the butt of the weapon, which had an artificial shoulder of leather to take its recoil, could sight their prey from the firm ground in sufficient light, and they did not miss.

Their sudden disastrous volleys broke into the ordered columns of flight from which units began to fall, the giant bombers looking no larger than wild birds winged as they turned and sank through the heights of air, and then increasing, enormous, menacing, as they rushed downward upon the trees.

There was none that fell on the little wood, neither the rifles nor the heavier artillery being pointed directly upward, but the next minutes saw the fields that sloped gently downward on each side of the wooded knoll littered with the huge wreckage of dismembered, shattered, or blazing planes.

Overhead, the regular lines of flight became confused, congested, as those that followed swiftly into the circle of death, flying as they were at over three hundred miles an hour, parted somewhat to left and right, and aimed at the same time to plane steeply upward to safer heights. Their tired pilots, who had been flying homeward with the skill of practice rather than present alertness of mind, were not all equal to secure their own safety from collision in the sudden flurry that broke their midst.

With their bomb-chambers emptied now, they were as impotent to reply as if they had been no more than columns of flying duck. It was in speed alone that their safety lay, and, filling the sky as they did, it was little less than two minutes before the last crippled plane, with one engine stilled, and a leaking tank, struggled out of the four-mile range of the deadly rifles below.

By that time not less than five hundred explosive shells and cartridges had been aimed with deadly deliberation into the crowded columns of flight, and though little more than one in ten had done fatal harm, yet there was a total of nearly sixty bombers that lay flaming or shattered wrecks within eight square miles of Balsham and Linton fields.

In assessing the military significance of this incident, it must be observed that every circumstance combined to favour the ambushed battery. The fleet of the German night-bombers came directly overhead, and flying much lower than they would have done had they been suspicious of danger lurking below. Their holds were empty of bombs, so that the riflemen not only remained unsilenced, but were able to direct their fire with the coolness which security gives. The pilots, being tired from a long and nerve-straining flight, may not have been as instant or intelligent in their reactions as would have been the case under more favourable circumstances. The skies had been clear of cloud, giving the air-fleet no cover into which it could make speedy retreat.

But when the event has been discounted by these and other considerations which fall into the same scale, it remains a convincing argument that St Paul's Cathedral might have been standing today; that the British Museum might have been something better than a ruined heap into which men would dig for such treasures of art, scorched or charred, as survived the destructions of fall and fire; that the Abbey might not have sustained the loss of its northern wall; that the vast storage of wealth that lay in the warehouses of the Thames, and the contents of fifty thousand humble homes that were blown apart, or swept through by the hot tempest of fire, might have stood when peace came again to a ruined world, had England spent for her own defence from her stored surplus of idle wealth with but half the freedom with which she lavished fantastic funds on petrol, garage, and road, on compensation for deaths and wounds, and on five million cars which would be on the scrap-heaps of ten years hence.

Major Aitken, having ordered that his men should have a quick meal, which they may be said to have earned, considered what he should do. It was easy to think that the place in which he now was would not long be safe for him if the German air-fleets had won control of the skies, as he had some cause to believe. He supposed that he might soon see the high approach of such bombers as would still be fecund to drop eggs of death on the little wood, or of fighting planes, low-swooping and swallow-swift, such as would rake it with deadly hail, to be the ending of him and his, even though he might bring some of them down to an equal fate.

But he was not therefore instantly sure that he should withdraw. He weighed, in a cool mind, his battery's loss against that it would be likely to cause under such circumstances of attack, and resolved that he could use it to better ends. "He who fights and runs away," he said cheerfully to his next in command, who proved to be of the same opinion.

He retired on his Kettering base, considering that, though his ammunition was still unexhausted, there would be some gain in replacing that which had been so fruitfully fired, and that it was there that it could most surely be done. If the Germans had won the skies, as he had enough reason to fear, he could do them more harm by a second judicious ambush, cunningly laid, than by exposing himself on the open road. He was of good courage, as he had shown, but he knew that it is to kill, and not to be killed, that is the successful business of war, which all brave men are not equal to learn. For a dead man is of no avail, and a wounded one may be worse than that.

He sought, therefore, to make speedy retreat, and his glance searched the skies, in which cloud rose from the south and west, rather to see what there might be time to avoid than as one seeking a further prey. There was once only that he had sight of an enemy plane, and that was one of the scouting type, such as were swiftest of all, and that crossed before him too small and distant a mark, and too quickly gone, for his riflemen to get their weapons to work.

He was vexed at this, when he came to the village over which he had seen it fly, for it had scattered leaflets along the air, printed in English, though it could be seen that they had come from a foreign press. They said:

> People of England!
> Germany fulfils her destiny!
> Thrones and dominions fall!
> Face realities, and accept the peace which may yet be yours.
> Cherish illusions, and die.
> The time has come when the German spirit will rise, and its culture will rule the world.
> Submit, and live.
> Resist, and your end is sure.

Major Aitken read this, and reflected that the proclamation showed little knowledge of English character. It seemed to imply a boast which was at least made somewhat soon, and on which his own battery had been having something to say, even while it was being scattered about. He said aloud that there was a proverb that the longest laughter comes at the last.

Yet as he spoke, he had a cold doubt that the proclamation would not have been worded in such a way had not those who sent it out felt very sure of themselves, and of their power to possess the world, and then, in the next instant, rebuked himself as having been already influenced by that which he contemned as ill-worded to frighten men of his English blood.

"It is deeds," he said, "not words, that will win this war." He spoke as one who would convince himself by making assertion aloud. Yet he saw that words had their power too. And as he thought he turned over the sheet, and observed that the frugal German mind had not been content to send it out with a bare back, but that there was more there in a smaller type.

"These," he said, "should be gathered and burned. They are foolish lies. Those who are confident in themselves are less quick to boast." He had halted his march to see what the papers were, and was now in the midst of a little crowd that had gathered in the village street, less concerned to read than to see the strange arms that his lorries bore, and the men he led.

Now the soldiers jumped down from their seats at his order and mixed with the civilian crowd, gathering up the scattered sheets to be burned, and as they did so they told of the German bombers that they had brought to ground. Major Aitken did not doubt that they would, and thought it as good a reply to the German threats as the village would be likely to hear. So it was; and it had its natural effect, though most of those who listened thought that the soldiers bragged, leaving the truth as far behind as will a fisherman's tale.

And while they mixed together and talked, he read that which was on the back of the sheet, liking it less than that he had seen before:

> WARNING to all men of Nordic race and of goodwill to the German Reich.
>
> Tomorrow, if there be any part of the British Isles which has not ceased to resist, it is there that Germany will REVEAL HER POWER.
>
> Before doing this, centres of safety will be announced where those who will may swear obedience and faith to the German Reich, and they, and those dependants that they may bring, will be secure from the FREEZING DEATH, which will spare neither man nor beast, neither woman nor child, in the path it takes, destroying all foolish men, and those of a stubborn will. MERCY WARNS ONCE BUT NO MORE.

He read this twice over with care, before throwing it to the wet street, which had ceased to freeze under the pale rays of the rising sun and a temperate southwest wind, and trod it down with a gesture of contempt, which was for others to see. He gave no sign of a cold doubt which had crossed his mind, turning into the bitter hate which is the offspring of fear. He recovered the cool, confident poise he had known before with the thought: "They may win England or not. It will soon be seen. But when they boast they will rule the world—well, it is a large place, and it may not be easy to do. And even England will have some strength which is scattered abroad, so that it will not be spent or won on the first day. And she has kinsmen in distant lands."

CHAPTER XVI.

THE dawn moved on, crossing the Irish Sea. It parted a clouding sky to shine faintly into the Dublin room, spacious and high, where the head of the Free State Government sat, as he had done through the fearful night, and where none thought to switch off the electric bulbs as the daylight came.

Two months before, a German Envoy had been received in Dublin with no evident purpose except to demonstrate the contempt of the Irish Government for the terms of the treaty on which its security depended, and its rights were based, and this violation of contract, wanton as it had appeared, had been accepted in London without public official protest, whatever representations may have been privately made.

But three weeks ago the peculiarly Irish determination of the Dublin Government to retain the advantages of membership of the British Commonwealth, while rejecting its logical implications and denying its responsibilities, had been roused to frenzies of excited protest by the terms of a Bill which had been introduced into the House of Commons, the effect of which would be to make aliens throughout Great Britain and her colonial empire of all who claimed citizenship of the Irish Free State, so long as her treaty obligations were neither observed, nor modified by mutual negotiation and consent.

Now Dr. Baumer, the German Envoy whose appointment had been the immediate cause of this somewhat belated bill, and whose clothes, like those of the Irish President, had not left his back since the previous day, had come at his own request to receive congratulations upon the success of the German arms as they appeared from the news that the night had brought, and to give guidance to the head of this liberated State, as the occasion obviously required.

The President was an appalled man, his feelings being like to those of the fabled dotard who protested desire for death, and found the arch-enemy at his side with a ready scythe, and with a purpose to grant his prayer. He had discretion to remain silent at first, letting Dr. Baumer expose his mind.

He was informed that the blight of half a millennium of oppression would be lifted at last, and that Ireland would rest secure in the future days beneath the shadow of German power. For this happy consummation of liberty, there would be a price to pay, as, indeed, most things require.

Ireland should be prompt to cleanse herself of the superstition of Christianity, unworthy of men of a Nordic race, as Germany, with some generosity of interpretation, would acknowledge the Southern Irish to be. The President might prefer to institute this religious purgation at once, so that it would be evident that it was an act of Ireland's own volition, in the first moment when freedom came, rather than under compulsion of German will, as it must otherwise be; for the President would not suppose that Germany would tolerate the practice of Christian superstitions in any land that accepted her Führer for guide and lord.

He would also require that the Free State Army should give any assistance that might be required for the occupation of the sea-bases that were still in English control, and for the subjection of Northern Ireland should there be resistance to German occupation there.

As present indications were that there might be considerable fighting on land and sea before a settled peace and good government should be imposed on the world, and as it was Germany's will that this strife should be quickly done—an end which could be most surely gained by using her utmost strength without initial delay—it was proposed to open recruiting stations throughout Southern Ireland where men could be enrolled for the German Army, and those so enlisting would have advantages over any whom it might be necessary to conscript later in the week.

To assist the President in such hurried hours, he said courteously, he had had orders already drawn up for his signature, to operate these immediate necessities. He had proclamations already drafted—he drew the documents out as he spoke—which he would thank the President to sign, and to have issued at once through the usual channels.

"We recognize the loyalties which you have shown," he said in conclusion, "through years during which we have not been able to give you the assistance which we should have wished to do, and it is our present purpose to do nothing except in your name, so long as you remain loyal to us, as we do not question that you will be."

The President was singularly destitute of mental agility. His mind may be appositely compared to a boxer whose feet are clamped to the boards. He may neither follow nor turn. Neither may he retreat, even though his safety require. But he may deal a hard blow at whoever may come within the swing of his arm, and he may have an honest belief that those who can sidestep are of a lower order than he.

But obtuse and inductile as he might be, he was yet annoyed at the greater density of the man who faced him now with these smoothly confident words, and of those whose instructions supposed that Southern Ireland would cast her British freedom away to become the lackey of German power; or that she could be indifferent to the fortunes and lives of her kinsmen in British lands, actually more numerous than those who still dwelt on their native soil.

Southern Ireland was of the Catholic Faith. She had no sympathy with the crude paganism, sinister if not childish, which Germany had professed to an amused or indifferent world. It was not likely that her religion would be changed at a German's word. She had little sympathy with German culture, no kinship with German blood. Berlin had been invited to send an envoy to Dublin with no larger purpose than to flout the British Government at a time when it was busy in other ways. Irishmen must quarrel, as the world knows, if they are to have any comfort in life. Has it not been truly written of them that they are:

> The men that God made mad.
> For all their wars are merry,
> And all their songs are sad?

How could they quarrel with other nations while they lay within the compass of England's peace? If she were frugal of wars to enlist their mirth, what remained but that they must quarrel always with her?

The Southern Ireland of those days may be compared to a shrew who will curse her husband to all the world. But a bully who judges therefrom that she will leave him, to be beaten to humbler ways, may find that he have made no more than a bad guess.

Dr. Baumer finished the proposals he had been instructed to make, and the President was not quick to reply. He had no will to assent, but some doubt of the position in which Ireland might stand on the next day. Yet he considered with some relief that if Germany, even with Russia to aid, were taking on the whole world for the coming bout, as she appeared willing to do, her air-fleets, secret and immense though they might be, would have calls upon them too numerous and too urgent for any leisure in which to drop bombs on the Dublin streets.

He saw it also as a wanton folly which even she might hesitate to commit. He thought with some increase of courage of that mobilization order which had stirred the United States during the night, of which he had heard in the last hour. He could no more than guess what its full significance might be, but he knew how large a proportion of American citizens are of Irish descent, and that their political power is far greater even than those numbers could justly claim.

If the United States were in a mood to watch the strife for a time, standing by with a bare sword, it might well be that a threat to Dublin would bring her hustling into the fray. Or if she were coming with no clearer call than the sight of a mad dog breaking loose to run across the face of the globe—well, all the more was it true that Germany would have no breath to spare from the wrestling-match to which she had called the world. There must be a hundred cities in greater peril than any in which Dublin would be likely to lie.

Magnifying his own part in the drama in which he found himself cast to play, as did many in East and West as morning moved over the world, he thought of New York again, and that the destiny of mankind might hang on the words that he paused to speak.

Dr. Baumer observed his silence, and drew conclusions which were partly correct. He did not doubt that the President would give way, for (he thought) what else has he left to do, having made England his foe? "But," he thought, "the man sulks. Who does he think that he is? Does he think to sit with us in equal seats? Are there to be two Führers in Europe now? The man is crazed with his foolish dreams. He must be removed on a near day, and by such a mode that he will not vex us again."

He thought it well to give the screw a turn more, though it was still done with suave words, and with lips that smiled: "As we do not know what measure of resistance there may be, either from Belfast or Cobh, and as it may be necessary to land German troops, either by water or air, I suggest that you should appoint an officer of sufficient rank, whose name I will supply in the next hour, so that he may take general control. You will agree that it would not be well that such operations should be under dual commands."

The President checked words which he had become ready to speak, and answered this point alone. "You mean," he asked, "that our Irish troops should be under German command?"

"It is a point," the Envoy replied firmly, though still in a courteous tone, "on which I feel bound to insist. For we have officers of higher rank than your own, and of better training in the methods of modern war."

"You are aware that you ask much—and that you assume more?"

"I do not assume. I observe evident fact, as I trust that you also will be equal to do. For those who fail in that will be very likely to fall in the coming days, as you will have wit to see."

"I am to take that as a threat?"

"Not at all. We would have your help, if you will see facts as they are."

The reply which the President would have made can be only guessed, for they were interrupted by his secretary's entrance. He had a typed sheet in his hand, which shook slightly, showing the nervous tension which he endured. "Pardon, Excellency," he said, "but there is that here which you should see. Am I to let it out to the press, or shall I wait till it be confirmed?"

The President took the sheet, which was a record of the news of the last fifteen minutes only, for it was a day on which it came fast.

His eye ran rapidly down the page, digesting each item in turn, and stopped at that to which his attention had been directed. He read:

> It is reported via Madrid, on the authority of the Argus International News Agency, that a combined squadron of Russian and German bombers flew over Rome at an early hour this morning, and descended to drop a large number of bombs upon St. Peter's Cathedral and the Vatican Palace, both of which are in flames. The Pope and a large number of Cardinals and other dignitaries of the Church are missing, and are believed to have perished. Having completed the destruction of the Papal City, the squadron left without inflicting any further damage, and without encountering resistance from the forces of the Italian Government. The event appears to be of political rather than military importance, signifying the extinction of Christianity by the forces of rationalism which aim to control the world.

"There are items here," the President said, making no effort to read beyond that, "which may be of some interest to you, if you have not heard them before you came. There is a report that Toulouse was heavily bombed at a late hour of the night. You will know better than I if there be any special meaning in that. And it is said that your army has entered France, and is making ground between

Hüningen and Sedan. There is also news that Yugoslavia, when it heard a report that France was attacked, did not stand on its defence, but was instant to take the air. It appears that it attempted to reach Berlin by a surprise attack in the night, but was intercepted while some distance to the east of that city, where there was a battle with heavy losses on either side, but with the result that the remnant of the Yugoslavian fleet has retired or been put to flight. That is the tale as it is said to have come through Switzerland from Berlin."

"It is likely enough," Dr. Baumer answered easily. "Yugoslavia would have been dealt with in due and orderly course, but I suppose that our fleets were largely engaged elsewhere during the night. It seems that her airmen must have been somewhat hurried to die. But there is something else, which you regard as of more importance than that?"

"There is a report, which I will not lightly believe, that the Vatican has been bombed, and that the Pope is missing or dead."

The statement did not disturb Dr. Baumer's serenity, but he looked interested, and not as one who hears that which he knew before. He said: "Well, it has a probable sound. And, if it be true, you must agree that our High Command are efficient in what they do. For if you cast off the head, the body will but flop about in a blind way, and will soon be stilled. Christianity has been finished for fifty years, if not more. Its trouble is that it does not know it is dead."

The President made no answer to that. He turned to his secretary to say: "Davitt, before you came in, His Excellency was explaining that London burns, and that we should thank his country for that. I would have you say what you think."

Mr. Davitt stared at the German Envoy. The Southern Irishman may be shiftless, and hard to bind, but neither friend nor foe has said that his wits are few. He thought: "Does the slow-brained hog—?" He said aloud: "Perhaps they will burn Liverpool next, and ask us to thank them more."

Dr. Baumer took this literally. He considered that Liverpool is the nearer to Dublin, and that when the Irishman visualized the hated Saxon oppression, it was that city that might first come to his mind.

"If England be slow to yield," he said, "I suppose that that may be by tomorrow noon." But as he spoke, being something more than a fool, he sensed the hostility in the eyes of the two men that were fixed upon him, and it bewildered his mind.

He had been prepared for some reluctance, even some obstinacy of resistance to the instructions by which Germany proposed to take control of the Irish State, though he had supposed that firmness and reason would bear them down. But that Irishmen should resent the fall of the Power against which their clamours had deafened the ears of the world...!

The President said his bewilderment and contempt gave him confidence in defying the menace which lay behind the smooth-spoken, insolent requisitions he had heard.

"Tell him, Davitt," he said. "Don't mind me. Let yourself go."

Mr. Davitt needed no second word. The astonished German heard how he, and how his country, appeared in the eyes of all decent men. The restraints of diplomatic language were forgotten in many of the chancelleries and legations of Europe during the sixth day of February, 1938, but in Dublin they had been little studied, and there was no bondage of traditional usage to be broken through. Tim Davitt let himself go.

Dr. Baumer heard that the planet stank with his country's crime, but that its folly outweighed its sins. England did not wholly escape, for when Germany had been on her back, the English (the doddering fools!) "Had pulled you up, and helped you to dust your coat." It appeared that it was England's weakness that she was unable to hate in a lasting way, or to understand that there could be others who hated her. And it was by that fault that London burned at this hour, with the loss, it was a sure guess, of thousands of Irish lives, and of property that was Irish-owned which might run to millions of pounds, and on which the insurances (it was as safe a guess as the last) would be devilish hard to get. *Thank them* for that treacherous, unprovoked attack in the midnight dark—and his own cousin in the London Rifle Brigade, and might be dead at this hour!

Mr. Davitt finished at last, having said much more than need be recalled, and the dignity remained with the duller man. Dr. Baumer said only that he would advise his Government of the opinions which he had heard. He rose to go.

The President remained seated, and did not respond to the formality of an offered hand. He said: "I will hold back the news of what is said to have happened in Rome for the next half-hour, which will give you time to clear out, if you know how or where you can safely go. I cannot promise your life in this city for a longer time. For when tempers rise, a shot is soon out of an Irish gun."

Dr. Baumer made no reply. He muttered "swine-hounds" (which is supposed to be a sensible word in the German tongue) as he went down the stairs, for which he had some excuse.

He found the street to be filled with a restless, murmuring crowd, from whom he heard expressions he did not like as he got into his car. He decided that there would be little safety upon the sea (which might still be in English hands), and that it would be more prudent to drive out of the city and take refuge in some quiet place until Germany had demonstrated her power to a crouching world. He was never heard of again, which, in that week, was the fate of millions of better men.

CHAPTER XVII.

THE winter dawn moved on. It left broad day over a Europe raging in the sudden bewildering grip of disastrous war, and chased the retreating night beneath grey Atlantic skies, and over waters restless with rising wind, and somewhat flattened at times by the flail of the falling rain.

It saw the black smoke-trails of hurrying, distracted shipping, of cargo-boats that put about in terror of the condition of Europe's seas, or that cried distractedly for orders to owners who did not reply.

It saw the Queen Mary lying-to, as its boats transferred to the *American Banker* the half-dozen passengers who were still resolved to land on their English shore, while it would return to a safer land, as most of its passengers would prefer. The *American Banker* would venture on, with its cargo of typewriters, chewing-gum, surgical instruments, and Californian fruits, only diverting its course from Thames to Mersey, as prudence plainly required.

It saw a British destroyer, grey and low in the mist, that had left Devonport for the West Indies two days before. Now its engines throbbed in the thin shell of the straining hull as it thrust its bows deep into the swelling waves. It drove for home at a faster pace than the following wind, so that its ensign blew backward into the west.

The hours passed that were so swift in the frenzied chaos of war, and the slow dawn broke on the long low coasts of the newer world. It came to where the President of its great Republic sat at his desk, as he had done through a sleepless night.

For twelve hours there had been laid before him, with each moment that passed, some fresh item of news that told of a shaking world. He sat with a map of the Old World spread on his desk, and Senator Ramsden, in whose counsels he had found it safety to trust, bent over it at his side.

The senator said: "It would make Europe and Asia a single power, against which we should not endure for a year.

"They would have Africa at their feet."

"It would be a recruiting-ground if the hordes of Asia should be too few."

"Yet the war is not ours, nor does it yet appear that it is directed at us. It may exhaust itself, and we may remain having kept our strength, and guard the civilization which would drive to wreck if the whole world should be involved."

"So we said before, but we were drawn in at the last; though it was a smaller thing than this is likely to be."

"Our people were not all of one mind at that time, and there was a general reluctance to be brought into Europe's wars."

"But you were not President then."

"And you think that I can lead them a better way?"

"You will not speak with the words of Cain."

The President pushed back his chair. He rose, pacing the length of the room.

"Ramsden," he said, "I can see what you would have, and I do not say you are wrong. I will not decide in more haste than I can avoid; and while mobilization proceeds there is no loss of time, even though we should use our strength at the first moment we may. But do we gain by such haste? By the news we have, Europe may be down in two days and its war done. Can we help that, though we may bare the sword in the next hour? Should we not talk first, and perhaps bring the world to better peace than would come from a wider war? Would there not always be time to fight if all else should fail? And shall we not learn much, standing aside, so that we might use our strength at last in a better way?"

"They are questions," Senator Ramsden allowed, "which are less easy to answer than ask, but I should say that the war will not cease in two days, nor perhaps in ten, even though we declare that it is no business of ours. But if there were a chance that there would be such swift and entire collapse, I should say that it is in our power to prevent, even though we should not have fired a shot or dropped a bomb in three days from now. For if it be known that we are coming in, it will prolong and stiffen resistance on every side."

"And prolong the torment of those who have no strength to prevail?"

"So it may. But we must look further than that. And there are some factors upon our side. Germany has the hate of Jewry throughout the world, and it is a great, though a scattered strength. I should say we shall keep the seas, which may be to hold Africa, if no more. And I suppose that England is not yet done."

"Yes.... And there is something more, which you overlook. There is the power of the Christian Faith. Have you thought that this may take the shape of a Holy War?"

Senator Ramsden looked doubtful. He was a man of vaguely materialistic beliefs. He had been heard to say that religion might be good enough for women and kids, but that it cut no ice with a practical man. He supposed that most men felt more or less in the same way, though he knew the President to be of a different mind. Was it a statesman's judgement, or a personal feeling that prompted this thought of a Holy War?

Yet if the President felt so, there must be others—how many?—who would feel the same. As an electioneering expert, he knew that the power of the Christian Churches in his own country was very great, if they were roused to use it in an organized way. He remembered the news that had come through two or three hours before of the destruction of the headquarters of the Catholic Church. In his mind the idea grew.

"It seems," he said, "that the Germans see it in the same light, or they wouldn't have thought it worthwhile to blow the Pope into the air. But what fools they are!"

"Yes. Unless they are very sure of their strength. 'Only eyes to weep with,' you know. Frightfulness has been their trusted weapon before. I suppose they impute themselves, as we are all likely to do. It is their nature to bully or cringe. I suppose we have come to the days of the last Crusade."

He remembered that the Crusades had not been conspicuously successful as military operations. But he put this thought resolutely aside. He said: "You had better see what the news is now," and Senator Ramsden reached for the telephone at his side.

CHAPTER XVIII.

THE President had given instructions that he was not to be disturbed under any pretext whatever during this time when he was directing his mind, with Senator Ramsden as his sole confident and adviser, to resolve the attitude of reserve or of instant war which his country should present towards those who had so wantonly disturbed the peace of the world.

Only, all the information that could be gathered concerning the events that moved in Europe with the terrible swiftness of warfare among the clouds, and of the reactions of farther lands, was to be held in readiness to be supplied whenever he should inquire, which Senator Ramsden had done two or three times during the hour.

News there was without stint, of war that waged in Europe from West to East, for the day that dawned in Washington was at noon in England by now, and farther East, on the frozen Danube, the twilight fell.

The senator listened for some minutes, and laid the receiver down. He said: "There is little that might not be known or surmised from that we have heard before. Beyond the destruction of the Papal City, Italy has not been attacked, and while that condition remains it appears that she will not move; or she may be waiting to choose her time, or to make her terms, as she did in the last war.

"Paris remains unharmed, though the French air-fleets are said to have been so shattered that they are practically out of action, and she is only protected now by her ring of surrounding batteries. But the Russo-German bombers appear to be concentrating upon the destruction of points of military importance. It is said that ten or more motorized divisions, moving with great rapidity, have already crossed into French territory, and the Germans claim to have isolated Metz, while the bombing of railways and roads behind the front line of the French armies has been, and continues to be so heavy that reinforcements will be difficult to move up. The British claim that the German losses in the air have been far heavier than their own, which is probably true, for on such points their bulletins have been straight enough in previous wars, but they do not say how many planes they still have—or how few. They claim also that the attack on the Midland industrial area failed to do any vital damage, and that the invaders who were not shot down were mostly outwitted by their defence. But they admit that eastern and parts of central London were set alight, and that the fires have not been put out, though the wind and weather have changed, and there is some help from the rain. If the wind continue from the southwest, and there be no further attack, it is thought that the eastern parts of the city, and much of that which is south of the river, may be saved. Farther east—"

The telephone bell rang, and the senator paused in midsentence.

The President said sharply: "I was explicit that I was not to be called, except as inquiry was made by you. Tell Potter—"

But Senator Ramsden was already listening, and the President checked himself, hearing him say: "Yes. Quite right. Go ahead."

A moment later, with the receiver still in his hand, he turned to explain: "It is a call for you from Ottawa. The Governor-General wished to speak to you, and being refused at first, he gave a message the importance of which he thought would justify intruding upon you. The British Government is proposing to remove to Halifax. Lord Tweedsmuir inquires whether he can rely upon our co-operation for their protection by sea and air. If not, he will advise that they move farther inland. He believes that Britain may continue to hold the seas, but he is less sure of the air."

"I will speak to him myself."

He stepped quickly over to take the call. He saw that the moment for decision had come. Senator Ramsden heard his voice, incisive even to curtness in his reply: "That you, Tweedsmuir? You can inform the Government of His Britannic Majesty that any place on this continent where they may be will receive our utmost support."

After that, the conversation continued for a few moments with mutual cordiality, but it was soon done, for it was no time for the wasting of needless words.

The President turned to his companion to say: "It appears that the British are resolved to continue the war, though they should have but one city that stands unbombed. The Royal Family have decided to remain in the British Isles. They are removing to Ireland."

"Ulster, of course?"

"No. Farther south. Lord Tweedsmuir mentioned that it was a place where they would be secure, and which would not be easy to find. Naturally, he was not more specific than that. It seems that the war is already at the doors of the New World. If we do not seek it ourselves, it will come to us."

"Well, I do not know that we need be overfearful of that."

The senator thought, with a sense of power, of the vast extent of the New World, and of the wealth which it contained, besides its millions of men.

He thought also of the ten thousand million dollars of hoarded gold that his own country held, the most huge mountain of gold that had ever been drawn together by mortal hands.

Two years before, it had been removed from its concrete vaults in New York and elsewhere, to be buried in a remote, far-inland spot in Kentucky, beyond the barrier of the Appalachian Mountains. It lay deep and safe, and strong batteries guarded its grave.

The senator thought of it as giving his country a splendid strength, but there followed a doubt. Would it have value at all, if the whole world should be joined in a final war? Had it even a value now?

It had been dug or drained or crushed from river and stubborn rock, it had been gathered with hardship and toil, and at heavy cost, and when it was returned to the ground, as it now was, did not the very act proclaim that it had proved useless to men? Was it symbolic of the fall of the civilization that had chosen it for its god, that men had reburied their foolish gold?

His wandering thought was broken through by the President's voice: "You will let Harcroft know? I will trust you to take such steps as the occasion requires. I must have some sleep. Tell Potter I will hold a Council at one o'clock, which General Veigt, and perhaps Simmons, should be required to attend."

It was less than half an hour later that the morning electric sign in Times Square, which tells the tale of the world's events to those New Yorkers who lack the cents that a paper costs, caused a roar of excited cries to go up from the Broadway pavements. PRESIDENT — DECLARES — WAR the moving ribbon spelt, without haste or pause in its steady course, RUSSIAN — AND — GERMAN — AMBASSADORS — TOLD — TO — LEAVE.

In New York there was daylight now, and a rising sun. A bitter wind blew from the north, freezing the central streets in spite of the high heated buildings on either side. The dawn moved on over the wide plains of the Middle West.

CHAPTER XIX.

THE dawn moved on—the indifferent, godlike dawn—serene again in the pale-gold haze of its winter light, chasing the darker hours across the immense vacancy of Pacific seas. It rose on Shanghai harbour at last, a red-barred menace of coming storm, where the British light cruiser *Balin* lay cleared for action and with a full head of steam, and Commander Trowbridge stood on the bridge, watching the flag-signals that showed darkly against the dawn from the mast of a Japanese cruiser, twice the size and far more heavily gunned than his own, which lay, equally alert, in the outer harbour.

The signal-lieutenant stood at his side. He saluted, and said: "It is to you, sir. From Captain Kato."

Commander Trowbridge read the slip of paper that he received. He frowned over it for a puzzled instant. *English they be.* What could be the meaning of that?

"Shall I ask them to repeat it, sir?" Lieutenant Hopkins asked. "It might be plainer in Japanese." He had some knowledge of Eastern languages, and the intended courtesy of communications in doubtful English often gave him more trouble than he would have when men confined themselves to the use of the tongues they knew.

But the Commander's hesitation had already passed.

"No," he said, "I should have understood it at once. It means that we can join Admiral Rogers at Singapore, if he will be still there." He gave the order that hauled the anchor aboard, and turned the *Balin*'s bows to the harbour mouth.

He remembered dining in Captain Kato's cabin ten days before, and the Japanese sailor, who, like most of the better-educated of his countrymen, had taken a course in English literature, had quoted *The Three Sealers*, stressing a line to which he had attached no significance at that time:

"English they be and Japanee that hang on the
brown bear's flank."

Now he understood. But was it a thing of chance, or had the Japanese captain foreseen the use which he could make of it on so near a day?

It was vain to ask; but he was clearly informed that Japan's hatred of Russia—jealous hatred and fear—had brought her into the war upon England's side, and that the information had been given to him in such a way that it was private from all the frightened, curious, many-nationed shipping the harbour held.

Knowing that, he knew also that Russia's left flank would be kept busy enough without vexation from him. He knew that there would be little peace for any ship flying the Russian or German flag where Japan policed the Pacific seas. The bows of the *Balin* drove hard through the back-flung foam. Clear of the land, her helm came round to a southern course. She had become part of the great movement which stirred the world and the farthest seas, as men of British blood rose up and turned their faces to home at the call of their country's need.

Over the wide chaos of Asia the slow dawn moved. It lighted the front of war that lay stretching from East to West like a zigzag lightning streak across the continent s breadth, where the unleashed Siberian hordes clashed with Chinaman and Tibetan, with Afghan, Persian and Turk, while mechanized Soviet armies at half a dozen strategic points drove spearheads of uncountered strength southward through the rabble of meaner strife.

Dawn—the only dawn that had been since primeval mist steamed upward to let it through—came once again, bringing the name of another day to a Europe which had become a vast confusion of strife, a welter of blood and tears in which men strove with frantic or ordered haste to destroy their foes, knowing that the next hour might be that when themselves would die. It came to the streets of Nürnberg, quiet and quaint in the peace and beauty of older days, and to the great aerodrome that stretched far out from its southern side.

BOOK TWO.

CHAPTER XX.

PERDITA WYATT stood in a Nürnberg street, among a crowd which took no notice of her.

Three days before she had been a welcomed guest at the British Legation in Prague, in a security which might have been considered as absolute as that of her English home.

In the next night, she had escaped from the burning city in the company of a Legation servant and a German officer whose plane had been brought down as it had bombed the Czechoslovakian capital; and the German airman, Captain Karl Dürer, before returning to duty, had left her with his sisters at his home in Nürnberg.

Yesterday, she had learned that Germany and her own country were at war, and that her new friends—as they had seemed a few hours before—were reporting her alien presence to the police authorities, by whom, she vaguely supposed, she would be arrested for removal to jail or internment camp, with indignities from which she shrank no less because the limited, gracious experiences of her twenty years of leisured and cultured life had not adequately equipped her imagination to guess what they would be likely to be.

She had observed that the necessity of reporting her presence without delay had seemed to the Fräulein Dürer so fundamentally obvious that it neither required discussion between themselves nor explanation to her.

As she had walked out of the house a few minutes after realizing this position, with no more of her possessions than her handbag held, and intent only on obeying a blind instinct of flight from the instant fear, she had wondered whether she would have acted in the same manner had her brother brought a German girl of good credentials to her own door, and half-persuaded herself, in a mind that strove to be fair, that perhaps she might; but there was still a difference that remained.

She would have done it, if at all, as a course of action justified by the requirements of patriotism to her own mind, and probably with explanation and expressions of regret to her guest. But these women had not doubted or thought at all. The fact was, they were not their own. They were possessed by a power beneath which their individualities were submerged. A ruthless, inhuman power. The power that had ruined Prague.

The younger girl had told her that she was engaged to a Nürnberg lawyer—or at least provisionally engaged; but it appeared that the consummation of this, as of all German marriages, must be subject to the consent of the medical officers of the State, although (she said confidently) they themselves had little severity of inquisition to fear, he being a contributor to *Der Blitz*, a periodical the professed aim of which was the destruction of Christianity, and he would be favoured on that account by the officers of the State.

The lovers had applied for permission, and had received application forms issued under the 1935 Nürnberg law, the details of which, when completed, must be verified by medical officer.

Profile and full-face photographs were to be attached to the forms, which must include descriptions of the applicant's body, habits, and physical history, in minutest detail. Perdita's knowledge either of the German language or of human obliquities had been insufficient to expose some of the filthier suggestions of this inquisition to her astonished mind, but she had understood enough to be as amazed at the servility of those who would submit to such legislation, as at the obscenity of the minds that were responsible for its composition.

Even in England in 1938, little of personal liberty had survived, and a large part of the population had become unfit to endure the severities of its bracing atmosphere. It was also true in that country that the counsels of the birth-restrictionists, openly proclaimed, had befouled, at its very threshold, the ideals of natural marriage. But human degradation sank here in a lower slough.

And if they would subject their own people to a tyranny so absolute, an inquisition so coarse and vile, with what scorpions would they be likely to chastise the alien races who might prove unequal to resisting their military machine? The machine which a frightened Europe had watched them construct during the last four years, and had lacked foresight or resolution to check while the balance of strength had still been upon its side.... For four years, under the darkening cloud of the coming war, England had cried peace where no peace had been, and what price would she have to pay, now that the ashes of London smouldered beneath the rain?

Perdita did not analyse the causes which stirred her instincts of fear and flight, but it may have been that form of application to marry (which might result in blank refusal, permission to wed at your own choice, or to marry only some "unfertile person") that, more than all else, had caused her to walk blindly into the streets, rather than remain to encounter the police of this hateful land. And she had been attracted to Captain Dürer! Had had a hope that she might see him again before it would be necessary for her to leave his home. Would he have expected her to be questioned and measured and weighed? To submit her body to the examination of German doctors? Surely there must be many, even in this country of docile serfs, who would have personal dignity enough to decide that permission to marry may be bought with too high a fee!

So she thought, but she may have been largely wrong, for the people among whom she moved had been mesmerized to belief in the profound lie that they existed not for themselves, but for some abstruse entity called The Third Reich, which was, in fact, nothing more than the ambitious greed of those who had laid their hands on the country's helm, and welded them into an evil, pitiless sword to subdue the world.

Even a few years before, Nürnberg had been a city of very leisurely ways, as though aware of its moss-grown age. Its citizens had become obese on a diet of sausage-meat, and of mugs of beer that were often emptied and filled. Its bankers had provided newspapers for the use of the leisurely customers who had strolled through their doors to make a deposit, or cash a cheque. But there was little either of obesity or of leisure now in the excited crowd among whom Perdita moved—a crowd of women and fewer men, mostly in uniforms of the earth or air, and too absorbed in the news that the morning brought to take much notice of her.

"London still burning. French army surrenders before Sarrebourg. Sweden declares for Germany. England given twelve hours to yield. Insurrections in Pennsylvania. Copenhagen occupied. Reported annexation of Switzerland."

These and a dozen other reports of a rocking world were the burden of bulletins continually issued, of newspapers constantly published and snatched hastily from hand to hand, and of swift rumours that came at times in advance of the published fact.

Perdita heard and read and understood enough to perceive that Germany boasted of a wide success before which Europe stumbled upon its knees. Courage, placed as she was, and amidst that jubilant crowd, was not easy to keep, but she remembered being told that

English prisoners during the last war were depressed by reports of more decisive victories than Germany actually gained, and she resolved that she would believe nothing from German lips, waiting to learn the truth till she should be back in her native land.

Yet that which she had seen in Prague less than three days before made the reports around her at once more vivid in horror and more credible than they would have sounded before she had encountered that dreadful experience, and though there were errors and exaggerations of fact, and suppressions of adverse items of news, there was little of that she heard which was not substantially true.

It was true that several of the smaller European states terrorized by the fate of Prague, observing the inadequacy of the English airfleets to preserve their own cities from destruction, and faced by the appalling alliance of the German and Russian tyrannies for the domination of Europe, had either (as in the major case of Poland) hurriedly professed fidelity to the German interpretation of existing treaties, and added their military forces to the strength of the aggressors, or (as in the cases of Switzerland, Denmark, and Holland) yielded in sullen shame to the military occupation which was the alternative to a resistance which, it seemed, would lead by a path of blood to no other end.

It was true also that the German Government had presented an ultimatum to Britain to which there had been no reply, and which was destined to prove as abortive as that which had commenced the war. It had offered twelve hours in which to discuss terms of capitulation, with the alternative of experiencing attack with new and more dreadful weapons than those which had already been directed upon her. It professed to be dictated by considerations of humanity, as though reluctant to use the extremity of what it knew to be invincible power; and it was true that, though no truce had been arranged, or even suggested, and many isolated acts of hostility were still being committed by either side, the interval was free from any major act of aggression by the German fleets of the air.

But it would be a misconception to conclude that the delivery of this ultimatum was either impulsed by humanitarian considerations, or had the military effect of giving to Britain the respite of one avoidable hour.

The fact was that the High Command of Germany was momentarily confused, if not exhausted, even by the magnitude of its own successes. A few hours' interval, in spite of the meticulous care with which the details of its aggressions had been previously planned, had become an imperative necessity, if it were to direct its further efforts to their deadliest possibilities.

And there was a further consideration, which might alone have been of decisive weight. The successes of the past forty-eight hours had equalled, and in some respects actually exceeded, anticipations; but the losses incurred—particularly those of the air—had also far exceeded the calculations that had been made. It had been demonstrated, in particular, that even the swiftest and most powerful of night-bombers was helpless against attack by the newest patterns of fighting planes, if these machines were handled in the spirit of desperation that the British Air Force had exhibited in the fighting over the London area, when they had appeared to be indifferent to their own destruction, so long as they could inflict far heavier losses upon their foes.

The anti-aircraft batteries, both of England and France, had also proved more destructive—and effective at higher altitudes—than had been anticipated; and though the devastation of London might seem inconsistent with these conclusions, yet the cost at which it had been obtained had been so heavy as to cause anxious calculations to be made of how many of such successes would be the end of the Russo-German air-fleets as an immediate striking power.

The air-fleets of Britain and France were supposed to he exhausted, if not utterly gone, but their land batteries largely remained.

The swift decision of the United States to enter the war had been a point on which the German miscalculation may be compared to that which had brought England into the field twenty-four years earlier, but it had some explanation in the constant protestation of the former country that she would not involve herself in the misfortunes of Europe a second time—a protestation which had increased in vehemence as her armaments grew—and it might be thought that it would be an interference less decisive in prolonging a war which was not to be fought with trench mortar and hand grenade, but with the deadlier weapons, and in the freer range of the air. Not again, the German Staff might confidently assume, would there be time for new armies to be arrayed, new munitions factories built, while the combatants remained in a long-drawn deadlock of fruitless strife.

But the menace of this new foe, which had been expected to wait aside until destruction should reach its shores, was a factor rendering it desirable that the Russo-German air-fleets should conserve at least a sufficient strength to outnumber anything which could be launched against them from the New World, and by doing so render it at least less probable that America would risk offensive action upon an arena so distant from her own shores; and this alone was a sufficient reason for desiring that the conquest of Great Britain should be completed with all possible economy of material re-sources, and with the surrender of the maximum quantity of unex-hausted armaments, such as could be used against Germany's foes of the next day.

Considering these arguments, and calculating that even if Great Britain should be too obstinate yet to yield, the confident and terri-ble warning which the ultimatum contained could not fail to intimi-date and divide counsels among those who were weak of heart (of whom there are too many in every land), the German High Com-mand may be acquitted from having deviated from its own ruthless standard of international conduct in giving to England this second opportunity of capitulating before loosing the extremity of chastise-ment which must be hers if she should be contumacious beyond the allotted hours.

The report of insurrections in Pennsylvania, although magni-fied, was also founded on a substratum of fact. The population of the United States was so heterogeneous, and so ill-assimilated, that it would have been difficult for it to declare war against any nation of the Old World without rousing the animosity of those of its citizens whose ties of sympathy and blood still held them more strongly to their native than to their adopted land. The deep-eating cancer of Communism (for the growth of which the blind selfishness of many of the leaders of industry and finance must be accounted primarily responsible), fostered during the last three years by liberal subsidies of Russian money, had prepared the mines which were now sprung for the embarrassment of the American Government, and for the pa-ralysis of its munitions supplies.

Disturbances which would have been described more accurately as riots than insurrections broke out so instantly, and in such widely separated districts, upon the declaration of war, as to make it evident that they were already organized in advance of the occasion which they professed They were not openly allowed to be in the Russo-German cause, which would have alienated more sympathy than it would have gained, and justified more drastic measures of suppres-sion than the Government might otherwise be immediately likely to use. More cunningly, their violence was said to be in the cause of peace: a protest against the country being involved in a distant war in which it had no concern.

There had been, for some previous years, a cunning Communis-tic propaganda in many lands, which had painted, in colours lurid but not untrue, the evils and degradations of war, and then asserted, as though it were a logical deduction therefrom, that it could be pre-vented by the simple method of refusing to fight. This confusion of fact and fallacy, as though a man could dismiss the danger of storm by the simple expedient of selling his overcoat, had been heard in Britain also, but had taken little root in a more difficult soil, and the stark reality of war had descended upon that country with too sudden a violence for such delusions to raise their heads.

CHAPTER XXI.

BUT there was another event of this noon, which occurred while Perdita wandered in undecided misery among the Nürnberg crowd, an event in Berlin that was not made known till a later hour, which, though it was no more than a single death, was more momentous in its results than anything which had yet occurred over the whole wide area of the war

For nearly two years past, the German air-fleets had been organized and developed to their gigantic and secret strength under the direction of an Air Minister, Prince Nicholas Alexander von Teufel by name, who had gained an almost idolatrous loyalty from the service which he controlled.

During these years he had shown no personal ambition, he had worked smoothly and amiably with his military and naval colleagues. He had appeared loyal to the Führer and the regime of the Third Reich. His sole interest had appeared to lie in the perfecting of the arm which he controlled for the day when Germany should assert her might.

Meanwhile, he had surrounded himself with subordinates on whose unscrupulous personal loyalty (with the opportunities of gratified ambition which he would be able to offer) he felt that he could depend when his hour should come, but even among these he had no confidant, nor was there one of them who guessed the purpose that filled his thoughts.

When the Russian and German General Staffs discussed the military directions of the attack upon the world's civilization which they had resolved to defer only until the opportune time should come, the question of unity of command was naturally raised, and as naturally proved to be one which could not easily be resolved, neither of these great and jealous allies being willing to submit its military forces to the control of an alien commander.

In the end they agreed to say, though they may not have thought, that the vastness of the battle-fronts which would be engaged, with other cognate considerations, rendered it a counsel of doubtful wisdom to place the whole under the control of a single mind.

But Germany had urged, with good reason and final success, that these objections did not apply with equal force to operations in the air, in which the battle-fleets could be moved over the whole area in a few hours, and in which the main enemy strength would be upon the right flank of the allies—that is, at her own doors.

In the air, she had urged, it was vital that the operations should be under single control, and on this point she had had her way.

When she had gone on to propose that the combined air-fleets should be under the command of Prince von Teufel, this nomination had been accepted without demur or even with satisfaction, he being of Russian descent on his mother's side, nor had the German Government hesitated to place in his hands so entire a power. He was regarded as a man whose whole heart was in his profession, and who took no more interest in the political arena than loyalty to those who ruled his country required.

The Air Minister had derived from his Prussian ancestors the military instincts, the industry, the ruthless brutality, the careful attention to detail, the ability to plan and the patience to wait, which constitute one of the dominant types of German character. But beneath these lay the sombre, visionary, dreaming mind which he had inherited from his maternal grandfather, Prince Alexander of Kov. A very large proportion of the world's greatest men, both best and worst, have been of mixed nationality, the blending of diverse characteristics giving the unusual quality which is most likely to deviate from the common path, and being often supported by a body of more than average vitality.

In the case of Prince von Teufel, the disposition to brooding and melancholy imaginations, in which the Russian mind so often reflects the cold monotony of its frozen plains, was strangely allied to the more virile and practical qualities of his father's race.

It was a combination that might be potent either for evil or good. With von Teufel, the prospect of controlling destructive forces vaster than had ever before obeyed the orders of man had an effect of moral intoxication, so that he had seen himself in imagination as the dictator of a trembling world, even from the moment when he had been appointed Minister of the Air, with the secret knowledge that he was to be permitted to build and organize battle and bombing-fleets four times as numerous as would be publicly admitted, or than would be possessed by the other Great Powers of the world, whose jealous rivalry, as the German people had been taught to believe, denied her that "seat in the sun" which, for some inscrutable reason, was the natural privilege of people of German blood.

But von Teufel had been too wary, too cool in judgement, to allow such thoughts to appear at a time when he might have been removed from office as easily as he had been raised at the Führer's nod. With silent, patient tenacity, he had kept his dream ever before his mind, but without exposure by glance or manner, by word or act.

His colleagues spoke of him as one entirely absorbed in the development of the Air Force which was his charge, as in fact he was. He obeyed at this time the wisdom of the Divine precept, the source of which, had he heard it, would have been occasion for easy scorn: *"If any man would be first among you, let him be the servant of all."*

He had his reward when he found himself nominated to the command of the combined air-fleets of the allies, and when his name was accepted by the Russian Government as one they would be pleased to approve. From that moment, he had no doubt of the great destiny that the future held.

During the two months that elapsed between the conclusion of this arrangement and the outbreak of war, which placed in his hands the actual power that had been till then no more than a paper pledge, he had considered and made his plans. The secrecy with which his air-fleets had been built and hidden had rendered it natural, if not inevitable, that their control should be in his single hands, and that no one beside should have more than partial knowledge, or only such as came from himself, concerning their organization. At the end of two days of aerial warfare waged over the breadth of two continents, and (with the exception of some separate minor commands in Southern and Eastern Siberia) entirely under his supreme direction, it might have been a disaster of the first magnitude had he been suddenly removed from that position, at a time when the dispositions of a few hours might change the fate of the world.

While being thus in supreme control of the operations of the air, it was von Teufel's obvious duty to act in conformity with the policies of the Allied Governments, and in military co-operation with Field-Marshal Wertner, who was in almost equally absolute control of the land armies of the Third Reich. But what might have been a difficult collaboration had proceeded, during the past three days, without a note of discord, Prince von Teufel accepting the plans of the War Council, and supporting Field-Marshal Wertner's dispositions without demur. It was shortly before noon on this day that a

War Council was held in Berlin, at which Herr Guttman presided with his accustomed dignity, and with the colourless but efficient neutrality which made his position secure among men of stronger wills and more turbulent ambitions than he would ever be likely to show.

Field-Marshal Wertner was there, with General von Hoffmann, his Chief of Staff, Admiral Saarbrück, and three other of the principal Officers of State whose names it is not necessary to record. The first business which engaged the attention of the Council was the unexpected promptitude with which the United States had entered the war and its probable consequences, regarding which the Council naturally desired the opinions of the Commanders-in-Chief of the military and aerial forces of the Reich. Following the established custom by which an officer will deliver his opinion, if at all, before his superiors have spoken, so that he may not be placed in the position of contemning the opinions of those of higher rank than his own, General von Hoffmann was the first to speak, to be followed by Admiral Saarbrück and Prince von Teufel, the final word resting with Marshal Wertner, as being the head of the terrestrial army, which still ranked as the senior service.

CHAPTER XXII.

GENERAL VON HOFFMANN spoke briefly, and as one to whom the problem was simple, and its solution beyond dispute. If the war were pushed on with sufficient energy, the intervention of the United States could, he considered, make little difference, except that that country would have anticipated a fate which might have been delayed to a future year. Providing only—which was already beyond reasonable doubt—that the allies could maintain supremacy in the skies of the Eastern Hemisphere, they should have Europe, Asia, and Africa in their hands before the armies of America could arrive to obstruct their advance, even if (which, for various military reasons, he was disposed to doubt) such an attempt would be made; and, after that, America could be subdued at leisure, as had been intended before. But he thought that there was now additional reason for intensifying operations against Great Britain with every weapon at their command, for if she were definitely out of action, not only might her Dominions desist from the efforts which they were said to be commencing for her support, but the United States would be far less likely to adventure a landing in Europe, losing at the same time much of the incentive for such an attempt, and the base from which operations upon the Continent might have been advantageously organized.

Admiral Saarbrück followed, and spoke in general support of the opinion of his military colleague. He dwelt with some seriousness on the naval position, pointing out that, while the allies might possess themselves of the three continents of the Old World, they would have no freedom upon the seas so long as the navies of Great Britain, the United States, and Japan should be unsubdued. And he drew attention to the fact that the subjection of Europe would not necessarily result in placing its fleets at their disposal. He instanced the action of Denmark, whose tiny fleet, before she made formal submission to German power, had sailed for Rosyth, with or without the connivance of her Government, and had sunk a German destroyer, besides capturing two cargo boats on her way.

But his argument led to the same point: the necessity of chastising the British Isles with sufficient severity to ensure their speedy surrender; and he proposed that it should be a first condition of making tolerable terms that her fleet should be handed over in good condition. It must be clear that Germany would not be flouted after the fashion of Scapa Flow. But even if the British fleet should escape to the shelter of American ports, the British sea-bases would be obtained. He emphasized the primary importance of these, and in particular of Gibraltar and of the Suez Canal.

"If we have these," he said, "the Mediterranean will he ours, and can be held against all the fleets of the world. And, with that, we have Africa for a plum to pick at what time we will."

He suggested further that peace should be made with the Japanese and their alliance bought, which itself would be enough to immobilize America's Pacific fleets. This, he said, could easily be done by offering them Australia as a colonial empire more suitable than the already crowded territories on the Asian continent, possession of which they had been disputing with Russia for the last forty years.

It was an island immense and empty, and suitable in climatic and other conditions for Japanese settlement. It would be an act of world justice also, for it was already evident that it would never be populated by people of British stock, for their immigration had almost ceased, and the women of the new land were failing to increase their breed.

Prince von Teufel was next to speak. He did little more than approve the opinions already expressed. Even the idea of making terms with Japan had his blessing, only qualified by a doubt (in which he showed a sounder political instinct than the previous speaker) of whether the astute Japanese statesmen would enter a trap baited with such suspicious liberality. His private thought was that, when he stood secure on a conquered world, he could give or take back as he might prefer.

He agreed that Britain must be eliminated without delay from the tale of Germany's foes. He proposed to ensure this, if she should not have surrendered during the day, by loosening upon her every weapon which a diabolical chemistry had prepared against such a necessity, and he had no doubt that they would be more than enough. He suggested that, had this been done on the first day, the question would have been answered now.

As to maintaining supremacy in the air, he spoke with the confidence which he felt that the occasion required. There were still large fleets that had not been used upon any front. Every European state that surrendered increased their material strength. More important, there were thousands of capable pilots in reserve who could take control of the machines that were still being built in haste, or that were surrendered to them. Within forty-eight hours (they might agree) it was probable that the air-fleet now stationed upon Italy's northern frontier would be released, and, at the same time, the air-forces of that country would come under their control. But he was not depending upon that. Come what would, the Russo-German fleets of the air would be more than equal to hold their gains.

Marshal Wertner was last to speak. He commenced in a tone of friendly moderation, complimenting those whose opinions had been already heard, and expressing agreement on points of detail, while leading up to an opposite conclusion.

He spoke with the quiet assurance natural to one holding a position the supremacy of which, in its own sphere, had not been challenged since he had been appointed to the high place he held. He felt that he gauged the position with greater accuracy, with more comprehensive vision, than the three previous speakers, and that the last word was properly his. After that, the civilian members of the Council who were, under the Führer, the actual rulers of Germany, would decide upon the measures necessary to implement the expert advice which they had received.

In a word, his advice was that the Russo-German allies should offer terms of peace to the world while their arms were supreme, and that these terms should be of sufficient generosity to make their acceptance probable. It should be done in the guise of a gesture of magnanimity, as from nations conscious of an invincible strength, but willing to give the world an equitable and enduring peace so long only as their own positions were made secure—such, at least, was the word he used, for which supreme, as he visualized the event, might have been a more accurate description.

He spoke of the military situation without alarm, but yet as one that should be very carefully weighed, not merely as it now was, but as it might develop if it should prove to be beyond the strength of the allies both to hold down the Old World and to conduct a successful campaign in the skies, and on the surface, of the New.

He agreed with what had been said respecting the necessity for controlling the Mediterranean, as a preliminary to the occupation of Africa, and that this could not be permanently secured unless Gibraltar should be in the hands of the allies, and the Suez Canal either occupied or destroyed. But he raised a doubt as to whether Gibraltar would be voluntarily surrendered, even though Britain should be unable to continue resistance on her own shores.

He said that its present Governor, a soldier of reputed valour and patriotism, was reported to have exclaimed, when the terms of the first ultimatum had reached his ears, that he would not have surrendered the fortress to German hands though every bloody politician in London had begged it upon his blasted knees. The rock of Gibraltar was understood to be well-provisioned, and might be very difficult to subdue, either from sea or air. Its capture, even with all the chemical resources at their command, would be a military and naval problem of the first magnitude.

Yet its possession, unless the allies should be in unchallenged control of its approaches on the Atlantic side, would (as Admiral Saarbrück had so clearly explained) be an essential preliminary to the conquest of Africa; and an Africa unsubdued might be a gathering-ground for the enemies of the allies, as well as a vast reservoir of human and material power.

For the moment, the blows which had been dealt from the air, and the rapid advance of the allied armies under the shelter of these successes, must have struck terror throughout the world. They could make peace at no better time. In the last war, more than once, they had made the error of underrating their foes. They had disparaged the military strength of the British Empire and the effect of the hostility of the United States. It was a mistake that should not be made for a second time.

He concluded quietly, without effort of peroration, as one who discussed matters too vital for any flourish of words, and it was evident to Prince Nicholas that his opinion had not only impressed the civilian members of the Council, but had raised such doubts as might soon be turned to assenting votes in the minds of the Admiral and the Chief of Staff. If he himself should be silent now, the whole stupendous adventure might collapse in a peace which, whatever it might do for Germany, might easily leave him a man of less account than he had been before. He saw that the moment—not of decision, for that was already made—but for decisive action had come.

He said curtly: "You remind us that Germany failed before, but you are wrong as to the cause. We failed, as men ever do, from a craven fear. Had we used the U-boats as quickly as they were built, and for all they were meant to do, we should have ended another way."

The argument was not new, nor was its conclusion one that could be unwelcome to German ears, but it was clothed in unseemly words, and stated in a manner, and with a voice, which was an insult not lightly to be ignored.

Marshal Wertner looked his surprise. His thought was that the younger man was breaking down under the strain of the colossal responsibility that was his. If so, there was reason for him to be answered with patience and self-restraint. He said mildly: "It may have been less simple than that. But shall we not do well to confine dispute to that which must be decided today?"

Von Teufel answered with a contempt which he had become careless to hide: "So I do. For you would urge us to fall again in the same way. Had we struck two days ago with all the weapons we have—with the blindness that eats the eyes, with the plague, and the freezing death—even those who trust in the ocean's width would have been slower to join our foes."

Herr Guttman made an effort to interpose in a soothing way, as a chairman should: "But, von Teufel, you will not forget that the Leunawerke was destroyed by fire on the night that we bombed Prague, and that our chemists asked for a space of days before they would have fresh supplies in the quantities which—"

Prince Nicholas broke in abruptly, but turning his words upon Marshal Wertner again, for he had no intention of quarrelling with the Chairman or the other members of the Council, if, as he believed, he could prevail on them to do his will: "Do I forget?" he exclaimed. "From what other cause could I have kept silence when it was resolved to strike with but half our power?"

Marshal Wertner still looked at him with doubtful eyes, as a physician might regard a sufferer from evident but as yet undiagnosed disease, and Admiral Saarbrück was quicker in reply: "It is tomorrow, not yesterday, on which we have to decide, and on which I trust that we shall not fail to agree. There is this question of how we should stand in a few days' time if Gibraltar declines to yield, and if it proves too hard to subdue. Would you tell us, von Teufel, how you advise that we deal with that?"

Von Teufel turned his glance on the Admiral, and his reply was in a more temperate tone, though he still spoke in a curt and masterful way, such as he had not used to his colleagues before: "Yes. I will tell you that. If we have England beneath our heel, and Gibraltar will not submit, shall we not hold hostages enough to assert our will? How soon would Gibraltar's Governor haul down his flag if he were told that a hundred English women would be hanged each day till the news of his surrender should be received?"

Marshal Wertner asked: "You would do that?"

"It would not be needed to do. It would be enough for it to be known that we were so resolved in an inflexible mood."

"So that, if we should prove wrong on that point, it would be done?"

"And do you say you would not, though it were that upon which might hang the result of the war, and the ascendancy of the German race?"

"No, I do not think that I would."

Von Teufel rose in his place, quickly enough, but without haste, in a deliberate way, and in the same action, coolly and yet in a second's beat, he drew a small automatic from a side-pocket, and shot Marshal Wertner, the bullet entering his left cheek (for he sat on the other side of the table, but not directly opposite to the Air Minister) and penetrating the base of the brain.

Marshal Wertner made no sound. He sagged sideways in his chair. His jaw dropped. A hand that had lain on the table slid off with a sound that could be clearly heard through the room, which had become quiet as the report died.

The men who looked on were not cowards, but they were unarmed, and the sudden tragedy stunned their minds. The next instant might have been vocal enough, but von Teufel was the one man there who had foreseen what he would do, and prepared what it would be needful to say.

"You will bear witness, Herr Guttman," he said, "that we had no option in what we did, for he was a man who was placed too high to speak such treason and live. Gentlemen"—he looked round as he spoke, as though sure of friendly support—"it was a necessity which we regret, but you are witnesses that there was no other way. The times are too pregnant with fate for us to bear with counsels of weakness here, nor can our armies be controlled by one of a maudlin will."

As he spoke, he put the pistol away, though it remained not far from his hand, and he did not resume his seat. He looked round on men who had been made familiar with assassination as a form of political argument by the methods of the Government of the Third Reich from its earliest days, men who, by their occupations, had become quicker in thought than action, and among whom none was in haste to be first to speak, either to condone the murder, or to condemn one who had not exhausted the conclusive arguments that his pistol held.

For the last five years they had upheld the pagan creed that ruthless violence is more admirable in itself and the fruits it bears than are the futile Christian virtues of pity and love. In the cases of Admiral Saarbrück and General von Hoffmann, there was consciousness that von Teufel had upheld the opinions they had themselves expressed, from which it had been made to appear that Marshal Wertner had dissented on mere humanitarian grounds. Marshal Wertner was dead. If his murder should he followed by von Teufel's execution or degradation, who would fill the double vacancies which would have occurred so abruptly in the supreme commands both of land and air? Who, in particular, could take von Teufel's place at the hourly changing chessboard of aerial strife in the stress of the middle game?—a game that was being played at such breathless speed, with half a world of the heights of sky as the arena in which it moved. Would his disappearance break the essential bond by which the Russian air-fleets had come under German control? What would be the effect on world opinion, if it should be announced that both commands had been changed in a single hour? Would it not bewilder and dishearten those who had been taught to regard them as supermen, by whom Germany would be led to the high place which was hers of right? Would it not be news to delight her foes?

These thoughts, with other more personal considerations of ambition or fear, were almost audible in the silence which had fallen upon the room.

Herr Guttman gave them voice, speaking first, as his position made it natural for him to do. He spoke tonelessly, preserving his usual dignified and impartial manner, his only recognition of the last moment's tragedy being in the somewhat increased formality with which he addressed the Minister of the Air: "Prince von Teufel, this is a matter which could not be long concealed. Would you tell us in what guise you propose that it be brought to the public ear?"

Von Teufel looked at the Chairman. He looked round at his colleagues. He sat down. He had seen that the game was won.

He answered: "There is no trouble in that. I will tell you what the proclamation shall be. If you will write it now, we will all sign, and it shall be issued at the end of the day, when men have been sated with news of greater events, among which it will scarcely be regarded

As he spoke, he saw Herr Guttman reach for a pen, and draw a sheet of foolscap paper towards him. The dead man still sagged in his chair. He slipped lower, as one might who lived and settled to more comfortable sleep. The other members of the Council looked on, watchful, doubtful, alert; but von Teufel, with a new confidence in his manner, a new dominance in his tone, looked already as one who expected obedience to wait his word.

Herr Guttman wrote, and von Teufel dictated clearly, without changing his phrase:

> "At a Council of War held in Berlin this morning, His Excellency Field-Marshal Franz Wertner, Commander-in-Chief of the land armies of the Third Reich, was charged with high treason, and convicted on his own confession.
>
> "He was executed under conditions that must prevail in a time of war, for the security of the State. He will be buried with full military honours, in recognition of his earlier services.
>
> "His Excellency General Ernst von Hoffmann was immediately appointed to the position of Commander-in-Chief rendered vacant by Field-Marshal Wertner's death."

Herr Guttman paused at this last sentence "Shall we say," he suggested, "subject to the Führer's confirmation?"

"That," von Teufel replied, "will be understood. But there should be no room for doubt in the public mind."

Herr Guttman's pen paused for a further moment, but went on. von Teufel reached over to take the sheet. He found it to be written as he had dictated. He signed it first, as it had not been usual for him to do. He was in a mood to assert the power which he had long purposed to seize. He had judged von Hoffmann to be the greatest danger he had to face, and he knew that there would be no protest from him, now that he had heard the last paragraph of the document which was to give him so great a place.

The proclamation came back to the Chairman's hand. It now bore the signature, boldly written, and too closely for any to be placed above it:

"Nicholas Alexander von Teufel,
Prince of the Power of the Air."

Herr Guttman signed, and handed it to the minister on his right. One by one, the members of the Council signed in silence and passed it on. It was passed in front of the dead man, but there was no protest from him. When it came back to the Chairman's hands, he rang for his secretary, who promptly entered the room.

"Thorn," he said, "you will have this printed, so that it may be issued at 6:00 P.M. You will see that it does not become known at an earlier hour. You will see what it says, and you will observe that Marshal Wertner is dead. You will remove him without delay, for the Council waits."

A moment later two footmen entered the room and bore the dead body out with less ceremony than expedition. In 1935, and more than once afterwards, they had been employed in similar ways, and they knew that it was more important to them to obey the wishes of those who lived than to show respect to the dead.

They noticed that there were a few drops of blood on the back of the chair, which was also splintered where the bullet had struck, after it had passed through the dead man's head. They dropped the body that they were dragging away, that they might draw the chair back to the wall, and place another where it had been.

As they left the room, von Teufel looked round on the five whom he had permitted to live. "If you will follow me," he said, "and will avoid dissension among yourselves, I will give you the world for a garden in which to play."

CHAPTER XXIII.

PERDITA stood on the pavement of the Haupt-market, watching the chaffer of the booths that were still busy with cheap-ware sales, as though unconscious that Europe was rent apart by the sword of war. She looked across at the quaintness of the steep-tiled roofs, and at the diverse spires of the ancient church, and saw it as a city she might have learned to love in serener days, and that might have been friendly to her.

She knew also that if but one half of what these German people believed were true, she was safer there, even in the midst of her country's foes, than she would be if she were returned that hour to her native home.

Yet the will to return was urgent within her heart, and the resolve that she would not be snared by the police of this hostile land. She thought, with the only reasonable basis of confidence that she had, of the store of German marks and English pounds that her handbag held. Surely there must be men in so large a city who would be her friend at a price? But how could they be found? How could she trust those of no faith to their own land, that they would be loyal to her? And she was afraid to utter a German word of the few she knew, lest she should expose herself for the foreigner that she was! And it was two hours now that she had wandered in these dangerous streets, tiring herself to no useful end. She had no more than a purpose without a plan.

Low at her shoulder a voice spoke in the English tongue: "Do not look round. You are Miss Wyatt, who was at the British Legation in Prague?"

She started slightly, controlled herself, and tried with a quickened step to lose herself in the crowd. She heard again: "Do not fear. I am friend to you. I am needing help."

The appeal for help, unexpected as it was, did more for reassurance than would any protest of regard for her. She slackened pace, and became aware of a private of German infantry who was at her left side, though avoiding appearance of walking with her. It was not the guise in which she would have expected to meet a friend, but those who are in extremity must welcome the slender chance. And what use would it be to deny her name to one to whom she was clearly known?

"Yes," she said, "I am Miss Wyatt. What do you want?"

"I want to aid your escape, as you will be helpful to me. Take the second street on the right. You will find a small restaurant there—number 17—a beer house, the door of which will be closed. Go in without hesitation along the passage, and enter the last door on the left. Take no notice of anyone you may see, but sit down and wait for me there."

The soldier did not give her time to reply. He quickened his pace, passing her, and then loitering at the window of a pastry-cook's shop so that she could observe him at leisure as she approached.

In that uniform he looked German enough, but he had spoken English as few of that race are ever able to do. The face was keen, lean, hard, and with a worn look, such as comes rather from stress of living than the mere passing of years. It gave her confidence in itself rather than as a protector to her. If he should wish to save her, she felt that it was what he would be likely to do. But her trust did not go on a willing path, nor any further than that.

As she drew level with him, he did not give her the opportunity to speak, even had she been foolish enough for the attempt. He went into the shop, out of which he came when she had passed, with a bag of biscuits in his hand, which he ate as he sauntered along the street.

Perdita went on, following the direction he had given, and found the beer house to which she had been directed. It was small and dingy, with windows on each side of a varnished door painted above her height a dull yellow colour, so that she could not see in. There were red curtains, soiled and faded, drawn back on each side of the windows, and painted lettering on the glass proclaimed the public character of the house.

Remembering the instructions she had received, she did not knock, but put her hand to the knob of the door, which opened readily. She stepped a few inches down from the street level as she entered a dark passage, the floor of which was strewn with sawdust not lately changed. She heard low voices from the room on her left hand.

Going on, she came to another door on her left, which she entered as she had been told. She found it to be empty, a small dark room with leather-covered seats around its walls, and narrow, marble-topped tables before them. She looked through a window not lately washed onto a small yard and some broken timber.

She sat down with reluctance and circumspection, for the leather seats were stained and soiled, and her only remaining clothes were those which she now wore. She had seen no one at all.

A few minutes later the German soldier came in. He entered the first door on the left, where there were others who sat and drank. He ordered a glass of beer, and talked and jested with the men who were seated there, in a German as good as the English he had spoken before. Emptying his glass, he got up to go. When he had closed the door of the room, and was in the passage again, he laid a hand on the outer door, opening it a little way, and closing it with sufficient noise for anyone in the room who had cared to notice to suppose that he had gone out into the street. But when he had done that, he went quietly down the passage and entered the room where Perdita waited.

He felt sure by now that she had not been followed, and that no one would suspect that he was meeting her there.

CHAPTER XXIV.

THE soldier seated himself opposite Perdita, and when he spoke it was again in the English tongue.

"You will want," he said; "to know who I am. I am an Englishman, Richard Steele. I am in the British Intelligence Service, but to them I have no name, but a number only, which would have no meaning for you.

"Until the night on which Prague was bombed, I used the guise of an employee at the British Legation there, though I was often away, and you would have had no occasion to notice me. But I observed Mrs. Langton and yourself, and I had a natural surprise when I saw you here, walking idly about, as you seemed to do. It was an extreme imprudence, as you would have found if everyone had not been too engaged with themselves and the world's events to take much notice of you. But you shall tell me now how you come to be here, in a brief way, for the time is short."

Perdita said: "No. I don't know you at all. I am almost sure that I have not seen you before. But there may have been servants I did not see."

"I did not look quite as I do now."

"Well, I will suppose that." She had an inward doubt, but she considered that she must not throw away the one chance that appeared. It was pleasant to meet with one who could talk her own tongue in a native way. And there was no secret in how she had come there, nor any wisdom in letting her doubt appear.

She answered frankly, telling him in a few words how Caresse Langton and Lawrence Norton had died, and how she had escaped from the burning ruins of Prague. She told him how Karl Dürer had obtained permission for their car to pass the Bavarian frontier, how he had left her with his sisters in their Nürnberg home, which she had preferred, at that moment, to the alternative of continuing the journey to England in the solitary company of Paul, the Legation servant who had driven the car, and who must go on with the dispatches that had been placed in his master's hands.

"I could not know," she concluded, "that England and Germany would be at war on the next day."

"No," he said, "I suppose not. You would have been safe with Paul. But I doubt that he will have got through. He would have thought of nothing but to get the dispatches safe."

"I did not observe," she replied, "that he was thinking of me."

"Well, I know Paul. You have not told me why you wandered the streets as though you were looking for someone to run you in."

"What else could I do? Captain Dürer's sisters were denouncing me to the police."

"You were awkwardly placed. I concede that."

He became silent. He seemed to have forgotten the shortness of time of which he had spoken before. She was aware that he was considering her in a way that she did not entirely like, though it was, or perhaps because it was, so impersonal in its regard. His thought was: "She may have courage enough, and perhaps brains. But are they brains of the right kind?"

In the silence, she remembered that she had not had food or drink for nearly six hours, and her breakfast had been a light meal.

"I suppose," she asked, "we can get something to eat? It will save time while we talk."

"It would be possible, but not wise."

She was not disposed to have her suggestion put aside in this casual manner. She persisted: "I have money with me. Surely we could get something. It must be a natural thing to do in a place like this. Will you not join me, and, if you will, order for both?"

"No," he said, in an absent-minded way. "Sleeping dogs should be let lie." And then, in an altered voice: "I beg your pardon. I forgot these." He pulled out the biscuits he had bought. The bag was half-empty now, and its contents had been crushed carelessly in his tunic pocket. But they were still food she was glad to have where no better came.

As she commenced to eat, she thought it time to come to the point of her own need. The mention of money had reminded her of the hope she had had before that she might buy her way through this hostile land. But she had become too cautious to mention how considerable a sum was in her own hands.

"If I could be got free," she said, "my father would pay well. He would honour any promise that I might give."

He put the suggestion indifferently aside. "It is not money will help you here. We must manage another way." He was following his own thought then he asked: "You are most anxious to get home?"

"Yes, of course."

"Even though I tell you that London was bombed two nights ago by some thousands of planes, and its eastern end is still burning beyond control?"

"Yes. All the more."

"And will you tell me how you thought that wandering the streets here would help you to do that?"

"I tried to think of a way."

"Such as—?"

"I had thought of stealing a car."

"You would not have gone fifty miles without being stopped, or shot in the back if you had gone on."

"Well, I could think of no better way."

He had put her method of flight aside, as the plain folly it was, but the fact that she had been willing for such attempt ended the doubt in his mind.

"If you will take a great risk," he said, "I can get you home."

"If you can promise that—"

"You had better hear what it is, and then say; and I will trust your silence if you refuse."

"You need have no doubt about that."

"So I believe. Have you ever flown?"

"Not much. I have been a passenger in airliners. I couldn't pilot myself, if you mean that."

"No. I was not thinking of that. You would be in an airliner again, though with less comfort than you have learnt to expect. There is a fleet of commercial planes assembled to fly to England tonight, to carry troops to be landed there. I am expecting to go with them, and if you will wear a uniform of the same kind I can get you through."

"I should be in England in a few hours? What is the special danger in that?"

"We shall have an escort of fighting planes, but we may be attacked in the air, even by larger forces than ours."

"I was told that the English fleets are entirely destroyed."

"Which is not true. But you must believe that I have reason for what I say, and not ask me to explain, which I shall not always be likely to do. There may be fighting in which many planes will be shot down. And if you land there may be another danger to face. You may be shot for the uniform that you will wear by your own friends, before you can explain who you are. You may even be abused by civilians who will not believe, for this will become a most bitter war."

She found it hard to believe that. "I would risk more to be home. I should have nothing to fear from English people when I had spoken a dozen words."

"Well, you may be right there. I have been mostly abroad since the last war. I may know more of foreign crowds than our own."

"But there is another danger you have not mentioned at all. Should we not be observed when we desert from the German ranks, and be shot by them?"

"No. There would be no danger of that."

"Can you tell me why?"

"I have said that I will not explain. You must trust me or not. I will tell you this, which it may be well for you to know. The Germans think that I serve them."

"What do you want me to do now?"

"I want you to go back. You will tell the ladies with whom you stay that you took a walk, and became lost in the town."

"As a fact, I am."

"Do you know the address?"

"I should know the house. It is near a Platz of the same name—Albrecht Dürer Platz."

"Well, I can direct you there."

He got up to go, but she was still in more doubts than one. She asked: "And if I should be arrested there?"

"You will not, during the day. I can promise that. Such visits are made by night, and before that I shall see you again."

"I suppose I should thank you for this. I cannot see why you do so much."

"You should not thank me at all. I have a reason for getting back to England which is more than yours, I might say by a million times. I will tell you this. If I could get there an hour sooner at the cost of your life you would not live till tonight."

Perdita laughed at that, though it was not said in a joking way. "It is nice to know. But if that be so, it is stranger still that you should help me at all. I must be an added danger to you."

"But you are not. You will help me here in a subtle way which I will not try to explain; and perhaps differently at a later hour."

"Very well," she said, "it must be as mysterious as you will. It is strange enough that you should have found me."

"So it is. But the world is a small place. And there are reasons why both Captain Dürer and I should have come here. And as I wandered these streets, you were plain to see. In our profession, those live longest who use their eyes."

He went at that, content with what he had done, but wishing that it could have been with some fewer words. He directed her to Albrecht Dürer Platz with particular care, not wishing her to become conspicuous by hesitation, or to make inquiries in her halting German. He told her to wait for not less than an hour after he had gone, so long as no one entered the room, which, for reasons he did not give, they would be unlikely to do.

CHAPTER XXV.

WHILE he was arranging with Perdita to assist her escape, Richard Steele, as he had given his name to her (or No. 973, as it was entered on the records of the British Intelligence Service, Private Eugene Gumpert, as he now was, or Adolph Zweiss, as he was believed to be by the German police), was the subject of an animated discussion at the Nürnberg police headquarters.

Colonel Wieck of the Military Police, a man of heavy Prussian features but with a slightly aquiline nose and a darkness of complexion which suggested a larger mixture of Jewish blood than could be explained by the records of his legitimate ancestry, sat with the brusque, bullet-headed Bavarian Chief of Police, and an officer, Captain-Major Lessing, who had been sent from Berlin with the dossier of the doubted man.

"I doubted him when I heard his tale," Colonel Wieck said, "and I am not sure but I doubt him now. But what could I do? The mole was there, and your instructions from Berlin were too explicit to override. Beside that, it is fair to say that we have found his tale to be true, so far as it has been possible to confirm it at any point."

"He has been seen," Major Lessing replied, "by two men who knew Zweiss during the war, and one says he will not swear either way, but he does not think it is he. The other says that he is sure that Zweiss was a larger and blonder man, but it is fair to say he is old and his sight is bad."

"Twenty years," the Chief of Police remarked, "will make a great change, for which these men may not have had sense to allow. It is often hard enough to get identification within a week! But it is for you gentlemen to decide. I have done my part. He will be here to receive his instructions at three o'clock." He glanced at a round clock on the wall, the hands of which stood at 2:55 P.M. He said: "Well, I have work that waits. I will leave it to you."

He went out, and Major Lessing was amused. He said: "He will leave it to us! He is too astute to risk a mistake which he need not make."

Colonel Wieck did not accept the plural. He said: "It is an honour you must not ask me to share. You come from Berlin because you are the most fit to judge, and have knowledge which is not mine."

Major Lessing became serious. He said simply: "We have our duty to do, and that does not include telling each other what it may be. I meant no offence. But I suppose that this is a simple thing."

"Well, so it may be to you. It was not to me."

They said no more, for at that moment Private Gumpert was shown into the room.

The two officers were not those whom he had expected to meet, and Colonel Wieck was an unwelcome sight. But he gave no sign of that as he said: "Good afternoon, gentlemen," greeting those who had been slower to speak to him.

Major Lessing asked coldly: "Do you not salute when you enter the room?"

"Private Gumpert does, but I thought that those I should meet here—" He stood to attention as he spoke, and gave the salute which their rank required.

"When you assume a part, it is well to maintain it in every detail."

The admonition brought a smile to the lips of a man whose thoroughness in the details of what he did was a byword in the secret service to which he belonged, and had already saved his life from those who were to examine him now.

But he said only: "I am rebuked. I was to come for instruction here, which implied that I should meet those to whom my status was known."

"Your instructions are that you will join the fleet which will leave at 3:30 A.M. You will be attached to the pilot plane, being rated as Air-Admiral Nachod's orderly, but your actual responsibility will be to guide the fleet to the landing place which has been already selected, as your knowledge of aviation, and of the country itself, should render you well able to do."

"I will do what I can. Where is the landing to be?"

"On the moors north of Sheffield, which it is our purpose to seize for our own use, rather than to destroy it with bombs from the air."

"I have heard that very skilful camouflages have been prepared for the protection of the manufacturing and mining areas."

"That is true. But they cannot hide every hill, every river's course. That is where we are depending on you."

"To do more than maps or your instruments of precision? Well, I will do what I can. What is to follow that?"

"You will be allowed to escape. You may be fired on, lest your going be observed from the English side, but you will not be hit. You will report to the English Intelligence Service."

"I may lose time in finding where it now is, if it has withdrawn from London."

"We can help you in that from the report of one we can trust. It has its headquarters in Bristol now. What we want you to learn is this: there is a British aerodrome which we have not yet found, where a large part of what remains of their battle-fleet is believed to resort and to get its fuel supplies. We have little doubt that it is in the Welsh hills, but we know no nearer than that. We wish you to learn where it is, as you should be able to do, and to report it without delay. You are sure that they do not doubt that you are loyal to them?"

"How can I answer that? I am safe unless they have spies in your own office, and you have been careless to let them learn. I have taken their pay for twenty years while you thought me dead that I might serve Germany now."

"Very well. We must hope you can. If you do, we shall not be grudging in our reward."

Private Gumpert made an impatient gesture. "It must be as you will. Do you suppose I risked my life in the last war for the sake of an airman's pay?"

Major Lessing was as near to a gentleman as a German officer of that day was likely to be. He was in doubt concerning the identity of the man to whom he spoke, but to doubt should not be to condemn, and, in fact, the doubt had lessened the while he talked. Yet he saw that this doubt had deflected both the manner and substance of what he said. He would not have spoken thus to one whom he recognized as the once famous ace of the air Adolph Zweiss, who had afterwards obliterated his identity for twenty years that he might do service to Germany in this war, which he had foreseen to be certain to come. Neither, it was very sure, would he have spoken thus to a most dangerous and impudent English spy.

Yet the man who faced him was one of these two. There was no middle way. He was not Private Gumpert in more than name, and in the uniform that he wore. In fact, and it was the most sinister of the admitted facts from which conclusions had to be drawn, Zweiss or Steele had strangled that loyal German soldier with his own hands. Major Lessing saw that while he admitted the man to be Adolph Zweiss, and accepted from him the most hazardous service that can be asked of any in time of war—that of passing from side to side—it was neither justice nor policy to address him as something less than he claimed to be.

"I meant no offence," he said, "and those who serve Germany now should not be overlooked when the war is done. She will honour herself when she honours them. But from the life you have lived in the last years, you must have seen that most of those who are engaged in the espionage services of Europe are people of mixed nationality and no patriotism. They have chosen or felt compelled to make their livelihood in what, for them, is a base way. We know that they are no better than that, but they are tools that we have to use, and must therefore buy."

"Yes, I have seen that. But there are some of a better kind."

"So I am glad to believe. Have you any questions to ask, or are the instructions all that you require?"

"They are quite clear. How do I report?"

"By the password 'Frankfurt,' for which our commanders will be alert, and which will be used in no other way. Anything else?"

"Only this. There is a young English lady in the town, Miss Perdita Wyatt. She was staying at the British Legation in Prague and escaped by car. I understand that she was instrumental in rescuing one of our own airmen, Captain Dürer, who came away with her in the car, which was driven by a servant of the Legation. This man went on, leaving Miss Wyatt at Captain Dürer's home here, that being, of course, some hours before the outbreak of war with England.

"With your consent, I propose to take this young lady back to her own country."

"Why?"

"Because, if I do this, it will be an additional assurance of my English sympathies, if any doubt should have arisen."

"It is a fine point."

"It is one of those trifles that are sometimes vital to turn the scale."

"How did you learn she is here?"

"I saw her wandering in the street."

"And she knew you, of course?"

"No. I knew her by sight, but I doubt that she had seen me before. If she had, she would not have recognized me in this dress. I was a mere chauffeur to her."

"How do you propose to do this?"

"I should disguise her in a uniform of the same regiment as mine. She would think that I got her through by that trick, as a member of the British Intelligence Service would be likely to do.

"I have talked to her in that way."

Major Lessing said: "Wait a moment." He went out of the room. He sought the Chief of Police, whom he questioned upon the accuracy of this account. He found it to be confirmed in all points, and the Chief, being asked, approved the proposed plan.

"I knew," he said, "that the young Fräulein was here, but there is no danger from her. I would have dealt with her when I could spare my men from more urgent needs. But her rescue will please the English authorities (if they have thoughts to spare for such matters as they are now placed), for she is a young lady of powerful friends. The idea is good, and I should say that Zweiss is still a most capable man, as he was in the last war."

Major Lessing allowed this opinion to outweigh some doubts that he had, and the more certainly so as he found that Colonel Wieck took the same view when he went back to give his consent, and to arrange the further details which it involved.

The proposed rescue of Perdita might or might not be essential to support the credit of No. 973 with the British Intelligence Service, but it had been of use in convincing the German officials of the genuineness of Adolph Zweiss's fears that it lay in doubt, which may have been the greater, as it was certainly the more immediate, need.

CHAPTER XXVI.

THE Nürnberg streets were still hard with frost, but the skies clouded during the afternoon, leaden and low. The Nürnbergers had long ceased to lift their heads to the noise of a passing plane, and during the last three days the roar of engines across the sky had been little less than a constant sound. Now they took little heed of a fleet that they could not see, when the roar of its passing was overhead, its course being above the low ceiling of cloud, where it had sunlight and open blue.

But men lifted their heads in a new doubt when, through the noise of the engines, there came the unmistakable spluttering sound of machine-gun fire. They looked up then, but there was nothing to see but the veiling cloud. They had ceased to think during the last day (if they ever had) that the war would come to their own doors.

The noise of machine-gun fire increased and was mixed at times with that of the bursting of heavier shells. They could make no more than a wild guess as to what the attacking force or the course of the fight might be, until a blazing plane tumbled out of the clouds and shot down like a falling meteor to crash across the narrow width of the Pergnitz Bridge. The frail structure broke to the blow. Its falling arch mixed in the stream with the wreck of the burning plane. The ancient houses that rose sheer from the waterside, with their straight-fronted, overhanging wooden balconies, that in summer days would be heavy with trailing flowers, were blinded with fumes of smoke and of hissing steam, till their dry wood caught and leapt up to a loftier blaze.

But it was not the only one to fall. One after one, French bombers and German battle-planes came down from the unseen fight, and, worse than they, there was a falling of bombs, heavy though very short, as the flying battle passed over the clouds and drifted westward to become no more than a distant and dying sound.

The fact was that the French Command of the Air, seeing its forces to be so greatly outnumbered by those of its Russo-German opponents, had resolved that its bombing squadrons could be better used in desperate efforts to destroy the German aerodromes than in attacks upon open cities or points of military importance of other kinds. A fleet of sixty bombers of the Amiot pattern, having a range of less than 400 miles and a speed of scarcely 200 per hour at 12,000 feet when carrying a full load of 2,000 pounds, but being built with two gunners' cockpits as well as that of the pilot, so that they were capable of some measure of self-defence, had been sent up with orders to avoid encountering enemy forces so far as their limited speed would allow, and to steer their course to any one of several such objectives, at their commander's discretion, or as the exigencies of the situation might permit.

Commander Despard, a man of courage and resolution and a skilful airman, had seen that he had an impossible task, unless fortune should be his friend. This being so, he had resolved that it should not be tempted too far. His fleet could only endure until the attention of a number of Germany's swifter and deadlier fighting planes sufficient for its destruction should be directed upon it. He considered that the longer he should wander about the skies, the more certain it was that such a position would develop, and that the better strategy would be, so to speak, to have none at all, but to take a bees' flight to the objective he chose, trusting only to such speed as he had to get him through before strong opposition could be marshalled to close his way.

By the boldness of this attempt, he came unharmed to the very doors of success.

He saw enemy planes crossing the skies, in large squadrons or small, and at times the swift transit of single scouts, but it was not until he had his objective in sight (that being the great Nürnberg Aerodrome) that a squadron of German fighting planes of a light build, which had been hanging on the right flank, though out of machine-gun range, for the last fifty miles, and which could fly three miles to his two, closed in to the narrow range which machine-gun fighting requires, at the same time that a larger number of German fighters of heavier pattern, armed with cannon to which the machine-gun could make no effective reply, rose through the clouds ahead, having been sent up from the Nürnberg Aerodrome to encounter him before he should be in a position to drop bombs where they would do serious harm.

Commander Despard, seeing the opposition he had to meet, saw also that his fleet could be saved only by such a miracle as he did not expect. He saw that he could order withdrawal before an enemy force so much more heavily gunned than his own, and that his action would be difficult to condemn. But in that case, he might expect that most of his own planes would be shot down, one by one, as they would be chased through the skies, whether he should order them to retain their formation or to scatter about, and that this might happen without their having done much to chasten his country's foes

He preferred, therefore, to order his fleet to advance boldly against their heavier and outnumbering opponents, which they did at such speed, and in such order, as the close-range fighting upon their flank allowed, and, believing that he was in the neighbourhood of Nürnberg city, though the carpet of cloud over which he flew hid it from sight, he ordered that they should commence to unload their bombs while they were still in a condition to do that which was the whole object for which they came.

This manœuvre, however costly, had its reward in the fact that his opponents who, in other circumstances, might have used their superior speed to direct their cannons upon him while keeping at a distance of three or four hundred yards, at which his machine-guns could have made no effective reply, were now unable to adopt a form of tactics which would have allowed him to fly directly over the aerodrome ground, dropping bombs as he passed. They must meet him in a frontal attack in an endeavour to head him off from that which it was their first duty to guard.

In attempting this, they found themselves under a further disadvantage, owing to the fact that the Amiot monoplane could soar as well, if not better, than themselves, and Commander Despard's fleet already was 500 feet above them when he first observed them rising out of the clouds. Commander Despard held this advantage with such success that there was one period when he was able to loose his bombs with the German fleet beneath him, so that they might protect the aerodrome if they could, by catching the bombs on their wings, which was not the method they had designed.

For a time, the tactical advantage was his, and had it not been for the dog-fighting in which he was engaged by the lighter squadron that had pursued him at first, which did not cease to worry his flank, he might have done even more, the close fighting which he had preferred having had the additional advantage that it had saved him from the aerodrome guns, which could not pick their aim through the veiling clouds, nor risk a random discharge which would have been as likely, or more, to distress their friends.

In the end, some of his fleet actually escaped, after their bomb-chambers had been discharged, and having done harm enough, though how much they could only guess. But we have no special concern with them, beyond the fact that one of the bombs which were first scattered over the town happened to fall on the house where Perdita was, so resolving the doubt of whether Gretchen

Dürer would be a fit wife for a lawyer of Nordic blood, or even worthy of an "unfertile mate," for her limbs were pitifully torn, and her head crushed by a fallen beam. Underneath, in the cellar's depths, Perdita and Eugene Gumpert (as he now asked to be called by her) faced one another under the light of an electric bulb which the serving-man would switch on when he came down for the wine, and heard the ceiling crack, and saw it sag at one end in an ominous way.

They had come down there, as to a secure and secret place where Perdita could change into the uniform he had brought (the details of which event may well be left, where there is so much of larger things to be told), and now they looked at the steps, down which there came a falling rubble of masonry, such as would be hard to surmount, even though there should be exit above.

No. 973 looked round coolly enough, having come through worse dangers than that, and even Perdita took it more quietly than she would have been likely to do a few days before, so adaptable is the human mind. He said: "Keep away from the steps. The rubble may slip again. It is good luck that the light remains. You had better change while you can, and we shall be ready for whatever may come."

He laid out the clothes on a trestle the cellar held, giving such explanations of what they were and how they should be put on as he thought she would need to know, and retired himself to a farther cellar, leaving her alone for the change that she had to make.

The clothes were clean but coarse, and she looked at them with distaste, both for what they were, and what they would make her to be. At a less desperate need, she might have refused, even now, to give up sex and identity thus at the bidding of a man she had met but a few hours before, and who offered her (if she believed him to be all that he said) a most perilous chance. But she had made her choice, and saw herself to be already started upon a path which she could not turn.

Slowly at first, and then at a better speed, she drew off a dress the fine texture of which she would have regarded so lightly the day before—had, indeed, regarded as fit for no better use than her escape from the burning city, and scarcely for that, and now recognized as identifying her with the secure status which she was casting aside— or had it fallen itself in the midst of a falling world?

Resolutely putting reluctance by, she clothed herself in the uniform of a German private, stifling a vague, fearful thought that—had she not heard it said?—anyone so found in a time of war would have earned death as a spy, without trouble of further proof. Yet she still had her passport, could show who she was, and by what chance she came to be there. Captain Dürer would be a willing witness of that!

Eugene Gumpert had come back, having given her so much time, and so noiselessly, that she had gone near to forgetting that he was there.

He said: "I made a good guess at the size. They fit better than I had feared. But if you walk with longer strides, dragging your steps, and in a less upright way, there will be fewer likely to look. You can be one who sulks to be called up, being young. You can think of me as No. 973 if you will, but you must call me Eugene, and you are Franz Hals for this night, that being an easy name which you will not forget. Berlin is your home—Danziger Street in Berlin, of which I can tell you as much as you need to know—but you will find your best friend in a quiet tongue."

"It is the friend," Perdita replied, "that I shall be most willing to have. How can I take this?"

She held the handbag that contained all her remaining possessions. She had left most behind when she fled from Prague, and the rest were in the ruins over their heads.

"That is soon said. You must not take it at all."

"But there is my passport here, and money, and other things that I need to have."

No. 973 took the bag in his own hands. "Listen," he said. "If I get you home, as I hope, it is all you must ask. As a German private, you cannot carry such things as these. I am thorough in what I do."

"I suppose I can keep the money?"

"Is it English or German?"

"There are English bank-notes, and five hundred marks in German money which Sir Geoffrey gave me when I was leaving Prague."

"And what value can they be now? I suppose none. The German money would have its use if you were staying here, which you aim to avoid. You can keep that if you will till you have got clear, but after that it will be the paper of which it is made. As to these," he had opened the bag, and had the English notes in his hand as he spoke, "I suppose their value is gone. They are paper too. But be that as it may, they are something you must not have. You must see the wisdom of what I do."

He tore the notes through as he spoke and pushed the pieces between the narrow bars of a drain that was in the centre of the cellar floor.

"You may be content," he said, "that what you lose will not be a German's gain."

He tore the passport up, and pushed the fragments down the same way. He looked at the remaining contents of the bag, which did not seem worth the trouble of such destruction. He smiled, as he rarely would, at his companion's half-troubled, half-angry eyes.

"Franz," he said, "I fear you must have pilfered a lady's things. You will give Danziger Street a bad name."

Perdita tried to smile in reply, but success was less than an attempt. It was hard to think that money had lost its power, frightening to think how absolutely she was in this man's hands; how difficult it would be, if circumstance should separate her from him, to explain how she came to be in a German uniform—and in a language she could not speak! They might shoot her at once as a very evident spy, without troubling about the explanation she could not give.

"Well," she said, "I suppose you know best. I am trusting to you. To what part of England are we to go?"

"Where would you wish?"

"Warwickshire is my own home. A few miles from Knowle."

"You may be fortunate in the place where we shall land."

"You could be more exact?"

"No. I think not."

"Do you think I shall find them safe?"

"Your own people? You may expect that. The world is large. It has a surface more than sufficient for many bombs. But you will tire if you stand, which there is no occasion to do."

He took her clothes as he spoke in a careless heap, and spread them upon the floor, making a clean place for her to sit.

She had a further resentment at seeing her garments treated in such a way, which her reason denied. But were no values left in the world?

As though hearing her thought, he said: "It is the last use they can be to you."

"Yes, you are right, of course. But should we make no effort to get from here?"

He answered easily: "How would you do that? There must come a time when they will dig. If you try clearing the steps, you may bring an avalanche on your head. For my part, I would rather live with my limbs whole."

She was puzzled that he should take their confinement in so light a way, but she was too completely under his guidance now to protest further. She must trust him, having done what she already had, or allowed to be done to her, and if he were indiscreet, she must pay the price of a bad guess. It was clear that he did not feel the need of advice from her.

So she sat down, and he took a place at her side.

Her mind went forward to the English home to which she was seeking return at so great a risk. Was it true, she wondered, that England was under the German heel, as she had heard it said in the Nürnberg streets? Had London really been served after the manner of Prague, where she had seen the streets burn and the houses fall? She put the question aloud in another form, as she had asked it before: "Can you say how it will end? Is it certain that Germany will win this war?"

He did not turn the subject aside with a brief reply. For some reason, he seemed willing to talk more than it was his custom to do.

"That," he said, "is a question I have asked myself for twenty years, as I have watched and waited for it to come, and now that the answer is near, I cannot guess what it will be."

"It has always been sure to come?"

"It need not have been. But Europe has been steered most blindly for the abyss."

Perdita made no answer to that. A week before she might have thought that the statesmen of Europe could survive the adverse judgement of one who, by his own word, was no more than an English spy. But sitting where she did, and after what she had seen three days before, their part stood condemned by the event.

As she was silent, he spoke again. "It is the looker-on, so it is said, who sees most of the game; and in my profession we see much, and have leisure to think.

"You see Germany loose like a savage dog, and Russia like a mad bitch at its side, and you may say that the guilt is theirs, and that there are no others to blame.

"But if you ask how they have grown to their present strength, and to the purpose they show, you find the answers to be of a more complex kind.

"The Russian tyranny must have broken down many years ago had it been faced in a bold way. It might have been trodden out with the world's strength like a dangerous fire, while the whole world was in arms; but that was tried in a weak way, which was worse than none, by men grown weary of war. Or it might have failed of itself, had the world been firm that it would not deal with men whose hands were black with innocent blood, who were assassins and public thieves. Had they refused Russia barter or loan until she had chosen men of less criminal kinds for her highest seats, or to be her envoys abroad.... So it was; but I do not say that there would have been much to fear from Russia alone. She might have been a curse to no more than herself, or to Asia rather than us; and it is true that she was ill-governed before, from which her later evils have sprung, though it was in a milder, less malignly intelligent way. But to treat Germany as we did was a deadlier fault, for which payment must now be made."

Perdita remembered the arguments she had heard at college and school, which, it seemed, were confirmed by one who had judged from a closer view. She said: "You mean that the Versailles Treaty was bad?"

"So it was. But not mainly as you may have been taught to believe, because it was too harsh to a conquered foe. Its folly was that it left Germany irritated rather than weak, and allowed her to return to her full strength while her irritation remained."

"It would have been wiser to treat her so that she would have become friendly again?"

"It is hard to give a certain answer to that. It might have been well either to destroy or forgive, but there could be no safety by a medium way.

"Was it wisdom to forbid Germany to rearm, and then watch her do it without prevention? To form new states that were small and weak, unless their protection were made secure?"

"But was that not America's fault more than ours? Would there not have been a real League of Nations if President Wilson had had his way?"

"Yes, that is a fair argument. It was Europe's tragedy that America came into the war, and that her Senate was what they were. But it would have remained true that the formation of those new states, with all the jealous problems and bitterness that they raised, was not to seek peace by a likely road."

"But surely the small nations have as much right as the larger ones to govern themselves?"

"I don't know that the question of right is worth discussion, when it was such an obviously impossible aim to reach. The races of Eastern Europe are too inextricably mixed for any geographical division to separate them, unless about two-thirds should be pulled up by the roots and removed into segregating territories, which would have little relation in extent or otherwise to existing boundaries. But there is a question that goes deeper than that.

"Suppose that Great Britain had been defeated in the last war, and that Germany had professed compassion for the Scottish and

Welsh peoples, and imposed separation upon them—I am not suggesting that there is any analogy between their present condition and that of oppressed nationalities in Eastern Europe; indeed, the less there is the stronger the illustration becomes—but would such divisions have made for peace, even between the friendly, highly civilized peoples of our own land? Would not tariff barriers have arisen, with all the frictions that they involve? Barbed-wire frontiers, perhaps, and armed sentries pacing where there is nothing now but amity and continuous fields?

"Might there not have been long dispute regarding the true boundaries of Wales—the line of the Severn, or the Malvern Hills? Would not Monmouthshire have been claimed both by England and Wales, with an almost equal balance of right?"

Perdita saw sense in this, and felt that she listened to one who had watched and thought, as he had had time to do. Hearing the conviction with which he spoke, his words had more force than when they are set down in a colder way. Yet she thought that it was an easier matter to condemn that which had been tried than it would have been to steer a smoother course through the problems that Europe had faced since the German armies had broken into confused flight, from Flanders to the Ardennes. She asked: "Do you say that things could have been done in a way which would not have had equal dangers, though they were of a different kind?"

"That is another question to which it is not easy to make reply. But there is one thing that is sure. There can be no lasting peace in a Europe that lacks a head. There can be no balance of power that will not lead to wars either of greed or of fear. That is a lesson that Europe has learnt and unlearnt for more than a thousand years—from the day when she shattered Rome."

"You mean one nation must be supreme?"

"Yes; or the states of Europe must be federated into one strength, which it should not have been beyond human wit to contrive, and it was clearly the hour when it paused from strife and looked down on its millions dead. Are Germans and French, are even Spaniards and Czechs, more diverse of race than Celt and Saxon, who dwell as friends in our own land?"

"And if all did not agree?"

"They would have had no strength to refuse, even had they been of a folly to shrink from a settled peace."

"You would have forced them all to come in, making war for that, if it could have been done in no better way?"

"It would have been needless, had such a federation been made of the countries of the allies, and of those that yielded to them. The others would soon have come within the bond of so sure a peace. But in the last resort, you must enforce peace with the sword. Can you tell me another way?"

Perdita puzzled over this, to which she felt that there was an answer the world had long struggled to find. She had come too close to war in the last three days to accept it as a tolerable method of settling the quarrels of men. She remembered things she had seen in the night, things she had seen in Prague in the flame-lit snow. She said: "I have been taught that war will ruin the world, as I suppose it is doing now. But there must be a better way. There are love and war. May not love prove to be the stronger at last?"

"So it may. That is the idea of the Christian faith, and it cannot be said that it has failed, for it would be hard to show that it has ever been fairly tried. But if you argue for that, you must be honest with your own mind. You must see where it would end, or perhaps, where it should begin. You need not shut the courts of law, but it is clear that you must pay off the police, and keep only such men in jail as are willing to stay."

"I don't see that. It is against criminals that the police act. It is nothing like two nations going to war."

"It is nothing like a war between two nations of equal strength. But if one be strong, and one weak—well, the weaker it is, the more the similarity is."

"But the smaller nation may have the better case of the two. It may not be a criminal at all."

"But suppose it is. Would the stronger nation be justified then if it should make war? Nations usually persuade themselves, or their rulers persuade them, that they have justice upon their side."

"But it must make a difference whether that belief be true or false."

"So it must. That is an oversight the pacifists often make. They say nations always contend that they are in the right, and then talk as though assertion and fact were one. As though there could be no distinction between righteous and unrighteous wars, because those who are in the wrong decline to admit their guilt. But you cannot alter the fundamental fact that it is physical force on which they rely, as the law does when a murderer hands.

"If you defend that, but say that war between nations is always wrong, you say that war is only justified when it is waged against those who are very weak, or are of your own blood, or when it can be waged without risk or discomfort to you."

Perdita did not willingly accept this, but her mind was sufficiently clear to admit that it was more logical than it had appeared at the first. She said that if the police were morally justified in arresting criminals at all, that right could not be lessened if the criminals should become a numerous and powerful body, nor even if they should dwell apart, providing that their crimes were against those whom it was the duty of the police to protect. She saw that all coercion by force is a form of war, its moral basis being only strengthened by the ethical standards of the tribunal which directs its activities. The tyrannies of Moscow and Berlin had made pitiless war on men of their own lands, before they gathered strength to extend operations beyond their own boundaries. Yet she saw war as the greatest evil which can fall on innocent homes, with a clarity against which no argument could prevail.

And as she was silent, the spy who had pondered long concerning this day which he had foreseen as certain to come, spoke again, as though answering her unspoken thoughts: "I'm not trying to tell you that war is a good thing. It was never that, and this one is likely to be the worst that the world has known. But, like most earthly things, it has two sides, evil and good, which you can't divide. And some of the pacifist arguments against it have not only been silly, they have been baser than that which they condemned.

"I mean, they have objected to war because of its hardship, danger, and dirt. They could have condemned pioneering, or exploration of any kind, for the same reasons, and perhaps some of them would. They didn't condemn it for killing people so much as for the danger of getting killed. Some of them talked in the name of Christ, but their arguments weren't Christian at all. Christianity doesn't put physical comfort at the top of the list of the things for which men should strive. It doesn't value life quite in the same way.

"The fact is that the pacifists were afraid of war. I don't say they were wrong in that; but it wasn't an argument by which war would be likely to be put away, because most men are made in a different mould. They love hazard of any kind. They want experience for themselves. You must stir them, in the bulk, by nobler motions than that. It was an argument that was bound to fail.

"And war has become a more dreadful thing because men have raised a devil they cannot rule. They took Science—physical science—for a very plausible god, and he promised them Comfort and Ease as men had never known it before. Then he told them to limit their children's lives while they burned corn, and ploughed cotton back into the ground, and they were bewildered, but still obeyed.

And now he has brought them here. It may be that it is a war that will clean the world."

He spoke the last words as though to himself, rather than her, and drew out his watch. Having seen it, he became content to remain for a longer time, and commenced again.

"There were times in the Middle Ages when men believed in a way that they do not now, and they saw death as that which you should not go too far to avoid. You can read Mallory for that, where its spirit lives.

"I have seen war; and I should say that men have not greatly changed, but that faith grows in a more difficult soil. In our wars there are no Truces of God. But I have seen that war exalts and degrades. It is a test of the soul of man, which the base cannot endure."

He became silent, and Perdita said nothing, seeing that he was immersed in his own thoughts. She was confused among arguments that she did not like, but could not lightly refute. She could not regard war as an abstract thought. She saw a present and frightful curse which had fallen across the fair face of the world, and was obliterating the gracious securities of the life she knew. *Give us peace in our time, O Lord.* That was the only sensible prayer, and it was one that it had become useless to pray.

He spoke again: "You could stop war if you would. But I suppose it is what you will never do. I do not say you are wrong."

She understood that it was not herself he addressed, but the womanhood that was hers, and again she had no reply.

He muttered: "If I can be in time!" and had she known him better she would have understood that he was under a tension of mind hard to endure, for spies do not cultivate habits of talking aloud; and, indeed, what he had been saying before might have been often thought, but it was that which those who knew him best (which may have been less than well) would have been startled to hear.

He looked at his watch again, and rose. "It is time to go."

He led the way to the next cellar, switching on a light there, and following a short passage to a flight of stone steps similar to those which they had descended before which were now blocked.

"Then you knew…!" she exclaimed, as he led her up as one who walks a way he has been before.

"Yes. I had a look round while you changed. In these old houses that are extensive above, there is often more than one way into the vaults."

"Then why did we stay there?"

"Because, speaking the bad German you do, you could have been in no better place till the hours of waiting were done. But I must ask you not to address me in English again, for it is a language I cannot speak, and one that you do not know."

She followed him silently after that through the dark portion of the house which was left unwrecked. No one saw them come out into the night, for there were many fires in the town which had been lit by the bombs or the falling planes, and such places as were merely wrecked and not burned were disregarded as yet, both by they police and the watching crowds.

She saw that he had commenced talking that he might keep her quiet in the cellar alone, and that he had not spoken as confiding to, or debating with her; and whether his arguments had been bad or good was more than she would have been prepared to decide. But it was no less true that he had revealed himself, and, with an instinct deeper than logic, she recognized that she had no longer a doubt of the side he owned, or the nation from which he came. He might be Adolph Zweiss in Berlin, and No. 973 in London, or wherever the British Intelligence Service might now be; but to her he was no more nor less than an English friend, and no less because he had said he would take her life with no scruple at all, if it should be of avail for the land they loved.

CHAPTER XXVII.

IN February, 1938, the standing army of Canada consisted of rather less than 4,000 men; her navy of half a dozen destroyers, sloops, and patrol-boats which were considered sufficient to police her divided coasts; and her air-service, which had been substantially augmented during the two previous years, of about 350 planes.

Contrasting the policy of the United States, which had been emphatic in her expressed determination to avoid becoming involved in the wars of the older world, but lavish in the establishment of military, naval, and aerial forces, Canada had continually visualized the possibility that she might be drawn into the vortex of Empire war, while making little exertion to prepare for such an eventuality. But this attitude, perhaps characteristic of the race from which the strength of Canada was most surely drawn, was not inconsistent with loyalty to the common Empire heritage, or the courage which rises higher as danger becomes more menacing and more near.

The additions to the Canadian Air Force which had been made during 1936-37 had been of fighting rather than bombing-planes, with good reasons enough. For Canada had no neighbours whom her Government conceived that she might ever desire to bomb, and it was also to be considered that the growing numbers of her commercial planes would be capable of conversion to bombers, or adapted for the transit of arms or stores, but they could by no possibility be transformed into fighting planes of the first line. They could be armed, as a merchant vessel may be mounted with half a dozen quick-firing guns, but she will still be quickly sent to the ocean-floor by a light cruiser of twice her speed and one-half her size.

The last additions to the air-fleet had consisted of six score of the Fairey Fantome single-seater, mounted with a motor cannon which would discharge incendiary or high explosive shells either singly, or at an automatic rate of 280 per minute, with an effective range of 500 yards. The weight of the gun was scarcely 137 pounds, and the recoil was absorbed by anchoring it rigidly to the aero-engine.

With an additional group of four machine-guns for closer fighting, these aeroplanes, skilfully handled, might be formidable opponents even to the newest patterns of the battle-planes of the German fleet, and would be likely to inflict fatal injury upon the most heavily armed planes of the bombing pattern, before they could be manœuvred into range and position to bring their own armaments into effective action.

Being biplanes, they had the disadvantages inseparable from that form of construction, but they were streamlined, lightly built, and capable of a speed of over 250 miles an hour.

Air-Marshal Dalton, looking forward to the European conflagration which became more certain as the years passed, had resolved that these planes could best be used as a striking force in its earliest hours.

He had formed his plan; and when the news came that London was under the hail of the German bombs, he required only the permission of his Government to translate it into effective action.

His theory had been that, if Great Britain should be engaged in aerial war, it would be useless to confine the Canadian Air Force to the protection of its own shores, for which it would be singly of no avail.

If the air-fleets of Great Britain should be destroyed by a stronger foe, that of Canada would be too small for its own defence when the battle-planes of Europe should cross the seas, as he did not doubt that they would be equal to do. It was a case in which the best defence was attack, and the value of the Canadian fleet depended upon the speed with which it could be brought into the front line of the war.

It is needless to ask whether he would have obtained permission for what he did, had the United States hesitated to declare its policy. The Ottawa Government heard that they would have the powerful support of Washington on their own continent; they heard that Japan would be no menace on their Pacific flank. They had at this time eighty-five of the Fairey Fantome biplanes under Air-Marshal Dalton's command stationed on their western coast, and thirty-five on their eastern. They ordered the force to transfer from the Pacific to the Atlantic seaboard, and gave Marshal Dalton permission to fly at once to the assistance of Britain at his own discretion, or in co-operation with the Air Command of that country.

There was at this time a large Danish aerodrome on the Greenland coast. German bayonets might shine in Copenhagen streets, but Greenland was far away, and there was no doubt as to the side to which its sympathies moved. Marshal Dalton made a long five hours' hop, and landed there in the late dawn of the Arctic day. Two hours later he took to the air again, leaving one plane, which had developed engine trouble, behind. He flew on to Iceland, and from there to a lonely landing-place on the Scottish moors, previously agreed with the British Air Ministry for such an emergency, where he arrived as twilight fell.

He had expected to rest his men till the next morning, when they would be fresh for whatever enterprise might offer, he having at that time no more definite plan than to strike swiftly and hard, wherever he might hear of congregation of the Empire's foes. He had no bombs to drop. He did not aim to attack the enemy's cities or camps from the air. Neither had he any troops to disembark. His numerical strength consisted of no more than eighty-two men (his fleet having now been reduced by two further planes, which had made a forced landing after their wings had grazed, with some damage to both). His sole object must be to attack and destroy the invading aircraft wherever he could find them vulnerable either by numerical or structural inferiority, or else to sacrifice his own fleet against outnumbering odds for the sake of the loss which could be inflicted upon his foes.

To gain the object for which he came, he must either be in possession of reliable information concerning the movements of his opponents, or he must accept the adventure of blindly cruising the skies, which, vast though the arena was, could hardly have been uneventful for many hours, if visibility were even moderately good, in view of the size and number of the hostile fleets that were in ceaseless operation towards the frontiers of Great Britain and France.

But his airmen had scarcely had time to stretch their legs on the misty, heather-coated moorland to which they had descended, and the work of re-fuelling was incomplete, when he received a message from the British Air Ministry, which was decoded to read:

> "Report from source believed reliable states that large fleet of military transport planes will leave Nürnberg at 4:30 A.M. (Mitel-Europa time) with escort of seven squadrons (forty-nine) fighting planes of type P2L P24. Reported destination, English Midlands, possibly Cannock Chase. Can you intercept?"

Marshal Dalton considered this, and concluded that he could not easily be better employed, and that his men must be content with a short night.

The P2L P24 was a single-seater, like those of his own command, but it was a monoplane, and instead of a single cannon anchored rigidly to the engine, and firing on the line of flight through a hole pierced in the airscrew boss, it carried two—one under each wing—of approximately similar calibre, muzzle-velocity, and trajectory to his own.

But it was at least doubtful that this double armament would be of substantial advantage in actual combat, and when he considered his own numerical superiority, and the fact that his opponents' freedom of manoeuvre would be embarrassed by the necessity of defending their clumsy convoy, he decided that fortune could not easily have offered him a better opportunity of proving the quality of the fleet he led.

He had no hesitation in replying that he would endeavour to intercept the invaders' fleet, and bring it to action. But when he came to consider at what point he should plan to meet it, he felt some difficulty of decision. For he thought first that every minute that he should remain in the skies would increase the probability that his presence would be detected, and that he might be attacked by forces which he would be too weak to endure. It appeared evident, therefore, that he should endeavour to intercept the convoy as it was approaching its destination. But suppose that this destination should be incorrectly reported or subsequently changed? Then the nearer to Nürnberg he should go, the surer he would be that the convoy would not elude his search in the wide waste of the air. He had still time to do this, if he should deny his men the rest which they had certainly earned.

He considered also the risk under which they lay that their presence would be reported to the German Air Service before they should take the air again, if they should remain long at that place; for in all he did he had to remember constantly that he operated against a foe of overwhelming strength, and that he could be engaged in no more than guerrilla warfare among the clouds.

But the officer who had welcomed him at this lonely aerodrome gave him some reassurance on that point. For the time, Northern Scotland had been saved by the vastness of the arena over which the war had developed. It had been undisturbed by more than reports and rumours of war, and the sound of guns at times from its misty seas. There were even quiet hamlets where paper money would pass seriously from hand to hand, as though its value remained unchanged while the Bank of England, whose name it bore, was a blackened shell.

Even as far south as Glasgow, the only bloodshed had been that of some Socialist members of the City Council, who had made themselves conspicuous the year before by refusing a monetary grant from the Air Ministry, which had been offered conditionally upon an equal sum being voted towards the provision of anti-aircraft batteries for the city's protection. Now their turbulent constituents had risen and battered two of them to death in a bloody way, and thrown others into the Clyde, from which they had not all been equal to swim ashore.

Admiral Dalton decided that his airmen should not go entirely without their much-needed rest. And this decision was approved to his own mind when he had talked with a young airwoman who arrived soon after himself in a scouting plane and brought some information that he was glad to hear.

Imogen Lister had spent most of her time in the air since she had escaped the fate of the squadron to which she had been attached by the fact that she had not been appointed to piloting one of the bombing-planes, as she had supposed she would, but to a single-seater scout, in which she had been required to fly ahead and give warning of any enemy force which they would wish to avoid.

In that capacity she had observed the approach of the fleet of battle-planes by which they were finally overtaken and shot down into the sea, and had given sufficient warning for them to have avoided the unequal strife had they not lacked the speed which safety required. By swift ascent and high speed of flight, she had evaded the host of their thronging foes, and returned alone to the Northfield base, with news of their successful raid and subsequent destruction.

Since then, like other airwomen of established reputation, she had been employed in reconnaissance and liaison work, piloting a light, unarmed scouting plane, and depending for safety upon swiftness and skill in skies which were seldom free either from single scouts or squadrons of foes.

"I am charged to tell you," she said, "that the German air attacks have relaxed somewhat during the day, and though this may be no more than a prelude to heavier invasion when the hours of a second ultimatum which they have sent have expired, yet it is thought that your coming remains unguessed, and that you may be likely to intercept the transport fleet before they are aware of any danger from us, if you delay until they are nearly here."

"Is it known at what point they are most likely to approach the English coast?"

"I am to tell you that they came at first over a part of the Norfolk coast which had been so heavily bombed that its permanent defences had been destroyed, so that it had become to them like a trodden road. But our mobile batteries, having been hurried to that part, have since done so much damage that there has been a tendency to come by a slightly more northerly route, which they may prefer, for it is thought that the transports will be heavily loaded and flying low, trusting most to speed, darkness, and cloud, and to the smokescreens that they are likely to use." She added, "I am to be at your disposal for any use I can be."

"You have wireless?"

"Yes. I can receive and transmit."

"Very well. We will have a code of our own. I will attack them, if I can, as they reach the land. I will not choose to fight with the sea below, unless for some evident cause. You shall fly out and give me warning of when they come. I suppose they will not be timed to land before dawn, though they may prefer to cross the coast while the darkness lasts."

CHAPTER XXVIII.

THREE hours after Perdita left the cellar of the Dürers' house, she sat in semi-darkness on a crowded aluminium bench of one of the converted airliners, which was now stripped of its luxurious appointments and loaded with troops and munitions. Her equipment, which she had been glad to slip from aching shoulders, was on a rack over her head, and she had a parachute strapped to her back. There was contrast here to the spacious comfort and light of the airliners in which she had travelled before, and she had been told plainly enough of the dangers which she would be likely to meet, but she was not greatly afraid.

She had gained some confidence in the man that she knew to be at her side, though he was not easy to see. She had confidence of another kind (which she hated to feel) in the strength of Germany in the air, as it had been revealed in the last three days, and which had become a more visual reality as she had been marched behind the endless-seeming rank of the huge aircraft that stretched in shadowy vastness over the aerodrome plain. She heard the officers' orders, brusque and confident, sure of Germany and of the huge fleets that she had brought out to defy the world. She heard their buoyant jesting among themselves. Even her alien spirit could not be oblivious of, nor entirely unstirred by, the optimistic excitement of those among whom she moved. But (she supposed) they did not know that they were likely to be attacked in the air. Or did they know, and remain careless, contemptuous of anything that England might attempt? And these great transports, loaded with troops and guns, were not dependent upon their own powers of defence. They were to have an escort of fighting planes.

She could not feel that she flew to a greater peril than she was likely to come through safely. She had the optimism of youth, and the good thought that she was making escape from an enemy land, and, in a few hours, if all went well, would be in England again.

An hour passed. They sat silent and still. Once a man spoke, and a sergeant's voice was curt and louder in its rebuke. At times the distant plain was lighted by signal flares that sank to darkness again. An officer climbed into the plane. He flashed a light along the rows of the sitting men. "Eugene Gumpert!" he called.

Her companion, who had not spoken for the last hour, answered to the name. After the exchange of a few words, he rose up, gathering his kit.

She had not understood what was said, but it was clear that he had received an order he could not refuse to obey. He said a few words in German as he withdrew, which she supposed to be meant for her. She caught the word *wacht*, but no more. The tone appeared to be intended to warn or to reassure. She wished she had understood, but how much could he have said in the midst of surrounding ears? After he had gone, she was conscious of a great loneliness, and a fear hard to subdue. She supposed that he had been called off the fleet by his German masters, and that she must go alone among these men to whom she could not attempt to speak without exposing the fraud she was. Under-officers who would shout orders that would have no meaning to her, and which she would be expected to obey without pause! Well, she must watch what her companions did. She must trust to numbers and night. After all, she was not alone. All of British blood that the world contained were with her, were at her side. They were one in a common cause. She felt some comfort in this, which is one of the subtle compensations of war.

And he might be coming back. He might have only been called away for some final instructions his German masters would give, such as were not for the ears of the other men. While they did not start, there was still hope. The idea gave her no relief, but rather the anxiety of suspense, and it died with the thought that, if it were so, he would not have taken his kit.

It was more probable that they had discovered the double part that he played. He might be confronted now with proofs of his treachery to the German cause. He might be tried—condemned— shot even now. She did not know just how quickly such things may be done, but she supposed that there was little patience in time of war, and the Germans had ruthless ways.

She was roused from her thoughts by a flashing light, and an officer's angry shouts. He called Franz Hals, which she was not instant to understand, or to connect with herself.

She rose, none too soon, with a hand she did not like on her collar, dragging her up. She felt a sharp kick as she fumbled to find her kit. She was hurried out and down the landing steps to face the colder air of the night; and a darkness less dense than that from which she had come showed her two soldiers who were bustled in, as she left, to take the vacated seats.

She took that to be final evidence that neither No. 97 nor herself was destined to leave that night, but she found herself led to a plane of another type, which she was ordered to enter, and as she did so the steps were pulled in, and the door closed.

Richard Steele was at her side, relieving her of the weight she bore, speaking in English without reserve.

"I'm afraid you must have had a bad quarter of an hour. We are in Admiral Nachod's plane. You'll find there's rather more comfort here. The Admiral knows who you are."

Certainly there was more comfort there, even though the luxury of the Air-Admiral's cabin, where he bent, with two military colleagues, over English maps, was not intended for her.

Perdita's place was with the Admiral's servants, of whom he had brought three, including the cook and the cook's boy. Steele was summoned into his private cabin at the same moment that she arrived, and the men with whom she was left regarded her curiously but did not speak, and she had neither ability nor desire to commence speaking to them.

Outside, the darkness was lessened by guiding flares and searchlights moved over the sky. Heavily, slowly, as though reluctant to leave the ground, a hundred of the huge-winged liners, loaded to the last ounce that they could be expected to lift, were taking off, and rising toward the clouds.

After them followed the fighting planes, to overhaul them almost at once, and divide into two columns that drew beside them to right and left, and then somewhat ahead.

The Admiral's plane was the last to rise. It followed the rear lights of the armada that it controlled. It soared higher and passed above them to take its place at the front, with some of the foremost of the battle-planes stretching forward on either side, like the antenna of some monstrous beetle that buzzed loudly among the clouds, of which Admiral Nachod's plane was the insect's insignificant head.

Here, in fact, was the directing brain. Admiral Nachod, a small man with close-cut grizzled hair, a tight, thin-lipped mouth, and keen, many-wrinkled eyes, was saying: "You think there will be landing space for the whole fleet?"

"Yes. It is the best place you can choose, except farther north than you wish to go."

"And you think that the English will not suspect that you are not faithful to them, even after you have guided us there?"

"I believe not. And it is a risk I cannot avoid. I suppose that my rescue of Miss Wyatt will be a straw in the right scale—which I hope that it may not need. By your leave, I would talk to her for a time in a useful way."

"Yes, you should do that. She should have no doubt in her mind. You can go to her. I will call you, Herr Zweiss, if you should be wanted again."

The Admiral spoke with a civility which he considered due to Adolph Zweiss's record when he had been an airman in the last war, rather than to the occupation of espionage that he now pursued, though he would not have condemned him for that. He would have regarded a foreign spy as one of the basest among mankind, but he accepted the creed of the Third Reich that there were few things that it would not be lawful to do that German *kultur* might win the world.

No. 973 went back to the cabin where Perdita was, with such ease of mind as his situation allowed. He had some reason to think that those who might overhear were ignorant of the English tongue. Certainly, they would not be equal to judge whether he talked it in a foreign or native way. He had Admiral Nachod's advice to make his conversation such as would leave her convinced of his loyalty to her own land. He did not think that much of what he intended to say would be overheard, even if it could have meaning for German ears.

"You can talk freely," he said. "I tried these men with English before you came, and it was clear that it had no meaning to them."

"They have been looking at me," Perdita replied doubtfully, "as though they know who I am."

"More or less they may," he replied easily; "there is no trouble in that. They know that we are to be allowed to escape after we land. I do not know how far they have been further informed. But there are things you should know, and the time may be very short. We are flying fast. We shall be over England before the dawn, if we get so far."

"You think there is doubt of that?"

"Nothing is certain in time of war." He sank his voice as he went on: "I will tell you this, which I think you have courage to hear. I informed London—I should say Bristol now—when this fleet would sail, and how strong, or rather how open to an attack of the right kind it would be likely to be."

"Although you were coming on it yourself?"

"In fact, I did not know that I was."

"And afterwards you found that they would compel you to come?"

"No. It was my own choice. I volunteered, saying that I could show them where best to land, and be of greater use after that. I would warn the Air Ministry not to attack us if I could, but there is no possible way."

"Not to attack us? Why?"

"So that I may save my own life."

"It is rather confusing—rather difficult to understand what you mean."

His voice sank again as he replied: "After I had sent word of when this fleet would sail, and of what strength it would be, I learnt something which made it so vital for me to get to England at once that all else became trivial. The need for haste is so great that I decided to come with the fleet if I could, even at the risk that I should not get through.

"We being in the same plane, it is probable that our experiences will be alike. It will be neither or both who will get safely to land. But even that is not sure. I want to tell you why I am here, so that you may do what you can, if you should be the only one to survive. Have you heard of the freezing gas?"

"No, I don't think that I have."

"Few people have. I was in Leunawerke when it was blown up and burnt a few nights ago. Some of this gas was released, and it killed about two hundred people who could not escape with sufficient speed. The next morning I went over the ground and saw what it had done. Germany might have used this on the first day of the war, but the loss of Leunawerke destroyed the main store that they had. It had only been manufactured there and in one other place, as they had been in constant fear that its secret would be disclosed to the world.

"Tomorrow night their bombing fleets are to visit England again, to release this gas over areas which are to be made examples to frighten the world."

"I could not have believed it a week ago. But I can believe anything now, after what I have seen in Prague."

"Well, so it is. You need not suppose that this war will be worse than many others the world has known, and may know again. But each is different from those that have gone before. They are much the same for those who are starved or tortured or die. It is the same thing, in new ways. Only, when wars have continued for many years, they have usually become more tolerable as their conventions mature. But it is no time for such talk as this."

"Many years?"

"We may hope that this will be a short war. But we have to think of today.

"The areas where the freezing gas will be spread are already resolved, and it is a choice which is unlikely to change, because there will be several parts of England where small mechanized forces such as this will have been landed, and they are to offer immunity to those around them who will surrender as to a conqueror's mercy. Clemency and chastisement are to be side by side for the world to see."

"It is certain that they will come?"

"Yes; unless Britain yield unconditionally, which the time is already almost past for her to do."

"You don't think that she will?" Perdita's voice, as she spoke, had become sharp with a new fear.

"Who can tell what politicians will do? But I hope and expect that Germany will get no answer at all. What I want you to understand is this: if I am killed or injured or hindered in any way, you must go to the first military officer you can find, or to the civil police, and say that you have information of the utmost importance for the British Government. You must use my number, 973, and when the Intelligence Service hears that, you will find that you will be put into communication with those in control without an instant's delay. It is a number you will not forget?"

"No. I will remember that. What am I to say?"

"You will say that the bombers bearing the freezing gas must not be attacked unless over the sea, or over some desolate area where the gas will do no harm as it drifts. For if they are shot down it will be released, and may do as much harm as though they should drop it at their own choice.

"The gas is heavier than air, but not much. If there be no wind, it will quickly settle toward the ground. Otherwise it will drift, spreading for a long time in the direction in which the wind moves. Its only effect is that, when it encounters the oxygen of the air, it freezes to an intense coldness such as no living creature—certainly no animal nor any plant—can endure. This extreme temperature is immediate, from which the atmosphere gradually recovers; its effect, in a still air, being entirely gone in about three hours. But before that time—indeed, in the first moments that it is loosed—it will have destroyed every living thing within the limits to which it extends.

"Of course, gas-masks are of no service against its attacks. They cannot raise its temperature, nor is it only by being breathed that it kills. It produces a cold the body cannot resist, which is said to be sufficient to freeze the blood.

"The areas which have been chosen for this destruction are widely separated. One is northeast Worcestershire. Another is a stretch of country south of the Firth of Forth. The third is to be south of London, in the district beyond Purley, the idea being in this case that the bombing fleet, heavily supported with fighting planes, will approach directly to London, as though that were its objective, but will then turn sharply aside, avoiding the London ground defences, which are now believed to be very strong, and will bomb the residential district to southward, the houses and bungalows of which are said to be overcrowded with population who have abandoned their London homes."

"Could I tell them of anything which can be done to prevent these attacks?"

"Very little, beyond what the Air Ministry and War Office will already know. I can suggest nothing beyond attacking the bombers while they are over the sea, for which I doubt whether a sufficient number of fighting planes can remain, or else vacating the threatened areas, for which there may still be time; for though the bombers will start during tomorrow night, they will not be timed to arrive before dawn, for they will aim to spread the gas with more precision than would be possible in the dark.

"It is true that this gas does not operate upon water or steam as suddenly or extremely as upon air, and at Leunawerke there was a system by which, if there should be an accidental escape of the gas, the streets could be immediately flooded with water of such heat as could be endured (having waded through it myself, I can speak with some I knowledge of this), and the water would be continually pumped out as it drained away, so that its heat would be maintained, and those who strove to escape must make their way through a thick steam.

"But the actual result of this protection could not have been very great from what I saw on the next day; and, even if it deserves more reliance than my observation supports, it would not be easy to improvise large supplies of continually heated water in which men could remain submerged, only breathing in its dense steam, for the time that the gas would lie."

"Then it doesn't seem that it's going to be much good letting them know?"

"With twenty-four hours' warning, much may be done. But I have no business with that. It is my part to give information, which is most often ignored. Do you suppose that if the advice of such as

I—of those who knew—had been asked, that England would have been left bare to invasion now? Though I do not say that there has been much which has not been commonly known, or could not have been guessed by one with the wits of a child of ten. For three years it has been Germany's open boast that she has been preparing for war."

They were interrupted at this moment by the voice of a loud-speaker which was tuned in to receive the bulletins which were issued at short intervals from Berlin, dealing with world events and the hourly changing course of the war.

"Did you understand that?" Steele asked, as the brief announcement was done.

"No. I'm not sure that I did. Something about Italy, and air-fleets being free. I couldn't get it clearer than that."

"It says that Italy has decided to support the Russo-German alliance, so that the forces of land and air which have been watching her frontiers will be released for service elsewhere, and her own air-fleets will be at the disposition of the allies."

"Is there any hope of how it will end?"

"Yes. There is always hope. We have come to that which must wake the world. There are the thousand chances of war. I will not say that we are facing less than a desperate cast. I will tell you one thing from which you must get any comfort you can. It is a nation's spirit, rather than numbers or strength of arms, that will most often determine victory or defeat. Nine times out of ten it is that. They defeat themselves. But there is a matter now which is of more importance to us than that Italy has the heart of a fawning cur. It is that we get some food with the chance that any moment may change."

He spoke with the lighter tone of one who throws care aside for a passing joy, putting the world's woes in the outer place to which, at such moments, they should belong.

"I did not think," she said, endeavouring to equal his mood, "that you cared whether I starved or not."

"You have those biscuits in mind? Well, if you have come through life eating nothing worse, you have had your share of the best."

He turned away as he spoke, and the smile faded as he wondered what her experiences would be likely to be in the coming days—in the coming years, if she should be one to survive the danger that shook the world.

He had had such a thought at times as he had looked at the play of a careless child. If he could look ahead through its life till its death should come, what would he be likely to see? It was a sombre thought, such as will be apt to end in a wordless prayer. That had been in times of apparent peace, when the world worked and bickered and played, married and bore and died, in its myriad continual way. But now, when its foundations slipped?

He brought some game-pie, and a wine which she would not drink. "There is no lack of food," he said, "where there is an Air-Admiral to be fed."

He seemed lighter of mood than she had observed him before, and she did not know him well enough to understand that it was because the hour of action, whether of air or land, could not be far, and his spirit rose, as will that of a good horse when it breasts a hill.

"I will go into the observation-cabin," he said, "when we have finished. But I expect there will be nothing to see. We cannot be far from the English coast, and when that is passed you may say you are home again. It is likely that England has become too weak in the air to molest our way."

She accepted this without knowing whether she were more heartened or grieved. No one wishes to be shot down when five thousand feet (or it may be ten) over the sea. But it was no pleasant thought that a hostile fleet could sail at will in the English skies. She would have liked to think of British battle-fleets, active and strong, and winning victories at some distance away. But her companion seemed to think that their absence could be explained by another cause. But in the observation-cabin, to which Admiral Nachod and his military colleagues had already gone, there was something to see, even before Perdita had finished her share of the game-pie and shaken its crumbs away. Something beside the headlights of the following fleet of the great liners that stretched far backward into the night, now shining clear, and now hidden in trailing mist. Something beside the taillights of the two horns of the fighting planes that stretched forward to right and left.

The fleet was moving over a drift of cloud that was not smoothed on its upper side, but banked in places, or broken through, so that at times they would fly over a stretching carpet of cloud beneath a heaven of frost-bright stars and the downward curve of a waning moon, and at others the grey vapour would close them in, so that they must fly blind, trusting to the warning their instruments gave, and with the caution that mist requires. And then at times the clouds would open below, and they would look far down to the restless waves of the shallow, unfriendly sea, and now to the dim line of the English coast, which was unlighted in time of war.

The observation-officer lifted his arm, and the Admiral adjusted his night-glasses. The officer's voice guided him, naming the stars.

"Yes," he said, "you are right. It is a scouting plane, very high. It is one which Lieutenant Mannheim will not catch."

"No," a staff officer said, "but we can judge something by the direction in which it retires."

"Yes," Admiral Nachod allowed, though with more doubt, "perhaps we can."

Imogen Lister, quartering the skies hour after hour like a questing hawk, had looked far down to the broken carpet of cloud, and seen the lights of the coming fleet, and at the same time became aware that one of its out-fliers was soaring to bring her down.

She had no trouble for that. She was far beyond the range of machine-gun fire. She had no fear that her pursuer would be lighter or swifter than she. She had not even the weight that a pair of machine-guns give.

She let the pursuer climb while she counted the twinkling lights, and read the number and strength of the coming fleet.

Then she turned and fled in a straight line for the southwest, as though it were there that her report must be made, or her safety lay.

She flew on for the next mile, making no effort of speed, till her pursuer, at 400 yards (being too long a range, but he did not know at what moment she might be greeting him in the same way), opened fire upon her.

Then she dived in sudden headlong descent, far down through the night-blue air and the ragged clouds, down with a heartbeat missed as the tossing surface of sea rose upward to meet a fall which was hard to stay, and then, skimming the grave she had missed by no more than a score of feet, she climbed upward again to the hiding clouds.

Admiral Nachod had seen the direction in which she fled. He turned his own fleet two points to the northwest. He was not seeking to fight, and he judged that he would thus be the more likely to evade the fleet to which he supposed she had fallen back.

A minute later he picked up the message that she sent out, but it had no meaning for him, being a code of arbitrary words to express how far he was from the land, and the direction in which he flew. It ended with a word to warn Marshal Dalton not to reply, lest his own position should be disclosed.

She repeated the message twice, to make more sure that it would not be lost on the air, and rose high for a westward flight to return to her Northfield base, for her part was done, and she was wearied by many hours of continuous flight in a sky where every cloud might conceal a foe. She was weary, but her heart sang with joy of success in what must ever be the greatest game that mankind can play, if it be played in a noble mode.

> What though the best of our wages be
> An empty sleeve, or a stiff-set knee?

It would be useless to ask now whether men approved or condemned war, and it would have been hard to find any on English ground who had patience for futile words. War had come, without asking leave. She was content that she did her part in her country's cause.

CHAPTER XXIX.

MARSHAL DALTON had made plans which, as the contrary is beyond proof, we may suppose to have been good. He relied upon the fact that the overloaded liners would be slower to turn or soar, and of inferior speed either to his own Fantomes, or to the German fighting planes which must make it their business to guard their convoy.

He planned to attack from above, and in such a manner that it would be difficult for any self-sacrifice on the escort's part to protect the liners from the full force of his cannonade. His own casualties might be high, but he hoped to inflict upon his fighting opponents as much as he himself endured, without counting the destruction he would deal to the transport planes.

But in the last hour, as he flew over the Lincolnshire fens and picked up the message which prevented him from taking a too southerly course, as he had been tempted to do, the clouds thickened and banked to a changing wind, so that he found he was flying blind, where he had sight of the stars and of some width upon either hand a moment before, and he was flying so when the roar of the oncoming fleet mingled with that of his own.

Steele had visited the observation-cabin, and returned to Perdita to say: "It was an English scout in the sky. There was a report that it had been shot down into the sea, but that has become less sure since some signal words which they cannot decode have been sent out very close to here. The Admiral has turned our course some further points to the north, as the scout retired on a more southerly line, but it was plain that he had some doubt, and I should guess it was what he was wanted to do.

"Will you come with me to watch? It is better than waiting here. You may be turned out; but the chances are you will not, if you come in a quiet and confident way."

The observation-cabin was glass-sided and roofed. Part of the floor was of the same unbreakable glass, giving a view of the depth below. When the cabin lights were screened, as they were now, much could be seen of the night while the stars were clear and the moon shone.

But now there were heavy drifts of cloud crossing the sky, reaching at times low down to the sea, and to a height that was hard to guess.

The lights of the great fleet shone far out through the night, and then would be hidden, near or far, as they drove into the mist.

Admiral Nachod had debated in his mind whether he should extinguish lights which were so broad a beacon for foes to see, either of the air or below. He would have done this before had he had no other than military planes in his command, but the transport planes were of a different kind, and many of their pilots had had no practice in formation flying at all.

In this gathering mist, he could not trust them to fly blind, relying entirely upon the sensitive instruments that they bore. He judged all with the caution good soldiers do not neglect, rather than with the apprehension of a strong attack, for which he thought the British air-fleets would be slow to waste their diminished strength, even if they should have known of his coming in time to assemble to close his way, which he had little reason to think.

They drove into denser cloud. Hail beat hard on the glass.

Admiral Nachod lifted his head in doubt. Was that the sound of bursting shells, of machine-gun fire? Next moment the answer came, as the air cleared on their flying course. For that moment he had a clear view to the northwest, from which came a great fleet of planes of a sort he had not expected to see. His own course was due west at this time, so that they came directly upon the right shoulder of his own formation. At that point, the foremost of his fighting planes were already engaged, having come into clearer air a moment before himself.

Perdita felt her heart beat hard, but it was with excitement rather than fear. She saw Steele look round in a keen, quick way, as though preparing for whatever the next moment might bring. He said: "There is little to fear, if you will be speedy to act should I give the word. You understand this?" He touched and slightly adjusted the parachute which was part of the equipment which had been served to her before she had come aboard. "We are over land now, and at a sufficient height. Those who keep their heads have really little to fear."

His words did nothing to reassure. She had a horror of leaping to empty air, and his caution seemed to make the vague dread a more imminent fear. But she made an effort to forget herself in the drama of what she saw.

The Admiral was issuing orders in a sharp, curt voice, to be transmitted to those he led. She could not understand what they were, and they may have had little influence on the course of events, for when air-fleets suddenly clash at a speed which every minute measures by miles of flight, there is little time for thinking of more than the instant's safety requires, or to make use of the fortune the chances send.

Perdita could see no more than the blur of a passing plane, and that the night was lit, near and far, as though by a million of meteor lights. The instant order that Admiral Nachod gave, which may have been the best that the position allowed, was that the transports were to continue their course ahead at the utmost speed they could make, while the battle-planes turned to occupy, and endeavour to hold off the foe. For this purpose, those on the farther flank were to rise and fly over the transports to engage the enemy on the northern side.

Whether or not these were the best dispositions that could be made, they were such as proved impossible to carry out with success.

The Canadian biplanes outnumbered the German fighting planes that they first encountered on the right flank of the invaders by more than three to one, and their own objective was the destruction of the transport planes.

They drove on to these with a stream of explosive shells pouring out upon their line of advance, as a swordfish attacks a whale. It was true that the transports were armed with machine-guns, and that many of them carried cannon also. But an airplane may be struck by scores of machine-gun bullets and keep the air. It is the explosive shell that inflicts the wounds it cannot endure and live. And the cannon the transports carried, not being rigidly mounted, were of little use for accurate firing at more than the closest range, their muzzle-velocity being too low for the flat trajectory that such fighting requires.

The transports fled, and the Canadian warplanes pursued and slew, and the German warplanes must follow and bring as many of their opponents to battle as they were able to overtake. The skies became a wild chaos of single combats and flight and chase, amidst which the loaded transports were shot down with a rapidity which their protectors were unable to stay. Perdita looked up and saw one of the German planes that were crossing overhead as they had been instructed to do. It descended sharply as it approached, having been winged by a bursting shell, and carried somewhat forward as it commenced to fall by the impetus of its flight. Then it fell headlong, turning in the air like a shot bird, seeming to descend upon them, monstrous in size; but they escaped by the rapidity of their own flight, and it went down through the clouds.

At this moment the Admiral's plane was not attacked, nor did it appear that he sought a foe. He appeared concerned solely to observe the course of the flying strife, as it was rightly his first object to do.

Yet the gunners were not idle, as chance allowed. Their machine-guns spluttered: the twin cannon which the pilot fired by tiny levers worked separately or together on the control-stick, poured out their deadly message of bursting shell when an enemy crossed their path within range, and flying clear of the friends that they must not wound.

The Admiral watched the rapid drama of death which he could do little to rule, and in which he saw that, whatever losses his own airmen might inflict upon the Canadian planes, they could not prevent the destruction of the transports which it was their mission to guard, to a point at which they would cease to be fit to fulfil the orders with which they came. A numerically small, highly mechanized force such as the transports bore is a single unit of which half could not be shorn away, as an infantry battalion might lose fifty percent of its strength, and remain no worse than of so much diminished power. It was hard to guess what vital portions of its equipment might not be sent to the shattering impact of earth with each transport that fell.

With bitter anger, but no hesitation in a very cool and competent mind, he sent out an order that the transports were to return to their Nürnberg base, the battle-planes continuing the conflict the while, as far as the convoy's safety could be secured.

While this order was repeated, time after time, to reach as many as it might of those who would give it distracted ears, the Admiral had to consider what his own action should be.

There was no sentimental tradition in the new service to which he belonged. He had no thought of perishing on the field of defeat, as a captain will go down with a sinking ship. He was a practical soldier, not one who dreamed a romance of war. But he had no thought for his own safety, or of swift escape from a losing strife

His duty of command being done, he looked round to see what he could do to vex his foes or protect his friends, and saw a battle that was already far-scattered among the clouds. Had it been no more than a meeting of battle-fleets, it is probable that the area of engagement might not have been widely spread, but the transports had been ordered to continue their flights, which, as they became desperate at the realization of their own impotence and the sight of their companions being shot down, they had not all done in the same direction. They dived from the path of the deadly shells; they sought to hide and scatter among the clouds.

After them came the swifter Fantomes, eager as hunting dogs, with no formation orders except to follow the transport planes—to follow and shoot them down. And after them, swift and deadly as they, came Admiral Nachod's less numerous fighting planes seeking to bring them to battle that the convoy might have time to flee.

The Admiral looked out on this wide-scattering chaos of strife which the starlight showed. Its gun flashes were many miles apart. Its general movement had been rapidly westward in the first minutes, but this had been checked by his last order, which had extended it north and south, as the transports which so far escaped came round for the homeward flight. Everywhere there was a tendency for the strife to sink into or under the clouds.

He gave an order that turned his course to where the fight was still most hotly maintained. His eye fell on Steele. He said sharply: "Zweiss, even a rifle helps." He looked at Perdita as though to address her with the same rebuke, remembered, and said no more.

Steele answered readily: "Yes, sir. So it does." He went back with Perdita to fetch the rifle which was included in Private Gumpert's infantry equipment. "Hals," he said, "you may bring yours. It will be no harm." He looked at its loading, explaining to her the use of the safety-catch.

She took it without gratitude, feeling it to be a heavy and awkward thing, which she was unfit to use, and unlikely to want.

"We must go back," he said. "We could not get out quickly from here."

The plane lurched sharply, so that they had some trouble to keep their feet with the aid of a friendly rail. Then it steadied again, and its cannon commenced firing from either wing. They were pouring out a continuous stream of shells, and the absorption of the recoil had a braking effect upon the plane, for which the pilot must allow if he should be firing from one cannon only.

As they regained the observation-cabin, one of the cannon jammed and its fire ceased. The effect, in the instant before the pilot had become aware and made the necessary adjustments, was to swing the plane sharply around from its line of flight.

Its position had been that it was on the tail of one of the Fantome planes, which was endeavouring to dodge the stream of its bursting shells, while another of them was approaching on its left rear in an endeavour to relieve the pressure upon its companion.

For one fatal moment, Admiral Nachod's plane was broadside to and well within machine-gun range of the second Fantome. It came under the rapid hail of bullets, and the scarcely slower stream of the deadlier shells from the single cannon the Fantome bore.

The bullets pierced the wings, with little damage in that; they punctured the thin metal hull; they shattered the glass of the observation-cabin.

Steele had said: "We are under fire. You can lie down if you will. But I should not say that there is much safety in that." He made a show of opening a slit in the glass, and firing upon the oncoming plane.

Perdita did not respond to words that she scarcely heard. She looked at the approaching plane, which showed dim and huge in a darkness that neared to dawn behind the winking flashes of its continuous fire. For a moment it seemed immense, imminent, a winged, fire-breathing terror that swept upon them to bear them down. The next, they had swerved and sunk from its line of fire, and were in the cloak of a covering cloud.

One of the military officers staggered to a seat, with hand pressed to a bleeding arm. The other went to his aid.

But Admiral Nachod called his attention away: "Colonel Heine, will you see what it means? Is the man mad?"

The plane had passed through the clouds, and was slanting rapidly down to earth. The officer went quickly out but was more hurried in his return.

"The pilot has been hit. He is dying or dead. I have levelled the course."

"Very well. You must take his place!"

Colonel Heine went back to the pilot's cockpit.

The Admiral looked out into the faint light of the growing dawn, his tight-lipped silence giving no indication of what he felt.

Grey in February mist, he saw the flat Lincolnshire fens. He saw no sign that the silent land was aware of the conflict, which was still scattered among the clouds, and from which his steep descent seemed to have brought him clear.

From the cover of a range of byres, which were themselves no more than a dark blur on the mist-grey fields, an anti-aircraft gun flashed upward, making his plane the sole target for its discharge.

He stepped quickly to the speaking-tube to direct Colonel Heine's course from this new peril, and as the plane came sharply round on a rising curve, it heeled over, with a jerk that jarred through its metal shell. From the starboard engine, the strained propeller, cracked by a fragment of bursting shell in its previous encounter, snapped and spun downward into the dusk.

It was a damage which would have been fatal to the planes of older construction, which would have been shaken to fragments by the racing engine, but here the breaking off of the propeller-blade automatically cut off the power. The plane could still continue its flight at diminished speed, but might be the simple prey of any foe that should observe it limping beneath the clouds.

Admiral Nachod saw that he could not hope to do more to aid the remnant of the scattered and flying convoy. He picked up the speaking-tube again, and ordered that the crippled plane should be headed back for its Nürnberg base.

CHAPTER XXX.

No. 973 heard the order, and it was one that he did not like. He had not understood the general instructions which had been sent out before, and not anticipated that the shattered fleet would seek to struggle back to its base, rather than attempt a landing on English ground.

There was too much at stake for him to consent to be carried back to land upon German soil, and with no certainty of when he would be able to come to England again. He looked down at the misty fields, now falling away as the plane struggled upward to the shelter of heavy clouds that were gaining shape in a windy dawn. There was already sufficient depth to make descent safe enough, which every moment increased. He said to Perdita: "You must be ready to jump, if you have no love for a German jail."

He did not see her face whiten at this idea, as he turned quickly and approached Admiral Nachod to say: "My orders are to land here. By your leave I will drop out taking Private Hals with me, as had been planned."

He did not anticipate objection, or that the Admiral would be greatly concerned as to what he did, having larger cares, but he spoke to a man whose temper was strained to the point at which opposition becomes the normal reaction to any proposition which does not originate with himself.

As he retraced the course he had come before in the higher skies, he looked down on black masses of wreckage, and on others that were pillars of glowing flame, and he knew that five out of six of these were transport liners that it had been his duty to guard. As most commanders are apt to do, he exaggerated the action in which he had been engaged, both in its intrinsic importance and its significance of other events on the wide front of the war.

He had been attacked by several score of a type of fighting biplane which he did not recognize to be part of the British Air Force as it was known to the world. He did not know from where it had come, nor how it should have been waiting so appositely to cross his way. He concluded that his country was faced by a British opposition previously undisclosed and more formidable than was actually the case. Perhaps Germany was not the only nation to spring surprises upon the world! Suddenly attacked, England had suffered before she could call on her secret strength, which was only now thrown into the scales of war.

"I do not know," he said, "what your orders may be, but you may do better to come back, as I am unable to land you where it had been arranged."

"But, with great respect, I must interpret my orders another way."

The Admiral was not prepared to strain his authority further in a matter which was not his direct concern. He said sourly: "Well, you have my advice. You may please yourself. But Private Hals will remain with me."

No. 973 recognized an obstinate man, and saw that argument might only increase the opposition he had to meet. A leap from a plane is soon done, if there be none who watches to interpose. He said easily: "That must be as you wish: it is little to me. It might be hard to explain, and of no advantage at all."

Admiral Nachod accepted this, and his mind returned to matters which were more important to him.

No. 973 went back to Perdita. He said: "I have told the Admiral that I will drop from the plane, as my place is here, which he does not deny; but he says that you shall not go. If you will do as I say, I think I can contrive that they will not attempt to interfere till it will be too late, and it is sure that they will not be able to fetch you back."

"You will think me a coward," she answered, in a voice she did not know for her own, "but I do not think I should dare."

He looked impatient, or even angry at that, which was a difficulty he had not expected to meet. He said: "But you must! There is no danger at all. But there may be much if they take you back and I am not there. With your passport gone, and in the uniform that you wear, they might do—there is no knowing what. Did you not say you wished to be home, even at a great risk?"

"Yes, but I was not thinking of this. I can believe you are right, but I am sure that I should not dare."

"Then," he said, with anger that was largely feigned, meaning to bring her to the resolution that the occasion required, "I must call you a coward indeed. It was a mistake to trust you at all."

"But how," she asked, "can you jump? Can you not see that we are over the sea now?" He looked, and real anger rose, though it was largely against himself for having overlooked how quickly they would have left the land, heading, as they had been, straight for the sea.

"No," he said. "It is ruined now."

She heard the bitterness in his voice, and said miserably: "You mean you have been ruined by me."

"No, it was my own folly I blamed. But it is too late to regret that. We must think of a better way."

He moved apart, as though from one with whom he had no further concern. He looked down on a sea which rose to the freshening wind. The clouds drove overhead, lower, denser than they had been during the night. He could see no more than half a dozen planes in the whole sky, either friend or foe. Those that there were flew low and scattered like birds blown apart in a storm. Were there so few that had doubled back and evaded pursuit? It seemed too much to believe.

But, be that as it might, his own course was clear. Even though the coast might be patrolled by planes which would shoot down one which was so clearly of German build, he must stake all on the desperate chance that he could turn back and land safely on English soil. For what could his own life be—or the girl's—against the importance of the information he bore?

It must be tried, and for that purpose, of what use would she be likely to be?

He considered this, and decided that there could be no reliance on her for such help as he needed now. Had it not been wisdom that had always kept women out of his life? He had seen that they had been the death of so many spies.

They differed, of course. He realized that. He did not hate or despise, but he saw facts, as it was his business to do.

They could be divided into the Delilahs who betrayed, the fools who talked (which was the same thing in such professions as his), and the loving women who clung and weakened resolve and made life too dear.

He could not say that Perdita would be any of these, by which his argument fell, but that "I should never dare," when he had told her that it was the safest thing for her to do! They were the words of a fool. There was no escaping from that, and now he had to ask her for help again, and in a more dangerous and more unwomanly way.

Well, he had made his plan while this undercurrent of thought had engaged his mind. He strolled back to her, as to one with whom he conversed in an idle mood.

"Listen," he said, "you know how much depends upon our getting to England now. How many—perhaps thousands of children's lives—may be saved if we can land in England today, and at the first moment we can.

"There is only one way. We must seize the plane. Are you too afraid to help me in that?"

There was a strange contrast between the casual tone and manner, and the import of what he said. It gave a note of sarcasm he had not intended to the final question, from which she did not flinch the less because she felt it to be deserved. She answered: "I am afraid I am not much use. But I will do anything that I can."

"Then listen closely to me without appearing to attend in more than an idle way.

"There are eight men here beside ourselves, including one who is hurt. These are not odds which are easy to overcome, but we have the advantage of surprise, and of the fact that I can pilot the plane, which some of them would not be able to do.

"We are armed, though not quite as I would have preferred us to be. Do you think that you could use your rifle if it should become necessary?"

"I can try. I ought to tell you that I never handled one in my life before. I don't even know whether it's loaded or not."

"Well, it is. But I don't know that you'll need to use it, if you can contrive to look as though you know how. You remember I showed you the safety-catch? Don't omit to slip it off at the right time. That'll look as though you're ready for what I shall tell you to do.

"But," he added, "you needn't do it too soon, and, if you walk behind me, you might carry it with the muzzle down."

As they talked, Admiral Nachod, after gazing for a moment at the low grey sky and the rising sun, had retired again to his private cabin, taking no notice of them.

There was no one left but the wounded officer, whose arm was now tightly bound, and who lay back as though more faint than aware of surrounding things, his hand over the wound. The bullet had pierced the artery of the upper arm, and the side of the seat and the cabin floor had been drenched with blood. There could be little to fear from him.

The wind drove in an icy gust through the shattered glass, and the roar of the remaining engine, which was subdued in the enclosed cabins, came in loudly enough to make hearing hard. It was the habit of caution rather than actual danger of being regarded with suspicion or overheard, by which Steele had controlled the conversation to a casual manner, and muttered words.

Now he said: "Follow me, and we will see what we can do," and led the way to the Admiral's cabin.

CHAPTER XXXI.

THE airplane which had the honour of Admiral Nachod's occupation was not of the P2L P24 pattern, as were the fleet of fighting planes which constituted his command, though like them, it carried twin cannon beneath its wings. They were single-seaters with little care for the comfort of their pilots, for whom sufficient provision was considered to have been made if they had a secure seat from which they could control their flight and discharge their guns.

The Admiral's plane had, as we have seen, a private cabin for his own use, an observation-cabin, a wireless operator, a kitchen and cook; and it had two engines instead of one, which had proved to be no more than its occasions required. It had a gun-ring aft where a machine-gunner could operate with a mind undistracted by a pilot's duties. It had been constructed with consideration both for the Admiral's comfort and speed and its own security, but its designer had not considered the possibilities of internal strife.

No. 973's first thought, remembering the narrow, crooked approach to the pilot's cockpit, had been that he had but to seize the seat which Colonel Heine now occupied, and a single rifle would be sufficient to hold off the crew; but when he considered that the rifle must be in the hands of a girl to whom it would be an unfamiliar weapon, he decided that the risk was too great to take. He must attempt a more absolute mastery of the plane before he could take the control-stick into his own hands, and, having some experience of what sudden, resolute action may accomplish against those who are unprepared, he did not think it beyond reasonable expectation that he could succeed in the attempt.

The wounded staff officer did not lift his head nor open his eyes as the two Franconian infantrymen passed out of the observation-cabin, with their rifles beneath their arms.

A moment later Admiral Nachod looked round as his door was pushed open without the preliminary knock that the etiquette of the service required, and Adolph Zweiss entered abruptly with Perdita behind him.

The Admiral heard a sharp command to put up his hands. He saw a rifle-muzzle rising in his direction. By all the laws of such situations he should have obeyed, and had he done so, his captor might have realized his intention of the single-handed capture of the crew, without the bloodshed to which he had an aversion somewhat incongruous to the occupation which he pursued.

But Admiral Nachod was a man habitually quick of action and thought, which qualities had brought him to his present command. He was of an arrogant disposition such as will not readily obey the command of a hostile voice, and he had a temper already frayed by the unexpected defeat that he had endured. As the rifle rose, his own hand dropped to the butt of the automatic in his belt, and wrenched it out with an instant speed.

Steele had no choice but to fire. His half-second's pause was too much. Admiral Nachod collapsed, but his pistol discharged as he fell.

The automatic was of a pattern recently served out to the officers of the German army, which fired by no more than a forward pressure of the thumb, and would then continue at half-second intervals till its ten cartridges were exhausted, unless a restraining pressure were applied by the trigger-finger beneath.

Admiral Nachod fell forward a dying man, the rifle bullet, at two yards' range, having pierced his neck, severed the spinal column, and gone on through the cabin wall to the outer air. As he fell, the pistol dropped from his hand, but it did not cease its discharge, and with every shot it leapt like a living thing. It had fired six times before Steele got his foot upon it, and held it down, struggling viciously to be free, as it completed its discharge, which was now directed, by the caprice of chance, into the body of the dying man.

Perdita, her mind made blank by the horror of what she saw, and stunned by the noise in the narrow space, was roused at once by the sound of approaching feet and the voices of men, and by the sharp admonition of her companion: "Do nothing but what I say. I may bluff it through: the Admiral killed himself."

The next moment they confronted four men who crowded the cabin door, and gazed with astonished eyes at that which was not simple to understand.

Perdita stood silent, vigilant, careful that her manner should indicate nothing until she should receive the cue for which she had been told to wait, hearing words which, in their guttural colloquial German, had little meaning for her, and watching the expressions of bewildered, uncertain men.

Steele had said sharply: "Stand back there! It will be better that no one shall enter the room. The Admiral has committed suicide. I suppose he could not endure defeat. I am taking charge here. I suppose you know who I am? I am a member of the Intelligence I Service."

He was answered by the machine-gunner from the gun-ring aft, the only air officer there, and a man of more shrewdness and resolution of manner than were the cook and the two mechanics beside him.

"I should like to know what Colonel Heine will say about that. If the Admiral is dead, we take our orders from him."

"I shall inform Colonel Heine as soon as I have locked up this cabin and you have gone back to your posts. He will then give you what orders he thinks best."

The gunner stood uncertain. The tale was plausible, for the Admiral had not been of the temper that finds it easy to face defeat, and there was no alternative, except of a far more improbable kind. Yet he had an instinct that something was wrong. He said sceptically: "It sounded as though he shot himself a good many times."

"He appears to have used an automatic pistol, which continued to fire after it dropped from his hand. You I can come in and look for yourself, if you wish, but I think Colonel Heine will say that everything should be left untouched for the military police."

The gunner accepted that. He knew how those automatics worked, and Steele had some reason to hope that it would be a case of a little truth going a long way. But the gunner did not retire. He still felt that he could know a little more, and not all. He looked at Perdita to ask: "And I suppose Franz there is in the Intelligence Service too?"

"It is a question you would be wiser to leave unasked."

One of the mechanics touched the gunner's arm, and said something which Perdita felt to be allusion to her, for she was conscious that all eyes were now on herself. Something—some hint or part of the truth—must have leaked out, as she had thought before from the manner of the same man, though it had not come to the gunner's ears. Now it had the effect, not of explanation, but of showing him that there was something here which it might not be intended for him to know, and which it might therefore be wiser to leave alone.

"Well," he said, "if Colonel Heine is informed, it's no business of mine. But it seemed strange hearing so many shots."

The little group withdrew from the door.

Steele looked down at the automatic, which he would have liked to secure and load, but he dare not delay. There were still four, including the cook's boy, who did not know what had occurred. There was the wounded officer; the wireless operator, who had not deserted his post; and Colonel Heine in the pilot's cockpit. Steele saw that he must not fail to lock the cabin at once, as he had said he would do, nor risk that Colonel Heine should be informed by other lips than his own. He said to Perdita: "It's all right so far. I've made them believe the yarn."

He took the key from the inside of the door, locked it when they were in the passage, and dropped it into his pocket.

"You'd better wait here a minute," he said. "They won't worry you, and if they come asking anything more, it will be safest if you don't understand."

"It won't be any trouble to manage that."

"So I supposed."

He went forward to the cockpit, where Colonel Heine, unconscious and unsuspicious of what had occurred, was still guiding the plane in its rapid flight backward to the Netherland coast. The cockpit was small but completely covered in, as was usual with the newer planes. The noise of the engine was not too loud for a raised voice to be heard.

He saluted, and spoke as though it were Private Gumpert who made report: "I'm sorry to say, sir, that Admiral Nachod has shot himself in his cabin. I have locked the door, so that nothing shall be disturbed. I thought that you would wish to know."

Colonel Heine accepted the report without incredulity and with little comment. It was to Adolph Zweiss rather than Eugene Gumpert that he replied: "That's a silly thing to have done. I don't see that there was much blame to him; but I suppose he thought his career was finished. You've done quite right to lock up the cabin. Zweiss, would you mind carrying on? I suppose that I ought to take control now. You're the only fit man left."

This was a position which Steele had not expected to meet. His plan had been to coerce the wireless operator to report that orders had been received that they were to land in England, so that Colonel Heine would feel compelled to return. But he might reach the same goal by another route, though it must be a harder matter if he could not keep the operator under his own control. He said: "Yes, I'll do that. But will you excuse me a minute first?"

He turned away without waiting for a reply, as though assuring an assent which could not easily be refused. He went back to where Perdita still stood by the cabin door. She had been handling and examining the rifle which had been her companion since the night before, and with the weight and construction of which she was gaining the familiarity which association gives.

"I believe," she said, "I could use it now if I were obliged."

"Well, don't try. What I want you to do is not to seem to have any understanding with me until I speak to you in English again. I may get the whole thing through in a quiet way. But be ready if I do call on you, all the same. You'd better go back to where you were sitting first."

She went feeling that she would have been glad to understand more, but having the sense to see that it was not a time for talk of a needless kind.

CHAPTER XXXII.

LEFT to himself, Richard Steele unlocked the Admiral's cabin and entered it again. He saw that, for the next few minutes, it was unlikely that there would be interference with what he did, and might have felt the relief of a leisured space had it not been that every moment the plane was flying fast in the wrong direction.

He picked up the empty automatic, sought and found ammunition, and loaded it with the relief of feeling that he had obtained a handier weapon than the service rifle on which he had been compelled to rely before. He saw that its absence might raise a puzzling doubt in Colonel Heine's mind, if he should make a close inspection of the alleged suicide, but that was a doubtful risk which was outweighed by the advantage the weapon gave. Dropping it into his pocket, he went on to the operator's cabin.

He saw a youth with a high, bare forehead above weak, receding features, and a thin, bony frame, who looked up angrily as he entered, to say: "What are you doing here? Don't you know that no one's allowed in?"

"There are no orders here. Admiral Nachod's dead."

"Dead?"

"Yes, shot himself, or been killed. You'll find yourself in jail when you get back, more likely than not."

"I? Why should I? I've done nothing."

"Probably not. But they'll arrest you all while they're finding that out."

"Why not you?"

"Because I'm a member of the Intelligence Service. My evidence will be about the only hope that you've got, if they decide that he did not die by his own hand."

"He might have got killed in the battle."

"So he might, but he didn't. You'll come unstuck if you all conspire to say that."

"I'm not conspiring about anything."

"Wise man. You'll come clear if you stick to that, and do what I tell you now, Fritz."

"Wilhelm's my name—Wilhelm Nord."

"Very well. Wilhelm. How long do you think you'll keep on at this game without being shot down? Don't you go cold when you think of that?"

"Well, how can I help that? I'm not here from choice."

"No. I suppose not. I expect you took up wireless to keep you out of the fighting services, and now it's landed you here?"

"Well, what if I did?"

"I can show you how to be safe in two hours' time, till the end of the war."

"What's the catch?"

"There isn't any, if you've got sense enough to keep a shut mouth about something you re going to do."

"What's that?"

"You're going to speak through to Colonel Heine in the cockpit to say that you've received a wireless order that we're to land in England."

"I'm not fool enough to do that."

"You'll be a fool if you don't, because you'll get shot."

Wilhelm looked at an automatic he did not like. He protested weakly: "That's not fair. You know I shall get shot if I do."

"Not at all. You'll be interned in England till the end of the war."

"In England? And how long should I be safe there? Half of it must be in German hands now."

"You think that, after what you've gone through during the night? England's just beginning, if you ask me."

"All the same, I should be in the soup sooner or later. Germany doesn't forget."

"Listen, Wilhelm. I had orders to land in England on a matter of the utmost urgency—the discovery of a secret aerodrome that they're known to have, and that no one's been able to locate. The Admiral knew this, and I told him that he ought not to have come back as he did, for that reason alone. I should have dropped out, if we hadn't been already over the sea. He must have known he was wrong, but he was too obstinate to give way. You'll be safe and live during the war if you're interned, and I'll see that you come to no harm after that. It's better than sitting here till the plane crashes. I tell you there won't be one of twenty planes left in the sky when the war's lasted another week. And it's a lot better than being shot now, which is what I should have to do, for someone's going to give the Colonel that message. I'll write down what you've got to say."

Steele pencilled a few lines on the operator's pad, and after a moment's hesitation the man took up the speaking-tube which communicated with the pilot's cockpit.

"Yes, sir," Steele heard. "Yes, sir. Wilhelm speaking. Message for the Admiral, sir. Yes, sir, so I thought. It reads, sir: 'Report of action received. All transports and fighting planes remaining airworthy must endeavour to proceed to rendezvous already chosen. Return explicitly prohibited. Adequate dispositions for destruction of enemy already made'."

After that there was a moment's interval. An expression of doubt, almost of panic, came into the man's eyes. He looked at Steele, and at the unwavering pistol-muzzle that covered him as he spoke. He said: "Oh, yes, sir, Frankfurt. The usual signature—9442."

"Well, Wilhelm," Steele said pleasantly, "you've done it now. You won't say that I forced you to give a number I'd never heard of before. But you'll be all right if you keep a shut mouth, which shouldn't be hard to do."

He saw the sunrise move on the horizon till it was behind his back, though he had not changed the position in which he stood, and he resolved that the man should come to no ultimate harm for what he had forced him to do, if they should outlive the day.

CHAPTER XXXIII.

STEELE went back to the cockpit with some confidence that Wilhelm Nord would not further compromise the position into which he had been forced by betraying what he had done to his new commander, and having formed that opinion, he resolved to risk the danger of a sudden attack upon himself rather than place Perdita on guard, which would be difficult to explain in a natural way.

He took the place which Colonel Heine vacated with a somewhat irritated reflection on the time he had taken before returning, to which he added: "We've just had orders to return to England. I suppose they don't know or care that one of our engines is out of action—and I suppose you know where we're to land? I believe it was understood that you know the country. I can't say that I've been there before."

"Yes, I know the country. There ought to be no difficulty in locating it during the day. I suppose you'll I wish me to take a route that's most likely to avoid meeting English planes? We shan't have much chance if we do."

"We shouldn't have any. We're not fit to return. But I suppose the High Command thinks it knows best. I suppose I'd better leave you to take the route you think safest."

Colonel Heine remembered that Adolph Zweiss had made a great reputation as a pilot of courage and skill in the last war. In more recent years he had seen much of England. He was clearly the most competent man to take the control-stick now.

As to the behaviour of the wireless operator, Steele had made a correct guess. He was one of those unfortunates who have a good brain, but lack the moral and physical qualities necessary for noble or successful living. He reflected, when Steele had gone, that if he should report what had occurred, there would certainly be trouble for him, possibly arrest, detention, court-martial. There might be final exculpation, but that would be no recompense for the unpleasant ordeal which must precede it.

On the other hand, if he kept a silent mouth, would he be blamed under any eventuality? Who could say that he had not received the order which he had reported, if he should not himself deny it? Was it a likely invention for him to make? Who could say that it had not been deceitfully sent out from an enemy source to which the code and system must have been betrayed? It was his sole duty to report the messages that came to him out of the air.

Carefully, methodically, he entered his records, setting out the invented message as one that had come to him in the ordinary course, and which he would have no reason to treat in a different way; and while he did it the low line of the English coast grew nearer, bolder, as they flew towards it under the clouds.

CHAPTER XXXIV.

THE occupation of an espionage agent, whether in peace or war, is one which must expect perils, and one that does not endure unless he be cool to meet and adroit to foil them.

Steele had had his share of such experiences, or perhaps more, but as he flew on steadily to the English coast he realized that he had taken a chance such as could be justified to his own judgement by nothing less than the extremity of his position and the magnitude of the stake at issue.

Every second he must remain alert against the risk that discovery of the ruse he had tried would lead to an attempt upon his life, or to arrest him, which would have led to the same end by a longer road. He watched always for the stealthy approach of one who might, if unobserved, have him at a disadvantage against which he could not hope to prevail. His ears strained for the sound which would be hard to catch against the engine's roar. His right hand seldom lost consciousness of the butt of the automatic with which he was resolved to shoot his way to control of the situation, if Colonel Heine's suspicions should be aroused.

But even if his bluff should succeed, he could not regard the course he had chosen as less than a most desperate chance. He was flying back in a crippled plane through skies from which the German squadrons had, for the moment, fled, and where every eye that was upon it from earth or air would be eager to bring it down.

If he should encounter English planes in the air, he would have no wish to fight, and no speed to avoid them. He would have no means of communicating who he was, and must either consent to be shot down without resistance, or use the cannons which were now under his sole control to the destruction of those of his own blood.

He was flying back in the direct path by which the victorious Fantomes might still be chasing their scattered foes, and he knew that he flew alone. Colonel Heine thought it to be no better than a desperate folly, although he supposed that all that remained of the German fleet were turning back on the same course, and with the assurance that "adequate dispositions"—was not that the expression that he had used?—were being taken by the High Command to destroy their foes. But he knew that that was no more than a baseless myth.

The weather was thickening, and the visibility no more than moderately good. Keeping under the clouds, as he had chosen to do, he found himself flying low over a turbulent sea. It was bare to his vision's range, except for a fishing smack hardily pursuing its craft in the midst of a world at war, until one of the transport planes came into view, very low to the sea, and, as it appeared, in some difficulty to maintain its flight.

Even as he saw it, it turned sharply to the southeast, as though bearing directly upon himself, and next moment he recognized the cause of this abrupt manœuvre in the grey, low-funnelled streak of a British destroyer that drove hard through the rising sea.

He saw that the labouring transport had cause for her sudden swerve, for even guns that could be thrown up to no more than sixty degrees would be a menace to aircraft flying as low as she. He looked to see the destroyer turn in pursuit, but she continued her course, as though content to observe the fear she had inspired in her aerial foe.

Rising slowly, and no more than a couple of hundred feet, as though struggling for a safety it was strengthless to reach, the crippled transport now held a course by which the two planes would pass at a distance of perhaps not more than a hundred yards.

Neither Steele nor the pilot of the approaching plane observed the periscope of the submarine that had been watching as the destroyer shepherded it to the spot where it lay await, and when it rose and threw up sudden guns from a deck that was still almost awash, Steele was so directly above that he thought he had reached his adventure's end even sooner, and by a different chance, from those he had feared to meet.

But it appeared that the submarine preferred to turn its fire on the larger game. As he swerved sharply to dodge the expected shells, and climbed swiftly to the covering clouds, he heard the rapid discharge of its dual guns, and saw the great liner heel over, seeming to leave a wing behind in the air, as it nosedived to the waiting sea.

The submarine was submerging again, and as he took a last downward glance while he gained the clouds, he saw the triangular wake that the moving periscope made, clear from that height even in the rolling lift of the waves. He saw that it must be quartering the seas like a submerged hawk seeking aerial prey, and coming to rest only when it had hope that its stillness would be unobserved from above by some enemy plane that approached in the distant sky.

He saw that, even if there were truth in the German boast that England had been overwhelmed by the power of the air which had been loosed upon her, she had still strength and will to bite at the crushing heel. But it was plain that there would be no safety for him, either low or high, till he came to ground. He flew on, seeking the shelter of denser clouds.

For the next hour he held an eventless course, his most immediate anxiety being caused by the erratic conduct of the remaining engine. The impartial elements were his friends in a boisterous, bullying way, for the wind rose to a western gale, bringing denser cloud, which was soon resolved into drenching rain.

To him, desiring neither to wander above the clouds, where he might be observed and shot down by those of his own blood, nor to be seen from below, which might bring the same end, there could be no better choice than to hide himself in the blinding, buffeting storm.

And while he flew thus, Colonel Heine, who had taken no more than one reluctant, perfunctory glance at the body of his superior officer (he was without experience in active service, having won his present position by ability in blackboard strategy, and he shrank from the sight of blood), was immersed in nervous speculations as to how he should acquit himself in the command which he supposed to have been thrust upon him, and by the doubt as to how many or few of the units of the great fleet that Air-Admiral Nachod had led would succeed in reaching the rendezvous of their first intention.

The gunner-officer, any doubt or curiosity he may first have felt having been discharged from his well-disciplined mind now that Colonel Heine had taken command, was in the gun-ring aft, which was his immediate concern, knowing that if at any moment they should stumble out of the storm into clearer air, and find themselves within the range of a British patrolling plane, their chance of survival, poor at best, would be slighter still if he should be less than instant in his reply.

In the observation-cabin the wounded staff officer had slipped to the floor, and Perdita, seeing him lying there, had given what aid she could to the comfort of one of the race which had been drilled and hypnotized to destroy her own.

In the kitchen, the cook cooked, as his duty was, and the two mechanics cut cards in a gambling game.

Having been in Germany since the war commenced, Steele had no exact knowledge of the extent to which the German air-fleets might dominate English skies, nor how far he would do well to fly inland before he could alight with security for himself and in a locality favourable for getting into touch with the military authorities with the least possible loss of time. He had heard only the German boasts, which appeared (even beyond the fact) to be discounted by the vigorous attack which had been made upon the fleet with which he had come, and he recognized the war to be one in which decisive changes may occur in a few hours.

Weighing the probabilities with the information he had, he decided that it would be best to avoid approach to the London area, around which it was likely that such defences of air and land as remained would be concentrated and alert, and that it might be equally injudicious to make a direct advance upon the Midland industrial districts, which had already been heavily attacked, and the destruction of which must be a primary object in paralysing England's power of producing the munitions of modern war.

Rather, it seemed expedient to fly midway between these two centres of concentrated activities and population, and to penetrate into the Western Midlands before coming to ground, so long as he could find an unmolested course.

His mind turned to the uplands of North Oxfordshire and the Berkshire downs, in the folds of which he had some reason to think that British infantry might be encamped, and where a safe landing-ground might be easy to find.

But after an hour during which he had flown with little sight of the landscape below, being less concerned to observe than to escape the observation of eyes that might be lifted to search the clouds, he drove into clearer skies, having, as it seemed, escaped the track of the storm.

There were spaces here where the trailing clouds were broken apart, and where he had no choice but to fly in open view both of height and depth. He looked down on green, undulating country, wooded with oak and ash, and with frequent columns of hedgerow elms splitting the fields. The height from which he looked flattened the trees, but he saw the difference from the barer Oxfordshire fields, or the wooded dips that break the sweep of the Berkshire downs.

The scene below was peaceful and quiet, and the skies were empty above. He saw men who worked in a field, where a cart stood. He was too distant to see what they did, but there could be no menace from them. At a more leisured time, he might have read from the scene the immensity of the peaceful earth, and the pettiness of the greatest war that men can wage to their own grief. For when it is done, there will still be some who remain, many or few, and the patient earth will yield the same fruits as before, with, it may be, some extra toil in the clearing of weed and ditch; and men who have learnt the values of life and love will revert to simpler, happier lives than the wheels of progress are likely to bring.

But, as it was, he listened to Colonel Heine's voice inquiring whether he knew the locality over which they flew, and how near they might be to the rendezvous which they were to seek in a hostile land?

He replied that he had little doubt about that, but he would like to have the confirmation of—of Franz Hals, who was a native of the county they sought. Could he be sent to the cockpit to give the required assistance?

It was a chance shot with no other object than to have Perdita at his side at the moment of landing, under circumstances which might be difficult in any of several very guessable ways. He half anticipated that Colonel Heine might make himself the medium of the suggested inquiry, but the Colonel's anxiety that they should find the appointed place was too real for any thought but of acquiescence to enter his mind. He said that Hals should be sent at once, and Steele put down the speaking-tube with the satisfaction of having simplified a problem which still had sufficient risks to be overcome.

A few moments later Perdita was at his side.

"Do you know," he asked, "where we are? I think I've come rather more north than I was aware, and made rather further progress."

She looked down on a landscape that had been familiar from childhood, but which she now saw from a new angle. "Yes," she said doubtfully. "I think—no, I'm almost sure. Yes, those must be the Lickey Hills on the right that we're leaving behind."

"Any military aerodrome that you know of near?"

"Yes. There's the new one at Northfield, not far away."

"I've heard of that. Should there be good landing without going too close? I don't want to be shot down now."

"There's the top of one of the hills. It's fairly level if I remember rightly. Not much but heather and bracken, and lots of bilberries."

"Then we're going down. Colonel Heine won't thank me for landing here. Probably engine trouble's the best tale. You'd better hold on for a jolt."

He had swung the plane round as he spoke, and, with the swiftness at which he flew, the level hilltop showed plainly no more than a mile ahead.

His hand moved among the complications of studs and levers which surrounded the pilot's seat, and the engine stalled abruptly, raced on for a moment, and stopped again.

He heard Colonel Heine's voice inquire with anxious anticipation what was wrong, and replied: "The engine's not running. And it seems to be a bad moment for it to stop."

The last remark, spoken with more sincerity than he had expected to use, was caused by the sight of three British airplanes, the engines of which had become audible as the noise of his own had ceased, and which could now be seen to be bearing directly upon him from the western sky. This was a complication containing little cause for surprise, but one which he had not calculated to have to face when his plan was made. He added, finding it no effort to speak with a genuine tone: "I'm going to plane down to the hill. It's the only chance."

His hand moved uncertainly towards the switch which would have given him the power he needed again, but he drew it back. If Colonel Heine should guess at the last moment that he had been fooled and betrayed, he saw that his own danger and that of Perdita would be increased in no small degree. He had enough to do without that.

The wind had veered somewhat towards the north, and he had used the impetus of flight that remained when the engine died to come round so that he could plane down against it. The three friends that supposed him foe were now approaching fast on the right at ten times his remaining speed. Any second they might open a fatal fire.

But it was from below that the bullets came. They were an easy mark as they glided down for the soldiers that lay in the withered bracken and scrubby growths of the lower slope of the hill.

Well, fate must have its way. His own attention must not be turned from the difficult feat of landing on level wheels. And, being boldly faced, fate retired its threats, as it often will.

The three pursuers, recognizing his intention to go to ground, did not fire, but remained watchfully aloft, circling the air.

Even the riflemen, observing that his engine was stilled, and the dropping of the retractile wheels, ceased to make a target of that which, it seemed, would surrender of its own will. Bumping, heeling, almost oversetting, the great plane came to rest on the rough hilltop, with no more hurt than a damaged wing.

CHAPTER XXXV.

CAPTAIN FELTON (15th Warwickshire, A.A. Brigade, 2nd A.A. Division, Territorial Army) advanced to accept the surrender of the German plane which had come down like a settling bird. It was his first experience of actual warfare, and it seemed to be even more of a picnic than a volatile imagination had led him to expect.

He came near to a disillusion which would have ended his career at the same moment that it began. For Colonel Heine, whose fear twenty-four hours before had been that the surrender of Britain would be too speedy and too complete to allow him the measure of fame which his deeds would otherwise be sufficient to win, and who still supposed that he had observed no more than the dying kicks of a prostrate foe, was in no mood to yield to half a company of riflemen on the hill when he remembered the armament which he had for his own defence.

The two cannon would be of little avail, being rigidly attached to the wings, and their mobility being that of the airplane's flight, but the machine-guns fore and aft were swivel-mounted, and capable of defending the hilltop from far more formidable assault than anything which Captain Felton appeared to have at his call.

Had Colonel Heine given the order which he actually commenced to speak, the position of the two English people who formed so considerable a proportion of the little crew might have been as bad as Steele's worst anticipation had feared, but at the moment of decision the Colonel looked aloft, and saw the three planes that circled above his head. The half-uttered words choked on a bitter curse.

"Well," he said, "it will be but, I suppose, for a few hours."

He could not bring himself to put up his hands, but he descended into bilberry bushes and heather that soaked him to the knees, and waited the approach of his too-confident captors.

Captain Felton saluted with the gravity which he considered appropriate to the occasion, and Colonel Heine responded stiffly.

"I am," he said, "for the moment, at your discretion, by the chance of war, and the accident of an engine that has broken down, but I am sure that you will not overlook that this position may be changed in a day, and that, while we talk, your country may have seen the wisdom of abandoning a conflict which she is too weak to sustain."

Captain Felton had studied many things, even including some Greek irregular verbs, but conversational German had not been included among them. But he supposed that the purport of the guttural sentences that he had heard could not be in doubt. The instructions that he had received to fit him for the command he held did not include the etiquette of accepting the surrender of officers of superior rank to his own, but he recalled very appositely a picture he had seen of Nelson with a sheaf of swords under his arm as he accepted numerous surrenders on a Spanish warship's deck, and held out his hand for the archaic weapon the Colonel wore,

Colonel Heine, who was equally unpractised in the aplomb which such occasions require, was yet able to understand the gesture, and though he reddened with anger at the impassive silence with which his protestation had been received, he surrendered his sword with a bad grace.

Captain Felton looked at the little group which had now descended from the plane. He asked: "Are these all?"

The Colonel, who believed that he had learnt English, failed to catch the meaning of the brief question, and a German infantryman interposed: "Perhaps I can help. These are all, except a wounded officer, and another whom I had occasion to kill."

Captain Felton looked his astonishment. He heard an English voice from an unexpected quarter, and that, with the equally unexpected matter of what was said, caused him to overlook the fact that he had not been addressed with the respect which captains require. He asked: "Who are I you?"

FOUR DAYS' WAR, BY S. FOWLER WRIGHT * 171

"I am Richard Steele, a member of the British Intelligence Service. This is Miss Wyatt, an English lady who has escaped from Prague."

Captain Felton looked and believed. He asked: "Then how the deuce did you get here?"

"I was, in fact, piloting the plane. I thought the engine could not stall at a better time."

"Then it was not forced to come down?"

"It has had one propeller shot off. The other engine is working, though not well."

"You had a brush on the way?"

"We were attached to a large fleet which was defeated on the East Coast. This, in fact, is the Air-Admiral's plane. It is he whom I had occasion to kill."

Captain Felton concealed some surprise. He had not thought that England had had forces in the air during the night sufficient for the destruction of any enemy fleet. But that was not to be spoken aloud. He said: "Well, that is pleasant to hear," leaving it to be guessed whether he were pleased by the German defeat or Admiral Nachod's end. He gave a sharp order to his men to disarm the prisoners, and march them to the regimental depot. He asked: "Then you could fly it to the aerodrome here? It is no more than four miles away."

"I suppose I could. But I have information of great importance: information of German movements which I should report without a moment's delay. It is for that that I have risked this method of getting here."

"There is a field telephone you can use."

"Whom can I get?"

"We could get General Yates, if I can say that it is of sufficient importance to justify being put through."

"Who is he?"

"He has the Midland Command."

"He will thank you for every second that you can save."

Captain Felton turned, with no further words, and led the way down the hill, with Steele keeping a rapid pace at his side.

Perdita followed like a forgotten dog.

CHAPTER XXXVI.

"GENERAL YATES is not far from here?" Perdita heard Steele's urgent question as she followed the two men down the hill, with the determination that, be she ignored or not, she would keep closely beside them while she remained disguised in the uniform of her country's foes.

"Probably not. But I'm not sure that I know where his headquarters are; and I couldn't say if I did."

"No, I suppose not."

Steele became silent. His experience approved the caution that Captain Felton's answer had shown. The position of the General Headquarters of an army in the field is a secret that cannot be too closely kept, especially when they are liable to be bombed from the air, but it gave him an unwelcome confirmation of German boasts, as though the defence of England, even in this inland county, had become furtive, a desperate broken resistance driven below the ground. And this impression was not decreased by the sight of a little army of men, mostly in civilian clothes of various qualities and cuts, who toiled to excavate the red sandstone side of the hill, at a point where narrow gauge lines had been laid down, evidently during the last two days, from the nearby railway.

It was as though men sought safety in burrows beneath the ground, as a rabbit will when the eagle's shadow moves over the land: as though they must crouch in caves and the deeper woods from the terror that held the air.

Yet he saw that they worked with a good will, and the words they called to one another were in confident, buoyant tones, with the sense of comradeship in common danger and common toil, the sense that they worked for something beyond themselves and their individual needs, which is one of the fairest growths that flower in the bitter harvest of war.

Perhaps even yet England might outlast this first shock of assault, though it was supported, as it was likely to be, with the resources of Europe and half of Asia beside, and armed with all the devilries by which science had cursed mankind; might have fortitude to endure until, as it surely must, the world's rescue should come.

And he saw that for any guerrilla warfare that might still be waged in the skies (and what he had seen at the dawn had been something better than that) the aerodromes, numerous and small, which the Air Ministry's policy had scattered over the land might be more useful than two or three larger, even though they had been better defended centres, and even though (as he knew too well) they were all marked on the German war maps with almost every defensive detail accurately attached.

But his thoughts turned back quickly to the more urgent matter of the warning he brought, as they came to where the field-telephone was set up. Captain Felton took the call first, and his statements that a German airplane was down, and that there had been an English officer upon it who had important information to give, were sufficient for him to be put through to General Headquarters without delay. He explained briefly what had occurred, and said to Steele: "They'd like to hear what you have to say."

Steele took the receiver, and said, without wasting words: "I have information of the utmost urgency. How can I get to you, and how soon?"

There was a moment's silence, and then: "General Yates will speak to you himself."

He heard a voice in which irritation was hardly controlled: "Well, what is it now? If it's urgent, you'd better tell me at once."

"I'm afraid it's too important for that. I ought to see you without a second's delay."

"Then you must tell me first something more before I—"

"Listen, General. It's a matter that affects London as well as you—London and elsewhere. It's not the kind of thing that can be discussed on the telephone. I ought to have reported direct to my own department, but I've just landed here, and don't know the quickest way to get in touch with them as things are now.

"I shot Admiral Nachod and turned his plane back to bring it here. He's here dead in his cabin now, so—"

"Wait a moment."

There was a pause of silence, and then it became evident that the graphic detail, logically irrelevant as it was, had brought conviction to doubtful minds. A fresh voice said, in a tone of curt instruction: "Please report at once to Commander Winfield at the North-field Aerodrome. A car is being sent to fetch you from there." The call was cut off as the words ceased, without waiting for his reply.

He turned to Captain Felton to say: "I'm to report to Commander Winfield at once. Can I get a car?"

"Yes. There is my own at the side of the road. You can have that. I'll detail a man to drive you."

"I suppose," Perdita asked, "I can come too?"

"Yes. You'd better come. I suppose you had," Steele said absently. And then, as they got into the car, in a more apologetic voice: "I'm sorry I almost forgot you. You'll want to get in touch with your own people, of course. I've no doubt that will be easy to do."

"Yes. I want to do a little telephoning myself. Of course, I understand that I mustn't hinder you now. But I couldn't wander about the country in this uniform."

"No. I'll explain to Commander Winfield. No doubt he'll arrange something."

He became silent again. He had succeeded, against almost impossible odds, in reaching England in time to reveal the German plan of attack, or rather of destruction, and with the knowledge that that was done his mind reverted to the question of what use the information would be, except to rouse an earlier terror in those who were doomed to die? What resistance could be made? What evasion organized in so short a time? If population could be moved, what security would there be that the Germans would not alter their plans, or even blunder in their attack, so that the warning might cause people to flee from safety to a place of more crowded deaths?

Commander Winfield received him as a man already informed. He said that a car from General Headquarters was coming for him, and would be there in ten minutes, probably less. This was Miss Wyatt? She had witnessed the destruction of Prague? He congratulated her on her escape. He suggested, on no evident ground, that she must have shown exceptional courage. Her father was Sir Reginald Wyatt? Yes, at Knowle. Of course, everyone knew Sir Reginald. She could use the telephone? Yes, of course. She should have no difficulty. Their calls had preference on the exchange.

Having disposed of her for the time, he turned to the matter on which his mind was more greatly concerned, to hear what he could of the action through which his ten-minutes guest had come. Steele told what he had seen, and was repaid with information of equal interest to himself.

He learnt not only the identity of the Canadian fleet, but that its own losses were reported to be nearly half its strength. Against that, and in addition to the German losses in fighting planes, it was already known that more than two-thirds of the transports had been shot down. It had been a decided German defeat, although dearly bought.

"It seems," Commander Winfield observed, "as though this war is to be fought out in the air."

"In which case we have no chance at all?"

"I don't think we ought to say that."

"Neither do I, though for a different reason from yours. I think all the air fighting we have had shows that every day the war lasts it will be fought less in the air and more on the land and sea. The casualties on both sides are too heavy to be sustained. The air-fleets have got to take a back seat, or to cease to be.

"Even if we can't meet them in the air, the land batteries will be always bringing them down. There was nothing in the last war like the guns we've got now."

Commander Winfield said he hoped that was right, though he did not speak in a hearty way, for he was one who had taught and believed that the supremacy of the air would be the decisive factor of the next war, and he had an indignation, bitter and just, against the Government which had left the Royal Air Force so inadequate to confront its foes. He added that, all the same, he was glad that Air-Marshal Dalton was to be attached to the Midland Command, with the two score of Fairey Fantomes he still commanded, which would be overhauled and re-equipped during the day.

It was a satisfaction that he was to lose at a later hour, when he would hear that the Air-Marshal had had explicit secret instructions from Ottawa, which had obliged him to notify the British military authorities that they could no longer expect his assistance.

There was to be a rumour also, as the day passed, that the Government of the United States had declined to allow its own powerful air-fleets to attempt the Atlantic crossing, as though it had been resolved that Britain was beyond salvation, and must be made to choose between destruction and shame.

But as Steele hurriedly left, the radio in Commander Winfield's office, which, like most others in England now, was continually turned on to receive the official news which was issued as it came from the censor's office, dealing with all the worldwide areas of the war, struck a cheerful note. It announced that mobile Soviet columns which had pushed forward to seize the oil-wells in Persia and Iraq had been foiled in both instances by the rapidity and thoroughness with which they had been destroyed.

"I'm sorry," Perdita said. "I'm afraid I shall have to be a bit more trouble to you than I expected. I couldn't get any answer when I tried to ring up my own people, and I've got on to a friend who thinks they have gone to Wales."

"Wales?" Commander Winfield queried, with ready sympathy. "That sounds rather a vague address."

"Oh, I know where they're most likely to be. The trouble is that knowing it doesn't get me there. And I can't go about in this uniform. And Mr. Steele made me destroy all the English money I had."

"I don't know that money would make any difference now."

"It can't really have lost its value? It doesn't seem possible."

"No. I don't say that it has. I don't know. I think that's the case with most people. They don't know. But they know one thing. They've no time to waste finding out. And, if you won't think me rude, I've no time really to give to you. But I've got to do something, all the same. There aren't many women about here."

The reflection appeared to remind him of a possible outlet from his dilemma. "Ruston," he said in a voice of relief, to a young officer standing by, "send someone to find Lieutenant—to find Miss Lister, if she hasn't gone off duty yet. There should just be time. Tell her I want her a moment here."

He hurried out as he spoke, leaving Perdita with a well-founded doubt of when or whether her existence would recur to his crowded mind.

CHAPTER XXXVII.

IT was a few minutes later that Imogen Lister entered the room, and looked round for Commander Winfield in some natural irritation that he was not there.

She had twelve hours' leave, after having spent the last twenty-four almost continuously in the air, and had been called back as she was on the point of leaving for her aunt's home, where she could get the rest she needed. She had reached the stage of nervous exhaustion at which even the stimuli of excitement and self-preservation falter, and returned in doubt that she might be required to undertake some further immediate effort such as it would be hard to refuse, and might be impossible to fulfil.

She looked at Lieutenant Ruston to ask: "Isn't Commander Winfield about? I was told he wanted to see me before I go."

Perdita stepped forward to explain: "I think it was about me. If you are Miss Lister? He thought you might be able to help me out of the mess I'm in."

The two girls faced one another in a mutual curiosity, and the instinctive sub-hostile doubt which is a woman's almost normal reaction to a first contact with one of her own sex and age. Each looked into a white, strained face, and eyes wearied from lack of sleep. Each had been through twenty-four hours of almost continuous peril and nervous tension, one in active self-reliance, the other in passive ways, which gave more leisure for fear. Each looked older than she would have done three days before, against which Perdita's slightly fresher youth may have put up the better fight, the fine lines round Imogen's eyes, which are the sign of those who take the ways of the air, being very plain in a bloodless face.

It was a position in which Perdita had the most to explain, all of which was not easy to say in a few words. But they knew more of each other at the first glances they changed than men would learn in a week.

Imogen said: "I'll do anything that I can."

Knowing that she had found a friend it was good to have, Perdita answered with comprehensive directness: "I've escaped from Germany, and I find my people have gone to Wales. I can't go anywhere in these clothes, and the first question seems to be how I'm to get any others."

"I should think the first question is where you can get some sleep. You'd better come in the car with me. I've got twelve hours' leave and we shall be home in ten minutes."

They went out together without regarding the fact that the radio had commenced another announcement, of which Lieutenant Ruston became the only auditor.

> "A statement was published in Berlin yesterday evening that Field-Marshal Wertner had been executed for high treason against the Third Reich, on his own confession, and that General von Hoffman had been appointed Commander-in-Chief in his place.
>
> "The significance of this event is not clear, but it is rumoured that Field-Marshal Wertner has been the victim of one of those political assassinations which have been common in Germany during recent years, and that its result will be to place von Teufel, who is already in command of the combined Russo-German air-fleets, in a position of almost absolute power."

There was a short pause, and the announcer commenced again:

> "During the early hours of this morning several attempts were made, with various degrees of success, to land highly mechanized German military units transported by air at a number of strategic points in England and Scotland.
> "One of these transport fleets was attacked, and with its escort was defeated and practically destroyed in an engagement which took place at dawn over South Lincolnshire.
> "Military dispositions adequate to deal with these invasions have already been made."

The voice paused, and broke out again:

> "The President of the United States has convened a meeting in Washington of the Ambassadors and Envoys of all neutral and friendly states to consider what he has described as the crisis of civilization.
> "He has also issued a proclamation, the full text of which will be given during the next hour, enjoining fortitude upon those nations of Europe and Asia which are enduring the first fury of the attack, and promising that those who endure will be quickly relieved."

It was almost at the same time in New York that the loitering crowd in Times Square, who endured the bitter colt of the night hours that they might learn the latest news of a world at war, watched the moving electric sign announce: PRESIDENT DE-CIDES — TO — ABANDON — EUROPE.!

CHAPTER XXXVIII.

IMOGEN said: "It isn't my own car. It's one that's lent for me to use. Do you drive?"

"Yes. Would you like me to? Really?"

"Yes. If you're used to this type of car, and you're not too tired."

"How far is it?"

"About six miles."

"Well, there's not much in that, if you'll tell me the way to go."

There could have been few cars of British make that Perdita had not driven at times, and none that she would have hesitated to take in hand.

But as she took the steering-wheel, and her companion got in beside her, the conversation reminded her of an idea which had come to her mind before.

"Miss Lister—forgive me asking—you're not Imogen Lister, are you?"

"Yes...I suppose you think I oughtn't to mind driving a car?"

"I didn't say that. In fact, I don't know that you do. You may have thought I'd rather drive than look on."

"But it wasn't that. You were quite right. I drive when I must. But I always hate it, and I think I'm rather afraid.

"It's the feeling of being hedged in all the time, with no space to turn except when a corner comes, and having to pass other cars, perhaps going at high speed with a few inches of clearance. It's so different from the open space of the sky. You feel that you can do what you like there with no danger at all."

Perdita considered this unexpected fact, that a girl whose air-manship had won the world's praise for heroism and skill should confess to nervousness in driving a car on a well-kept road.

"Well," she said, "I suppose it's what you're used to that counts. But when I think of that Polar flight...!"

"There wasn't anything really in that. I only did it because I was dared, and was too cowardly to draw back when I'd said I would. And after that I hadn't much to do but keep on. It was the engine-makers who pulled me through."

"It sounds surprising that it hasn't been done about twice a week," Perdita smiled in reply, and then, changing the subject with an instinctive feeling that it must be one of which its heroine would have heard more than she wished, she asked: "Do you think I shall have much trouble getting to Wales?"

"No, I don't see why you should. You'd get there best in a private car. I don't know much about how things are going on except from some talk I hear. I've been in the air almost all the time since the war began, except when I've been asleep, and I believe everything's changing about twice an hour. But the newspapers and the wireless are helping people to pull together as far as possible.

"You wouldn't get petrol without giving a good reason. That is, not from a filling station. You might get it privately. And I don't know anything about trains running to Wales."

"I've got no English money. The English agent who got me out of Nürnberg said it wouldn't be any good, and he burnt the lot."

"I believe it's a fact that it isn't much, though I don't think most people are quite as drastic as that. The trouble is that the trains are all under military control. If they think people ought to be moved into Wales, they'll provide the means, and if not, they won't. But there aren't any men wasting their time punching tickets now. People understand that it is a real war.

"I suppose that wars used to be between kings, and most people thought they were nuisances they ought to avoid as much as they could, like a bad storm; and the last war was a mongrel affair, in which the people themselves had some concern, though they didn't expect it to interfere overmuch with the ways of life that they'd always known; but this time—on our side, at least—we know that everyone's in it up to the neck, and we just let the small things go."

"You mean that if a train's going, I shan't need a ticket."

"Yes, but it's a big 'if.' I know you could have got to London if you'd a good reason to give on the ambulance trains that returned empty, but I believe the hospitals are all full in the Midlands now after what's happened round here, and the London ambulance trains are going much farther west. Probably they think it's safer to take the people farther away, and out of the industrial districts. And they say that the Germans have special orders to fire on the Red Cross, wherever they see it, because it's the Christian sign. I don't know whether that's true, or only a tale."

"Are the coaches still running?"

"No. They are all commandeered for moving troops, or distributing food supplies, except the small local ones that take people backwards and forwards to work. What part of Wales do you want to get to?"

"Cardiff. My father is head of a shipping firm there. I might have thought that he would be certain to go when the war began—but it wouldn't have made any difference really. I should have been landed here just the same."

Imogen heard without comment, but with a mental adjustment of her opinion of her companion's family. She knew that there had been a national appeal to the population to hold its ground, except as it might be advised to move, and that those who disregarded this request in endeavours to secure individual safety by flight into lonely places were subjects of occasional violence and more general contempt. But though there was no allusion to that, there was a different tone in her voice as she replied: "Well, I shouldn't worry. You'll find everyone will be anxious to help. But the first thing to do will be to find you some other clothes."

The conversation had been punctuated by directions as to the road to be taken, and was now abruptly terminated by their arrival at Mrs. Rowntree's house.

Mrs. Rowntree was in the garden using a spade. It might prove to be a short war, as everyone said it would. But she concluded that, even so, its consequences would take longer to dear away. Her knowledge of gardening was not great, and the spade was not the gardening implement she was most accustomed to use, but she knew that broad beans may be safely planted in February in the English Midlands, and this she was proceeding to do.

Imogen, considering the occupation in which she saw her to be engaged, the deafness from which she suffered, and the time it would take to explain the appearance of a strange girl in the uniform of a German private (especially as she was herself very slightly informed), decided that the weariness from which they both suffered was a sufficient reason for deferring such explanations to a later hour. She sought the cook, to whom she said no more than that she had brought a friend who would share her room, and that they would both be down for dinner at the usual hour, and would she please tell her mistress that when she came in from the garden? And the two girls retired together, for Perdita to reveal the completeness with which the methods of No. 973 had deprived her of everything which belonged to her self or sex, and for the recovery of sleep to lessen the effect of the experiences through which they had passed, and to prepare them or others that were to come.

CHAPTER XXXIX.

"THE plan," Steele said, "so far as I could ascertain without an appearance of curiosity which I dared not show, was, in the first place, to establish military centres at various easily defensible strategic points, such as that at Sheffield which was our own destination, from which the inhabitants of the surrounding country would be required to surrender the while—"

"Yes, we know that," Field-Marshal Blackstone interrupted rather brusquely. "We are moving troops already to contain those which have been established at Stirling and Durham and farther south. If you can give us any details of their equipment and strength—"

"I can give you some. But it is the second part of the plan which it seemed to me most urgent to let you have. As a means of terrorizing those who might otherwise be slow to yield, bombing fleets are to come over, timed to arrive at tomorrow's dawn, to destroy three selected areas, each of about eighty square miles. One is the thickly populated residential district south of the Firth of Forth, one a strip of country west of Birmingham, and one in Surrey, sufficiently south of London to avoid the guns of the anti-aircraft defences which surround the Croydon airport."

"*Destroy?* Do you mean by incendiary bombs?"

It was Mr. Ponting, the Defence Minister, who asked. The time was three hours after Steele had been picked up from the Northfield Aerodrome. The place the secret headquarters of the Council of Defence for the British Isles, in what was publicly supposed to be nothing more than a small underground aerodrome which had been enlarged from a cave in the Quantock Hills, to which General Yates had sent him at the fastest speed that a plane could make, after two minutes' conversation had convinced him of the deadly urgency of the tale he heard.

"No, I suppose they would hardly choose residential suburban districts for that. There is to be a systematic distribution of a gas previously untried in warfare, which will destroy all life by intense cold."

"Against which gas-masks would be of no use?"

"Not the least."

Field-Marshal Blackstone interrupted again: "How do you know that those areas will not be changed?"

"I don't. But it is improbable, if they have nothing to lead them to suppose that their plans are known."

"Unless they have given you this information with the anticipation that it will be betrayed."

"From the way in which I acquired it, I think that to be an improbable theory."

"But I think differently."

Without waiting for further reply, the Field-Marshal addressed his colleagues in support of the opinion he had expressed.

"Even assuming—and it is a large assumption—that attacks of such a character and on such a scale will be made during the next twenty-four hours, I suggest that this information is of an inherent improbability, such as in itself makes the conclusion almost irresistible that it is deliberately intended to mislead, and that areas have been designated which it is particularly improbable that the German High Command would select for such an attack. Few things are more certain than that, if further large-scale attacks are made from the air, in spite of the heavy losses which have already been inflicted upon the invading air-fleets, they will be made upon the industrial districts, crowded with machinery and manufactures, upon centres of storage, aerodromes, and railway junctions, rather than upon sub-rural areas less thickly populated, and in which the human and material damage would be much less in proportion to the bombardment expended upon it."

Mr. Ponting, the civilian chairman of this gathering of military, naval, and aviation experts, thought that he saw a flaw in the Field-Marshal's reasoning; or perhaps two; but he had no concern in an issue of such gravity to score a debating point. He thought it better to observe with what arguments the bearer of this dubious information would be able to make his own reply. He asked: "What have you to say to that, Mr. Steele?"

"I don't think it's very difficult to answer. The small military forces which have been landed at various points are surely a sufficient indication that a heavier attack of some sort will follow in a very few hours. Strong in artillery as they are, they couldn't hope to hold out against sustained attacks from the outnumbering troops you could have on the scenes within forty-eight hours, if not much less than that.

"But if the presumption is that the country will be demoralized by this time tomorrow, then it's evident that they will have been placed there ready to take over surrendered territory with the least possible delay, and before its resources can be destroyed.

"I suggest that the reason why they have selected sub-rural areas is about equally simple. They don't want to destroy stores that will be in their hands almost at once, nor to damage factories that will soon be turning out munitions for them.

"The fact that the New World and the British Dominions and Japan, and perhaps a few other countries, are coming into the war has decided them that they must use all their strength to subdue Britain at once, and in such a way that they can use it against their foes."

Mr. Ponting observed that the majority of the members of the Council appeared to be impressed both by the weight of these arguments in themselves and by the quiet confidence with which they were stated. He saw also that Field-Marshal Blackstone was unconvinced, and knowing from experience that that very able officer would be the slower to abandon an opinion the more emphatically he had been led to express it, he was quick to interpose with another question: "Do you know anything about this gas that, you say, kills with cold?"

"Yes, I have seen its effects. There was an escape from a damaged reservoir when Leunawerke was burned down a few days ago. They tried to neutralize its effects by instantly flooding the streets with hot water, for which the necessary apparatus had been laid down; and the people had been taught to escape at the first alarm by avoiding the way of the wind. Most of them succeeded, but next morning I saw the way the escaping gas had taken. It had killed everything. It killed men and women so suddenly that they were frozen into grotesque attitudes as they had been rushing to escape from it. It killed every insect, every weed. Nothing escaped."

"How does it do that?"

"Simply intense cold. You know how snow and salt make something colder than either alone? It's the same, only about fifty times worse, when this gas meets the oxygen of the air. I'm told that its own temperature isn't particularly low, but when the two meet they produce an air that no creature could breathe and live, even if the cold were not fatal in other ways."

"But there is oxygen in water?"

"Yes, but it doesn't combine in the same way. Even hot steam does much to neutralize its effects. But it's not easy to use on a large scale in the open air."

"Do you know the approximate strength of the bombing fleets that will bring this gas?"

"Only by inference. The intention is, if I was rightly informed, to destroy all life in a thorough systematic way in the three areas, each consisting of about eighty square miles—say eight by ten. The swift new type of German bomber which has been built so largely in the one pattern, and which is presumably the one that they will use—but that's no more than a likely guess—would carry sufficient bombs to drench an area of about thirty acres, so that in theory about twenty-one night-bombers would be needed for each square mile, or 1,680 for each fleet. But in practice, even with very low flying, it would be impossible to drop bombs with absolute regularity over such a space, and a larger number of bombers would be needed to avoid a merely patchy effect, which is what they particularly wish to avoid. They aim to make the freezing death appear to be a certainty wherever they decide to spread it, not merely an odds-on chance. I should guess that each fleet would consist of not less than 2,000 night-bombers, with a proportionately large escort of fighting planes."

"Proportionately large? What exactly do you mean by that?" Air-Marshal Stockdale asked sharply.

"I don't know. You can only judge by the composition of fleets which have come over previously."

The Air-Marshal did not appear to be encouraged by the reply. He said. "I suppose it won't be much use shooting down their bombers when they're once over the land?"

"No. The gas will be likely to be let loose where ever they fall. They should be shot down, if possible, over the sea."

Mr. Ponting raised interrogative eyebrows to the Air-Marshal, who shook his head.

"We've got some planes left, of course. Perhaps more than some people think. But we should have none left tomorrow if we were to encounter even one fleet such as those, and we should do well if we put twenty-five percent into the sea. We should do no more than that, and tomorrow there mightn't be twenty British planes fit to go up." He added, seeing the gravity of his colleagues' faces, and with a foolish momentary inclination to accept the forbidding odds: "Of course, the Navy would give us what aid they could; and Admiral Dalton, who did such good work this morning, has two score of his biplanes that will be fit again by that time."

"I'm afraid," Mr. Ponting said, "you mustn't count upon him. He had a telegram of congratulation from Ottawa this morning, but it ended with instructions for him to leave England without delay."

"To leave England? Wherever for?"

Mr. Ponting hesitated, even in that assembly, but decided on a frank statement of what he had learnt in the last hour, and of his own conclusions therefrom. "He has orders to proceed to a Portuguese aerodrome, from which he can operate in Gibraltar's support, or to Ceuta, if the former fortress should be in German hands."

"That means," Lord Vinton exclaimed, with a mingling of incredulity and bitterness in his voice, "that they're leaving England to drown?"

"I don't know what it means yet," the Defence Minister replied, "and perhaps I oughtn't to guess." He was the only minister of cabinet rank who had remained in England when the Government had chartered an airliner for Halifax, and he felt some hesitation in saying that which was rather intelligent anticipation than official knowledge as yet. But after a moment's pause, he went on: "I don't think it would be fair to say, even so, that they leave us to drown.

"But there was something like a World Council held at Washington in the early hours of today, at which Sir Edward White was present to represent this country, and the Ambassadors of other European Powers, including those that have been overrun by Germany so that their home governments are broken up, to decide upon a general line of military policy in which all those who oppose the Russo-German menace should be advised to unite.

"We've no official news yet of what its decisions were, but it is being said in New York that the President, in their emphatic journalese, announced his determination to 'abandon Europe.'

"I suggest that, even though there may be a sense in which that phrase is verbally true, its actual meaning is no more nor less than a decision of large-scale military strategy, which will adopt the north coast of Africa as the main line of resistance, with the Mediterranean as a protecting moat.

"If we can hold the seas, as we seem able to do, the Mediterranean will be a difficult barrier to surmount—at least so long as we can retain Gibraltar and the Canal.

"What is required is a line on which resistance can rally, and, unless the Old World is to be entirely lost, the North African coast appears to be the natural one to choose. Of course, you'll understand that what I'm telling you is no more than a likely guess, but the fact that Dalton has been ordered to Gibraltar gives it support, and, besides that, it seems to me to be the right strategy to adopt, even though, as you suggest, it should leave England to drown.

"If we haven't had sense enough to provide adequately for our defences, we can't ask that the rest of the world shall adopt a rotten strategic plan just to save us from the natural consequences of our own neglect."

Field-Marshal Blackstone considered this with a reluctant admission in his own mind that it was the probable meaning of the meagre facts from which it had taken shape in Mr. Ponting's notoriously fertile brain. He recognized also that it indicated a strategic plan such as was rendered almost inevitable by the nature and extent of the success of those aggressive powers who had broken so suddenly the peace of the world; and by the great distances of water and land over which the reserve strength of the world must advance to make common front against its gigantic foes.

He had wished and supposed that the resources both of the British Empire and of the United States would be directed to the support of Britain, regarding it not only for itself but as a sea-girt fortress vital to hold, within the shelter of which their legions of land and air could be gathered, and from which they could be launched when the moment to strike should come.

If the world's seas could be held—he recognized this to be the decisive factor—he had concluded that his military problem was no more than to hold his own for the few days that must elapse before the first reliefs would begin to arrive, perhaps with air-fleets even sooner than they. Patriotism and professional pride united in protest against the sacrifice of his country's freedom, and the ignoble part for which it seemed that he was to be cast in this drama of war. He said: "So you're telling us that we can as well throw up the sponge?"

Mr. Ponting observed a reaction that he had half-expected to meet and which it must be his purpose to overcome. He said quietly: "I didn't mean to suggest that."

"Perhaps not. But it's the plain meaning of what you said, all the same. We've just been told that the Germans control the air. We can't even put up a fight when we hear that the brutes are going to bomb our women with freezing gas. We're licked before we begin.

"It isn't we"—his glance took in his professional colleagues of sea and air—"who are responsible for that. It's you damned politicians who—" He checked a temper which he knew to be difficult to control if he gave it rein. "I beg your pardon," he said. "There's no use in quarrelling now. But do you think I've got men or guns to fight half Europe and half Asia as well, if they bring them over here at the rate of about fifty thousand a day, which they may be quite equal to do?"

Mr. Ponting would have liked to reply that the inadequacy of England's defences of land and air was not of his will; but a fine sense of loyalty to colleagues of narrower vision, and a realization that he could not avoid responsibility for the defaults of a Government from which he had not resigned, left the words unsaid. He answered: "No, there's no use in quarrelling now. But we'll hope it's not too late to save England yet. Do you know that the *Normandie* left New York nearly twelve hours ago?"

Admiral Crosshunter took the question to himself. "Yes," he said, "I heard she had left. Bound for Cherbourg with a cargo of munitions of war and an escort of U.S.A. destroyers. It's to be hoped she gets there before it's in German hands."

"I can tell you now what the Admiralty will be officially advised during the day. It's not Cherbourg, it's Southampton that it's aiming to reach, unless we divert it to come round the North of Ireland, and unload at Liverpool or Glasgow or even Belfast, according to what the position may be when it arrives.

"Well, the point is that it's loaded up with munitions till it must be a bit lower in the water than anyone ever saw it before, and the best part of its cargo is anti-aircraft guns and the ammunition that they require.

"I don't know enough yet about the President abandoning Europe to say more than I've done already, but I know that you owe this to him.

"The first moment that he decided to come into the war, he gave an order that every anti-aircraft battery that could be got to the dock should be loaded up for England without a second's delay. I believe they've even stripped their own coastal defences, to be replaced later from reserves. And that's what we've got to hope for now. We've got to fight the air from the ground, and I don't know that it's more than we shall be able to do.

"In a week's time, if they escape the German submarines, there'll be more of these guns landing in England with every tide, and they ought to be worth more to us than a million men."

The confident words brought a new hope to those who heard, who were not naturally timid of heart. To Admiral Crosshunter's mind there came a vision of the *Normandie* with a foam-white wake, and its long hull trembling to the pulsations of the rapid heart-beats within, its low bows driving hard through the grey wash of Atlantic waves, and the thin streaks of the destroyers, with their black smoke-trails on either side. Rapidly, he redisposed the naval forces at his command that he might send out a further escort for this vessel on which the fate of England so largely hung.

"She won't spare fuel," he said; "she ought to be here in four days, or perhaps less."

Field-Marshal Blackstone's jaw set with a determination more obstinate for the moment of shaken fortitude through which he had passed as he had regarded that which all his professional experience had told him to be impossible odds.

"Hold the air," he said, "and by God, we'll be enough for the devils yet."

He looked at Air-Marshal Stockdale, who was quiet, even gentle, in his non-committal reply: "You know that we shall do all we can."

No one doubted that, or failed to understand the courage that his demeanour did not obtrude. His thought was upon the men he had lost, and of those who remained, "the few that were alive to die" whom he must send to their deaths in the coming hours. There would be very few, he supposed, who would be alive in ten days from now. Or perhaps two.

But for the past three years he had looked for no other end. The utmost that any government could be even induced to discuss was that the world-scattered strength of the R.A.F. should be equal to the disclosed strength of neighbours whose fleets were concentrated at home. And how far behind that had the fact become! He knew, as all soldiers know, that if you stint metal, you pay in blood. And the time had come, and he said no more than "we shall do all we can." For what more was there to say?

Mr. Ponting recalled the meeting to the subject from which the discussion had turned aside. He said: "But there is this question of the freezing gas with which we have still to deal."

The thought reminded him of the presence of the intelligence officer who had brought the news, and who, sitting somewhat backward, had heard matters on the secrecy of which even the fate of England might ultimately depend. He observed it without alarm, having learnt something of No. 973 a few days before, but for which it is improbable that he would have been present at this discussion at all.

He said: "I needn't warn you, Mr. Steele, that nothing heard in this room is to be spoken outside."

"No, you needn't do that. It's my trade to find things out, not to give them away."

"So I suppose. You have done services to England that none of us will forget. I believe it was you who got through the first news of the burning of the Leunawerke?"

"I sent it. I didn't know it had got through. It was mere luck that I saw it burn, though it was through me, in a way. I had meant to get in and find out what was going on."

"Well, it was bravely tried. You look as though you're very nearly done in."

"I've had no sleep for two days. But I'm used to that at such times. I could do with a few hours, if you could find me a sofa of any kind."

"We can do rather better than that. You can have the use of my own room. We don't want you to go out of call. You have too much information on which we may wish to draw. Gentlemen, I propose that we have some lunch, and discuss what steps it will be possible to take. It seems to me that if we begin moving population or any-thing on a large scale at too early an hour, it will leak out into Germany, and we shall be wasting our time, or perhaps worse. But you may see it another way."

* * * * * * *

In Berlin at the same time, though it was a later hour of the day, Prince von Teufel frowned at a weather forecast which had been laid before him. It showed a cyclone advancing from the northwest on the British Isles. It foretold cold and probable snow.

"We shall make no change in the plans?" Baron Triberg asked, with an obsequiousness which would have amused or astonished those who knew him only in the habitual truculence of his army manner.

Von Teufel made an impatient gesture. "Change? No. We must have England by this time tomorrow."

He felt himself already to be as one seated on the roof of the world. He did not disregard the importance of the elements to assist or hinder the dispositions he made. But he felt that importance to be subordinate: an interference to be thrust aside by his inflexible will. And he had been angered in a cold way by things he had heard during the last hour.

The Crown Prince of Italy was reported to have escaped to Tripoli, where he had received the support of the Governor of that colony, and had issued a proclamation denouncing the surrender of his country, and calling upon all patriotic Italians to join him in what he described as a holy war for the Cross of Christ and the deliverance of their captive land.

And it had been found that it was easier to occupy Paris than to obtain possession of the French fleet, a large part of which now lay in Valetta harbour, or under the shelter of Gibraltar's guns, where its captains had placed themselves at the service of the British Admiral on the Mediterranean station.

Certainly, England must be subdued, that he might be free to deal with his further foes.

BOOK THREE

CHAPTER XL.

PERDITA waked, yawned, sat up, and lay down again with a sense of comfort not to be lightly left. Her mind, blank at first, gathered recollections of the events of the last week, with a sense of unreality hard to break, as though she wandered back into dreams that the night had bred.

From the high Legation window, she looked out over Prague, while the darkness was torn apart by the explosion that gashed open the city's midst. She waded knee-deep in snow while the loud bombs burst and the houses fell. She knelt in the snow by the side of a dying friend. She heard the petulant, futile cry from the lips of one who had always found that she could coax or cajole a complaisant world, as the blood pulsed from her unseen, unstaunchable wound: "God wouldn't do that to me!" She waked in the car in the faint light of the frozen dawn to find that her shoulder leant on Karl Dürer's arm. She wandered like a trapped hare in the Nürnberg streets. She sat in the mean inn-room, giving doubtful trust to one who was a stranger to her and with no claim beyond that he could speak in the English tongue. She stood, holding on to a supporting strap, in the observation-cabin of the German Admiral's plane, as it pitched and swayed, and its gun-flashes lit the clouds. She stood behind Richard Steele as Admiral Nachod fell dead to the cabin floor, and the automatic dropped from his hand and leapt like a living thing with the impetus of its own recoils, deafening her ears in that narrow space.

But under all these nightmare memories of the sudden storm that had swept the gracious security of her sheltered life, there was a feeling of satisfaction that had its roots in the fact that she was returned to her own land. Home was home, with the peace it brings, even though it lay under the red shadow of war.

Imogen said: "There's no need for you to get up, if you'd rather not. I think I've put out everything you can need. It's a good thing we're about the same size. I'll have some dinner sent up to you if you like. I shouldn't have minded lying a bit longer myself, but I've got to be back at ten."

Perdita sat up again. She saw that Imogen was already dressed, and that she had laid out clothes and articles of toilet of her own for the use of her guest.

"Oh, I'll get up," she said, yawning again. "I expect you're a lot tireder than I. Or anyway, you've got a much better right. Shall I be in time if I'm quick now?"

"Yes, I dare say you could. It's only half-past seven. Dinner's at eight. I'll turn on the bath, if you'd really rather get up."

Perdita had no doubt about that. She felt, apart from more serious inclination or arguments, that courtesy required that she should meet her actual hostess before the departure of the one who had brought her there.

She dressed quickly, throwing off some of the lassitude of insufficient sleep with the resilience of her healthful youth, and becoming more conscious of the time that had passed since she had eaten Admiral Nachod's game-pie; and of an ungrateful wish that Imogen, in addition to being of the same height as herself, had been two inches larger around the waist, and worn a size larger shoe.

She had been introduced to Mrs. Rowntree, and described something of her adventures in Central Europe without allowing conversation to obstruct the demands of appetite, when the radio broke out into one of those frequent announcements by which the Council of Defence communicated such facts or instructions as were of general importance; and which could be so worded as to convey no information useful to enemy ears.

"There is reason to believe that preparations are now being made in Germany for air-raids of an extensive character which will be directed against this country, probably in the early hours of tomorrow morning.

"All citizens are advised to remain alert for instructions which will either be broadcast or issued by local authorities at a later hour."

It was almost immediately afterwards that Imogen received a telephone call to say that she would not be required to report for duty again before 1:00 A.M.

"I don't know," she said, "that I'm very grateful for that. There isn't time enough to make it worthwhile to get back to bed, and it's mostly likely to mean it'll be a few hours later before I get off again—if I ever do."

The last words slipped out, and were regretted before their sound had ceased on the air. They were the natural result of the free talking of the last hour, and of the emotional strain of the life which all England was living now, and most of all those who sought to protect its safety above the clouds. She was glad to see that her aunt had not caught the concluding phrase.

Perdita asked, with a note of restrained anxiety in her voice: "There isn't anything special on tonight, is there?" and was aware of the banality of the words.

But Imogen answered seriously: "No, it was a silly thing to have said. I don't really do anything in which there's any danger at all. I'm not in one of the fighting or bombing-planes. I suppose I'm lucky in that. They say several girls who had reputations for flying have volunteered and are acting as pilots now. There was a report just as I came away that Ethel Mair has been killed in the Hartlepool battle—" She checked herself abruptly, and went on: "But we're not supposed to speak about that. Of course, the Germans are trying to bomb as many ports as they can, as well as the aerodromes and munitions works. We can't defend everywhere properly, when we haven't one plane in ten for those they can spare for attacking us, but we try to give them a surprise now and then.

"But I'm not asked to fight anyone. I'm just a specialist in the art of running away. I tried to be too clever this morning, and had about the nearest squeak that I ever could, and I expect that was what made me talk in that silly style."

"I suppose you mean you do observation flying, and have to take care not to get caught?"

"Yes, I do patrol work, and give warning of the approach of German planes, and all the particulars about them that I can make out. It's a girl's work, because she weighs less than a man, and weight counts. I've got a scouting plane that's all engine and flying speed. It's got no gadgets at all. Just space for one to sit, and a good wireless.

"I had the job during the night of putting the Can—the attacking fleet in the way of the Germans that came over Lincolnshire this morning—the one that got smashed. The one, I suppose, you were with yourself. I wasn't in any danger of being caught, but I tried a dive through the clouds, so that they shouldn't know which way I retired, and I didn't realize how low they were over the sea till it was almost too late.

"For the last two seconds before I regained control I thought I was booked to drown. But I'm not likely to make that mistake again." She turned the conversation to say to her aunt: "I wonder Eustace hasn't come before now. I hope nothing's wrong with him."

Perdita saw in the words the explanation of one of the two unoccupied places that had been set for the meal that was nearly done, and Imogen completed it the next moment, when she went on: "Mr. Ashfield's a friend who's been very kind during the last few days. When I knew that I should be free, I phoned him to come for dinner, and he said he'd be here for sure. The other place is for my brother-in-law, Captain Malins. We've no reason to expect him tonight, but Auntie has a place set for him for every meal, just to be on the right side."

Even as she spoke, there was a ring of the front door-bell, and a minute later Eustace Ashfield was shown into the room.

Perdita, before being introduced to a young man who looked tired and dispirited, but whom she felt it would be pleasant to know, had seen the look of depression pass transiently from his face, and his eyes light at Imogen's greeting as he came in. She saw with quick feminine instinct that there was an understanding between the two which went beyond casual acquaintance, and was as quick to see that though the additional guest might be not unwelcome to her, her own presence might give less satisfaction to him.

So, in fact, it was. He had a tale to tell which had made it difficult to come, and late before his resolution had equalled that which he knew it would be both cowardly and futile to delay.

"I'm ashamed," he said, "to come in so late. No, please don't trouble. I've really had—"

"Don't be absurd," Imogen said lightly. "I've not got to be back until 1:00 A.M., so it won't matter if dinner goes on for another hour. You can tell us what's kept you the while you eat. I suppose you've got the night-shift working by now?"

He hesitated in reply, and then said with more bitterness in his tone than he was aware—what did it matter who heard it now?— "I've been told that I might be some use at sweeping the office floor."

Imogen asked, with a quick, indignant sympathy in her words: "You mean that some fool's said that the gas-masks aren't any good?"

"Perhaps they're not. But it's gone a long way beyond that. I'd better tell it you from the start. I don't know whether you know that there's been a Control of Industry Board set up, with power under martial law to inquire into what every factory's doing, and put it on to any work and under any management it thinks best.

"I had a visit this morning from a man who called himself an Assistant-Controller. He asked what we were doing, and I told him that I was working on a War Office telegram which I received the day before war began, and that since then I had heard nothing, beyond receipt of a letter confirming the wire.

"He spent about two minutes inquiring what the gas-masks were like, and then said: 'Well, we've no time to waste on them now,' and began to ask me what technical manufacturing experience I had had, and how long I'd been in charge there.

"Then he went to talk to the men, and in about half an hour he came back to me. He said he was afraid I'd have to find a job that I understood better. He'd appointed one of the tool-makers to take control, and the foreman was to keep his position, but under him.

"All the gas-mask work was to be put aside, some of the machines were to be sent to another factory, and two new ones would be delivered during the afternoon. The whole place was to be put on to the manufacture of some small parts for an anti-aircraft gun.

"I said I supposed I should be allowed to stay in my own factory, and that I was willing to do anything that would be most useful, and he said he was afraid not. I should only be in the way. He didn't see what I could do beyond sweeping the floor.

"I said at least I could keep the books, and he asked, books of what? He said they would send in all the metal needed, and fetch away all the parts made. There wouldn't be much booking about that. Didn't I know there was a war? I heard him tell Bates to telephone for anything he required, and it would be delivered at once. He said: 'We shall fetch the material, but don't waste time having it weighed.' He told me to go to the Ministry of Labour this afternoon, and they'd find me something to do."

Imogen held to her point. "Why did he say the gas-masks weren't any good?"

"He didn't say that exactly. He implied that other things mattered more. And, if I'm fair, I can't say that I was much surprised about that.

"I've heard a good bit of talk during the last few days, and it seems to be the general opinion that the gas-mask's a back number, a sort of relic of the ideas of the last war.

"You know that the Defence Council has had about forty million of the standard pattern manufactured and distributed over the country during the last two years. I've been told that most of the local authorities haven't even troubled to give them out. They say that it will lead to people relying on a useless thing.

"I know the one we were making was a much better pattern, but the point is that the Germans aren't fighting with any of the gases that the masks are adapted to meet.

"Of course, they may start using them any time, but so far they've depended upon incendiary and high explosive bombs. And it's said—and the propaganda leaflets they're scattering say the same—that they've got new inventions against which it doesn't seem likely that masks would avail.

"Anyway, if my patent would have been any good, I can see that it ought to have been tried a bit sooner than this. And one thing's certain: gas-masks won't win any war. We've got to have something that can hit back, and if every factory's being put on to that, I'm not going to say it's wrong."

"All the same," Imogen said, "it's beastly bad luck for you.

"No," he said, in the tone of one who talks to convince himself, and expresses that which his reason approves, rather than that to which inclination turns, "I'm not sure that I ought to say that either. We've all got to find our own level now, and it's not easy to think of anything really fairer than that."

He became silent, thinking of that second interview which wouldn't be pleasant to tell, and Perdita said: "They didn't use gas in Prague. It was all burning and blowing up, just as you say."

The remark drew the conversation to her own experiences, and how she had seen a great city blaze to ruin in a few hours, as half London was to do on the next night. It turned Eustace Ashfield's thoughts from his own reverse to the larger issues on which the fate of his country swayed, and the feeling of bitterness against which he had fought during the last hours finally left his mind.

"I went," he said steadily, determined to complete the tale of his own discomfiture while this mood remained, "to the Labour Exchange in the afternoon, and asked what they'd got for me to do. I saw a man who asked a lot of questions and didn't think most of the answers worth putting down. He said I was like a lot of others who didn't know anything, though I knew about *quite* a lot. It struck me that he'd made that remark a few times before. He wasn't really rude till I said that even if I couldn't do anything else I thought I could drive a lorry. 'Drive!' he said. 'If you'd find me ten dolts in England who don't say they can do that I might think we should win the war.' And when I got up to go, I heard him muttering as I went out:

'Drive to hell! What do they think they're all going to drive, and where to?'"

"Didn't he suggest anything that you could do?" Imogen asked, feeling that there was an incompleteness in this account.

"I'm to call in tomorrow for that. But it won't be in the army, unless it's a labour corps. He said the army's only wanting skilled men, and it's too late to begin training them now."

"I'm not sure," Imogen said, "that he'd got overmuch sense himself. We can judge that better when we see what he's got for you to do. But I should think you're glad you've not got to spend your life any longer trying to get a profit out of things that other men make, and perhaps finding at the end of the year that you're no better off, or made a profit by paying wages on which men couldn't live decently. There must be better ways of living than that."

As she spoke, Eustace was aware that, under all the natural resentment which he had felt at being told to walk out of his own works, and at the contemptuous condemnation that his educational and business qualifications had received, there had been from the first a subconscious sense of satisfaction, of shackles broken and freedom gained, very different from how he or others similarly placed would have reacted a week before if their means of livelihood—all that divided them from the restraints and degradations of poverty—had been suddenly lost.

There was a sense of new values, new freedoms, a breaking of the old tyrannies, social and bureaucratic, that came as men turned from the rigours and the hard meanness of civil economic strife, to face death from an outer foe.

It was Imogen's judgement of the event, perhaps her condemnation, even contempt, for himself which he had feared—or pity which might have been worse than all. But if she thought he had been freed from an ignoble use of his days—well, it was not hard to see it in the same way. And who knew what tomorrow's proposal might be?

He put the thought from his mind, as he drew from a sidepocket a folded copy of the *Birmingham Argus*, which had been accommodated there more easily than would have been the case a few days before.

He said: "There's a lot of news you'll be glad to have, if you haven't heard it already. There's a rather queer paragraph here:

"The following was included among various items of propaganda issued from the Berlin (Funkstunde) wireless station in English this afternoon: 'The British Government is earnestly warned against the importation of cattle from Belfast, Dublin, or other Irish ports in view of the outbreaks of foot-and-mouth disease which will occur in numerous Irish agricultural districts and loading depots during the next forty-eight hours.' It is difficult to understand with what object the German Government can desire to give such a warning, even if it be true that they have been distributing the virus of this disease in Ireland, unless they are deluding themselves into the belief that Great Britain is on the eve of falling into their own hands, and wish to avoid the contamination of herds which they regard, so to speak, as being on their own farm. But there is a proverb which deprecates the allocation of the skin of a living lion."

The *Birmingham Argus* had been one of the most strongly established of British provincial newspapers before the days of the war. Curiously devoid of ideality (there may have been no comparable English newspaper by which current literature was so absolutely ignored), and having built its circulation upon a genius for reflecting rather than any effort to influence the opinions of those who read it, it now appeared, shorn of the pages of short advertisements which had been a mine of gold ever since the war of twenty years before, when newspaper proprietors discovered that people would still be obliged to insert them, even though the cost were increased by 300 or 400 percent, produced by a mere remnant of the more elderly members of its staff of the previous week, distributed under Government instructions to all who asked, without the obsolescent formality of the copper coin which had been formerly necessary for its acquisition—it still retained the solid, capable, pedestrian qualities which had rooted it so firmly in the affections of the Midland English.

It gave bad news and good in a stolid way, free from the hysteria of some sections of the London press; it was stubbornly—foreign critics of British character might have said stupidly—optimistic, but this also without hysterical enthusiasm: it accepted heroism as a routine that the time required.

It gave, in addition to its censored news, much commonsense advice on details of conduct to a population naturally patriotic, orderly, cheerful, and with much latent capacity to endure, but weakened in recent years by a policy of bureaucratic government which had discouraged individuality, crushed liberty under a contemptuous heel, discouraged the nation's cradles, and concentrated attention upon the comfort and sufficiency of its bath-chairs.

Its leading article, written in the commonplace phrasing and unemotional temper on which its readers had long learned to rely, contained one sentence of a profound significance when judged less for itself than by the position in which it had been allowed to appear.

The *Birmingham Argus*, in common with many other secular newspapers, while regarding sectarianism as news, had maintained an attitude of aloof reserve towards Christianity in its more absolute form. Now it showed consciousness, by no more than three tentative lines, that there might be something more than nationalism in the issue that rent the world, that it had become a struggle between the nations whose flag was the Christian cross, and those which still flew the eagle of pagan Rome.

CHAPTER XLI.

PERDITA yawned deliberately, but finding it quite easy to do. She said: "If you won't think me rude, I could do with some more sleep. In fact, quite a lot."

Mrs. Rowntree decided that it was also time for her own retiring. She remarked that she hadn't been asleep most of the day.

Eustace rose, saying that while they had been talking he hadn't noticed how late it was.

Imogen said: "There's no hurry. It's only ten." She turned the conversation quickly, to propose that Perdita should have the radio in her room. "There's the portable set," she said, "that someone could carry up. That is, if you don't mind being disturbed. But there's no knowing what you might miss, and Auntie's liable not to wake."

"You mean, my dear," the old lady said, with the frankness that crisis brings, "that I shouldn't hear if I did."

"If you're depending on me to wake!" Perdita exclaimed. "Why, I slept through it when the Nazis burgled our bedroom in Prague, and I wasn't half as tired then as I am now."

"Of course," Imogen said, "you needn't have it unless you like, but if you don't, no one else will, and I'd better have a new battery put in if you do. They soon run down now that we're leaving them turned on all the time."

The conversation recalled to Perdita's mind the terror which Steele had said was to come with the next day, and of which the government had issued a warning, probably based on his report. Was not this one of the areas which was to be drenched with the freezing gas? The thought paused on the edge of speech, but was withheld, for why cause needless alarm? The government had been warned, and would issue such instructions by wireless, or perhaps by the local police, as the occasion should require, and at the right time. Actually, it was hard, even after all she had seen and heard, to believe in the reality of such horrors descending upon herself. It blasphemed heaven and earth and her vital youth, and all the secure amenities that her life had known. But she made no further objection to having the radio in her room.

"I suppose," Eustace said, when they were left alone, "I'd better be going now."

"Yes, if you'd rather. But I thought you might drive me back, if you'd nothing better to do."

His eyes lighted again at a suggestion which invited him to remain for the intervening hours. He said: "Yes, of course. I'll be very glad to do that."

There was no doubt of the sincerity in his voice, but he did not offer to draw closer to her in this opportunity that the moment's chance, and the complacency of others, had given them amid the hard distractions of war. He commenced to pace the room restlessly, ignoring where she sat watching him with quietly observant eyes, in a silence she would not break.

"I never knew till today," he said, "what a fool I was. When I think of what you're able to do, and the risks you run, while men like I—"

"I don't think," she answered, "that there's much sense in that, though I can understand how you feel.

"It's just a chance that I'm any use. It's no credit to me. I never thought about doing anything if a war should come, and I'm not running into any more danger now, nor perhaps as much, as I did for sport.

"We've seen Germany arming day and night for the last three years, and making its people believe that the thing most worthwhile in the world is successful war, and if we've thought they were wrong, I don't see how you can argue that those of us were fools whose minds were on other things. Not fools in the way you mean, though I don't say it was wise. For that matter, it doesn't seem very wise, as we look back, that we ever let Germany begin rearming again after it had done its utmost once to destroy the world. At least, it wasn't how they'd have treated us, if they'd had the power.

"But that wasn't what I was meaning to say. There was a calculation in the *Birmingham Post* this morning of how many bombs it would take to cover the surface of the world—"

"Yes. I saw that. But that was if they were dropped equally over the whole surface. It's altogether different if they pick the places where they'll do the most harm."

"Yes, so it was. But it wasn't so very different from how they're likely to fall. It's always the thing they aim at that they're most likely to miss. If you think what the chances are of hitting anything when you're half a mile from the ground and flying at three hundred an hour—! And if they come lower down, they're just asking to be picked off by the guns.

"Well, anyway, bombing the earth is too big a contract for any nation to undertake. It just can't be done. And it couldn't be destroyed by gas. It's a case where God wins against—against all the devils of hell who discover the secrets of how He works, and then use them to destroy what He had used them to make.

"After the worst war that the world can know, it will still be green and the better things will remain; and if we believe that there are better things, we can't say that all men are fools who have given their time to them, rather than in learning how to make engines and bombs, or to throw hand-grenades into a trench thirty yards away.

"And besides," she added, coming back in a woman's way from abstract speculations to the personal question from which they rose, "you don't know what they'll offer you at the Labour Exchange tomorrow. And if they don't propose anything worth doing, you can always refuse."

"I'm not likely to do that. The war can't last long. Not at the pace that it's going now. I hate to think of the work I've put into getting those gas-masks out during the past two days, and how they were tossed aside. It wasn't only the loss to myself—I don't think it was mainly that. It was having the work stopped which I had been trying to do. But I'm not going to sulk over that. I don't mean to argue over whether there's something better or different that I'd rather be at. I'll do something, though it's only using a spade."

"I'm sure whatever you do will be done well."

"It's kind of you to say that."

They fell silent again. She was content to relax in the short leisure allowed by this stress of merciless war. The fire was hot. She could have become drowsy with ease. On the window a rough wind beat, threatening a night of storm.

He looked at her with longing, and a feeling of dissatisfaction with himself, natural after the experiences he had had, but which now came from another cause.

Was he no more good at making love than munitions of war? Would not other men have made more use of these midnight hours for which she had asked him to stay? To be silent thus, and with so many things that he longed—and was unable—to speak! He was inexperienced, inexpert, diffident—or was cowardly the truer word? A failure for love or war.

"You wouldn't rather I go?" he asked, seeing her eyes on the fire.

"Go? Not unless you want. I don't prefer being alone, if you mean that. I suppose I've been very dull. But I just felt content, having you here."

They were friendly words. It would be straining their natural use to give them more meaning than that. But they roused him to a sudden impulse of courage which deliberation might have denied.

She spoke without raising her head, and he stood beside her, leaning against the mantelpiece. Defiant of the cowardice of which he was self-accused, he stooped over her, kissing her neck.

He straightened himself again, and she sat silent, saying nothing, and without raising her head. The room became very still.

"I couldn't help it," he said. "I suppose you don't know how tempting you are. I hope you don't mind."

She lifted her eyes at that, and looked at him with a gravity which he found difficult to read.

"I don't know," she said seriously. "I think it depends on how much you meant."

"I meant everything that I could. If you knew how much—"

"Then I don't mind it at all."

An hour later they went out to the car, which it was some trouble to start. But they were not in a mood to be irritated by petty things. Life had become of a new meaning, a new value, a new hope, and at such times as these were, it must therefore be lived with a keener fear.

"I believe," Imogen said, "I can hear the wireless now in Miss Wyatt's room. It must be something rather important to be sent out at such an hour of the night."

"Yes," he agreed, "but it couldn't make any difference to us. It's important for some people, no doubt."

Nothing could alter the fact that she must be back at the aerodrome at 1:00 A.M., or that he must leave her there for long hours during which she would face the violence of the impartial elements, and the more direct malice of human foes. And with this thought of her separate perils filling his mind, there was no space to care for what might happen on the ground she would leave behind.

"But," he went on, with a doubtful hope, "I suppose you won't go up at all if the weather doesn't improve."

They were driving now through a fall of snow that showed where the car lights shone forward on the straight breadth of the road. It fell from a bleak sky in a thin, leisurely way in the pause of the northwest wind, as though aware that it would not be hurried in what it did.

"I don't know," Imogen answered. "Of course they won't want me to go up if the weather's too bad for there to be any risk that the Germans will be about during the night. As a matter of fact, bad weather's the best thing we can possibly have till the American air-fleets have time to get across, if they ever will. I'll ring you in the morning, if I don't go up, or as soon as I come down if I do. I ought not to have brought you out on a night like this and with no means that I know of for getting home."

She had in fact forgotten that the car was not one which he could use for his own return, but he made light of that, as he well might. To walk home a few miles on a good road, even though the wind were rough at times, and the snow fell—there was little man-hood needed for that, while the girl he loved might be flying blindly aloft in the black air of the gale-swept night.

So they broke apart from a moment's clinging of lips and hands, and with the mingling of joy and fear that those must know who find love in a shaking world.

CHAPTER XLII.

PERDITA waked reluctantly after three hours' sleep to the consciousness of a disembodied voice which was announcing stridently within three feet of her ear:

> "...is emphatically denied. She was torpedoed while about forty miles from the Galway coast, but was able to continue her voyage, and discharged her passengers this afternoon at an English port."

The announcement, momentous to those who had friends or relatives on the *Britannic* on its homeward voyage, and had heard the German broadcast a few hours before include that vessel in a list of British ships which had been sunk by their submarines, seemed to

Perdita an inadequate reason for disturbing her needed rest. But she did not fail to observe that she had missed the earlier part of the message, and that this might have been a critical loss had it dealt with matters of more direct concern to herself.

She slept again, but with a resolution that she would be quicker to wake when the voice should resume, and with more vigilant ears, and it was still dark when she was roused by a thrice-repeated "Attention, all listeners!" with sufficient celerity to hear with an alert mind the announcement that followed:

> "It is reported on reliable authority that extensive movements of German air forces during the early hours of the night have resulted in the assembly of three very large bombing fleets, one of which left Staaken about an hour ago, steering due west, and the others, at Nürnberg and Frankfurt, are preparing to take the air.
>
> "Two of the fleets consist of Vogel, and the third of Zeus night-bombers, with escorts of fighting planes, and their destination is believed to be this country.
>
> "The gas-masks which have been already distributed may be worn as a measure of precaution in all areas over which these fleets may pass, of the approach of which due warning will be given by the usual methods, but it is not advised that reliance should be placed upon the protection afforded by these masks or other respiratory devices, as there is reason to believe that the enemy will use a new gas, the effect of which is to produce an extremely low temperature, such as may be fatal to those who sustain it.
>
> "The effect of this gas may be mitigated by steam, but, as this form of defence is neither generally practicable nor certain in its results, those who find themselves exposed to aerial attack are advised rather to retire to sealed and heated rooms raised as far as possible from the ground, the reports which have been received indicating that the gas will be likely to lie low, and that its effects will gradually lessen, and normal temperature return within four or five hours."

FOUR DAYS' WAR, BY S. FOWLER WRIGHT * 205

Reluctantly, Perdita got out of bed. She was feeling rather more tired than when she had got into it about seven hours before, and it was more difficult to believe in the reality of such events now that she was back among familiar scenes, than in the strangeness of foreign lands. Queer things might be expected to happen there. Strange, horrible things. One knew that they often did. But in the secure, enduring peace of this English land... It had been peaceful all the years she had lived. It had traditions of peace that reached back more than a thousand years. In fact, since Ethelfleda had chased the Danes.

And when you looked at it in a reasonable, cool-blooded way, it was apparent that about forty million people would hear that broadcast warning and take it quietly, or fuss about it as their natures were, and thirty-nine million would find nothing happening at all, or probably more than that.

Looked at thus, it seemed an ignoble, certainly an undignified thing to crouch from an absent bomb, to run away from a foe that was not there.

But she dressed quickly, amid a confusion of wondering, fearful, half-incredulous thoughts, the while the radio became vocal again, repeating the warnings and instructions that she had heard, with no difference beyond the fact that the Nürnberg fleet had now also risen into the air.

She heard wind without, and wondered what the weather might be through which these heavy-loaded bombers must be forcing their rapid way. How did they hold their places in ordered ranks that must be near and must never touch, when they flew through darkness and storm? She had seen enough for the wonder to fill her mind; she knew too little to find the answer which it required.

The radio told much, but it said nothing of weather conditions now, or if it did, they would be those of the past day. It must tell nothing which would be of use to the enemy who was hearing all. Doubtless, that was why it gave no hint of where the bombs would be most likely to fall. To do that would be to invite the invaders to turn aside, perhaps to drop them upon the very place to which the threatened population had been withdrawn.

She did not think that she was greatly afraid, but the memory that this was one of the places to be attacked made the chance for her something different from forty million—or should she have said forty?—to one. It might be no more than an even chance. *It might be there was none at all.* That all who were living around her there were doomed to a dreadful death before evening fell. Would it not have been better than that to accept the indignities of a Nürnberg jail?

She would not admit to herself that she was sorry that she had come home. But she found, with some resentment against herself, that it was hard to restrain her voice to a casual tone when she waked Mrs. Rowntree and the servants, as, under such circumstances, she had promised to do.

But Mrs. Rowntree received the news with even less excitement than Perdita had been able to feel. She consented to rise, for which it was, in any event, near to her accustomed time. She listened to, and may have heard, a third repetition of the broadcast warning, from which it appeared that three fleets were now launched on their westward way.

But she declined to make any preparations for leaving the house against the possibility that there might be sudden warning to do so. "I'm not quite young enough," she said, "to be kept running round to avoid bombs, as I did on the first night. If I do, I may be blown apart as quickly as if I stay here, but I should say that pneumonia's the more likely chance.

"And if the Germans think that they'll win the war by killing people like me, they must be sillier than they were twenty years ago, and it isn't easy to say anything stronger than that.

"But of course you'll go, Miss Wyatt, though I'm sorry to say that I have no car to offer you, and cook and Clara can please themselves."

"They haven't asked us to go yet," Perdita said reasonably, "they've only given us some advice for being as safe as possible where we are."

"You can't go very high, my dear, in a two-storied house. But if you'd like to tell Clara to light one of the bedroom fires, I've no objection at all. The Germans are going to a lot of trouble for very little result, if they can be upset by a scuttle of coal."

Perdita gave no more than a smiling answer to that. She admitted the probable futility of the bedroom fire. "Anyway," she said, "we shall have time for breakfast before they come."

CHAPTER XLIII.

WHEN Imogen returned to the aerodrome she had reported at once to Commander Winfield's office.

Lieutenant Ruston was there, and explained why she had been notified that she need not return till the later hour.

"Commander Winfield said that he doesn't know that you'll be needed at all tonight, and if you are, it will be towards morning, when we've got information that there are some big fleets being got ready to come this way, and we're likely to be all up in the air together, and you're to be kept fresh till then.

"But they may not come, if the weather gets any worse than it is now. There was snow in Perthshire a foot deep some hours ago, and it's spreading south with a northwest wind. They say there's an absolute gale over the North Sea."

"Well," she said cheerfully, "the worse the weather, the better it is for us."

"Yes," he said dubiously, "that's one way to put it."

Better for England it might be that the wind should rise and the snow-squalls blow, or that the night should be blind with fog. Better for everyone if the weather should be so bad that the German air-fleets should remain in their own lairs. But if the weather should be foul without assurance of that? Was it better to have to strive at once with both elemental and human foes? To circle in the black air when the landing-flares would be blind with fog, or dimmed lest they should be a target for hostile bombs?

He left that question aside to say: "We've had your plane overhauled, as there was some extra time."

She thanked him for that, which was, indeed, no more than routine when she came to ground from many hours in the air. But she had reported some ignition trouble on her last flight, and asked that everything should be tested with special care.

"I'll have a look at it myself, all the same," she said. "It's a custom I've always had." She knew it to be a precaution which had saved her life once, if not more; and though that might not be a large percentage of the times she had gone aloft, it would have been sufficient to make an important difference to her. There was treachery also to be feared—a danger against which all flying officers had been warned; and though she might be of a temper to risk her life at her country's need, she did not intend that the hazard should be increased by lack of foresight or care.

The night was not very dark at this time, though the snow fell slowly between sudden gusts of wind which would drive it horizontally through the air. She walked quickly between the dark shadows of the hangars, taking a way she had been before, and answering the sharp challenge of a watchful sentry in a voice to which he responded in a different manner from that in which he had spoken before.

She found her plane at the entrance of the hangar ready to be run out, but with the doors closed to obscure the light by which two mechanics were still busy upon it. For the next half-hour she remained with them, till she could feel that every precaution of testing had been observed, and that she could subject it safely to any strain of speed or endurance that might be required before morning came. She was summoned back by a telephone call to Commander Winfield's office, where she found three flying officers assembled with her to receive instructions.

"We have information," he said, "that three fleets of escorted bombers will be leaving Germany during the night to attack this country, of which the objective of one, with which you will be solely concerned, will be this immediate district. This fleet has been assembled at Sakrow.

"The weather, as you will have observed, is not favourable for aerial operations, and it is likely to become worse. It is possible, therefore, that these fleets will delay to start, or will be recalled after they have commenced their flights.

"It is possible that information on these points may reach us from sources which are still not entirely closed, but accurate facts regarding the time and direction of their flights are too vital for any means of observation to be neglected. I have decided, therefore, that it will be necessary for you to reconnoitre the movements of the Sakrow fleet, approaching as near to its base as time and other factors will permit, this necessity being the greater because the atmospheric conditions likely to prevail during the latter part of the night may render it difficult to observe the approach of such a fleet from the coastal observation stations, particularly if it should be flying at a high altitude, as it is likely to do.

"You will take off at intervals of fifteen minutes, and, of course, operate separately.

"You will be recalled at once should reliable information be received that the Sakrow fleet is not taking the air, and you will similarly return if you are able to observe any conclusive evidence to this effect.

"Should you encounter the fleet, you will use your wireless code to transmit your observations of its composition and the direction of its course, and in a sufficient emergency, you may inquire as to your own position, but otherwise, and perhaps even then, you will receive nothing, lest guidance to the invaders should result.

"When you have done all that your instructions require, or when, from whatever reason, you are unable to remain longer in the air, you will land at the nearest aerodrome, or wherever considerations of your own safety I may suggest; but you may have to do this without guidance, and if you are able to remain up till the morning it may be the more prudent course to adopt."

He spoke in a matter-of-fact way, for what purpose was there in saying that he sent them to likely death? Except that they had less explicit knowledge of how bad the night was likely to be, they would know that without words from him. But when they had gone, he said: "Ruston, I should like to think I should see one of those four again."

Lieutenant Ruston did not deny the peril to which they flew, but he saw another risk of a closer kind.

"Yes, sir," he said, "but if we are rightly warned, there may be less safety here than above."

Commander Winfield understood, but remained outwardly unperturbed. "Threatened men live long, so it is said. And when the Germans say where their bombs will fall, we have not always found that they have made a good guess."

Reason might doubt, but instinct was more content with the solid earth, and the quiet lighted room where all who came were deferential of speech and prompt to obey his will, than it could have been in the black heights of the turbulent air, and with the knowledge that there was no lighted place under the clouds to which to make descent at whatever need. Beside that, there was the obligation upon his mind that must be felt by all men who are in control at a time of fear—the obligation to speak serene and confident words.

The aerodrome could not be removed. If the German bombers should come overhead, as they had nearly done on the first night, it must be destroyed. There was no choice about that. But, in fact, it was little more than an empty shell. The remains of the three squadrons that had been stationed there had been transferred to a last retreat, secret and deep, in the Brecknock Hills, which had been prepared in the last year. He had no more than a few old bombers which had been out of repair, on which the mechanics were toiling now, the four scouts he was sending aloft, and Admiral Nachod's plane, which had been brought in during the day, and had one propeller with which it could still fly.

But he must hold his post there unless he should have orders to withdraw, which were no more than a likely doubt, so he returned his mind to the duties that were still his, and Imogen, being the first to take off, left the ground behind and rose steeply, seeking the stars.

It was nearly half-past two when she took off. By six-thirty there would be the first light of the dawn—sufficient to enable her to find some place on which to land with no more than a moderate risk, if she could remain in the air till then.

The plane she flew was built only for speed. It was not intended to remain aloft for many hours while maintaining its swiftest pace. Its store of fuel was calculated to cover from twelve to fifteen hundred miles at three hundred an hour, but it could do over four hundred if it were flown at its utmost speed, and its power would be sooner done.

Imogen, soaring still through the driven clouds, which seemed as high as though they might have no ceiling at all, had a thought of regret for the very different machine in which she had made her Antarctic flight. It had had comfort and strength. It had had a speed which had seemed high enough, but she knew that it would have been useless here.

She had registered a height of 18,000 feet before she came to a clearer air, and flattened her course, flying due east, with the speed-ometer steady at 357 miles an hour. She would not reduce below that, which would have been to put her own safety before the success of that which she had undertaken to do

A fleet such as she sought, flying on a wide front, might not be easy to miss, but the nearer to Sakrow she could approach, the smaller the risk would be. She knew, and might have had some pride in the thought had she been of that temper of mind, that she had been sent first because she was the one on whom Commander Winfield most surely relied. The others, following at fifteen-minute intervals, were to ensure that, if she should fail, the fleet would still be discovered before its approach to that English shore. But the first chance was for her.

Such a fleet might not be easy to miss in a clear air, but flying blind as she must, or at a height beneath which it might pass unseen through the clouds, though at no great distance away (as distance is counted in the wide spaces of air), it was a more difficult chance.

When she thought that she was nearing the position to which they would have had time to approach, she commenced to fly in long, downward slants that cut obliquely across the probable line of advance, and then turned and mounted again on another slant as a ship might wear on the wind.

Flying so, and with seldom sight of the stars, she risked much, having to rely upon the unchecked verdicts of her instruments, not only for the altitudes which she maintained, but for direction, while her compasses might be swayed by the magnetic track of the winter storm.

Soaring into clear air at a time when she guessed herself vaguely to be over the eastern frontier of Holland, she saw, far off to the northwest, that which she had almost missed, by a light that twinkled a moment and then was gone.

She soared higher, making a direct line for a widespread fleet that flew over the clouds, and showed no lights beyond that which may have been a signal to those who followed, or perhaps of no more than a careless kind.

Flying four miles to their three, she rapidly overhauled a great regiment of bombers, with fighting planes guarding their front and flanks and scouts far out, which would have been a sooner nuisance to her had she not approached as she did, from a rearward angle.

As it was, she had time to observe, from the height she had soared, the great number of the invading fleet, by the light of stars and a moon which was now high overhead and still not far from the full, before she was aware that she was pursued by those against whom she had no weapon to use.

But she had no fear to be caught. The German scouts were no swifter than she, and were less lightly equipped. There was flight and chase, and a breathless moment when she must outdistance converging foes, that she might get down to the cloudy safety she sought.

Diving thus, and altering her course in the murk of the driving snow, she had no fear of pursuit, and could direct her mind to the sending of the message which a dozen stations on the English coast and farther inland would be waiting to take.

After that, she must rise again, keeping the fleet always in view, diving at times in the covering clouds, to appear, like a vexing wasp, at another place, but neither losing contact for long nor allowing the near approach of her angry foes.

The cold at that height was intense and hard to endure, even wrapped as she was. She could not remain long under the clouds, lest the snow should become too heavy upon her wings, in spite of a recently invented device be which they could be charged with the engine's heat.

So, for the following hour she held to the flank of the long advance, and sent out her frequent records of where she flew. And then, being betrayed by too audacious approach, or by the treachery of the storm, or being caught in a trap that her foes had planned, she found herself in a wind-torn clearing of upper clouds, with one of the major fighting planes crossing her way, and a scout too close for comfort upon her tail.

She took the one chance of a headlong dive, but the swift manœuvre was not single to her. To be caught within cannon-range of the larger plane would, she knew, be her likely end. To avoid that, she must remain, for five seconds' space of the downward spin, too near to the scout's pursuit, and it was time enough for her to learn that she was chased by one of as much skill as her own, or it might be more.

There came a moment when the stream of bullets beat upon wings and fuselage like a giant hail before she was able to draw away with her greater speed, and to hide in the gale-blown snow.

With some added caution from that event, she held for the next half-hour on the heels of the great fleet to which she was no more than a teasing fly, and then gave what was merely a routine glance at the petrol-gauge, and looked again with a heart-beat of sudden fear. For how could it be true? And if it were, what was the hope that she would be alive in another hour? When she had looked before, she thought it was lasting well. She had hoped to endure till the dawn in the windswept skies.

But now she saw, with would-be incredulous eyes, that her fuel was almost—in three minutes might be entirely—gone. It was a simple guess that the tank had been a target too broad for that stream of bullets to pass it by.

True, at the worst, there was the parachute on which to rely. It was not a choice to be cheerfully made, without knowing what might be below, but it was one to be taken now, if she were sure that it would be land, not water, to which she fell, and that she was at a sufficient height. She resolved to drop lower, to seek some knowledge of what welcome to earth she would be likely to get, perhaps to recognize some landmark beneath the clouds.

She became aware that she was looking up to a dim-blue sky, with no evident cloud. Behind her head she supposed that the sun shone, though she did not turn it to see. She was not anxious to move at all. She was stiff and cold, and her limbs seemed a long distance away.

There was no hurry. It seemed that time and place had become equally vague. She might lie there for a thousand years, or already have lain. There was even comfort of mind, if she could only hold consciousness back, if she could keep it at some distance away as, but for this maddening thirst, she supposed that she would have been able to do.

But the thirst would not be stilled. It was an insistent appeal which her wandering mind must be wakened to understand. Slowly, recollection returned. Returned, at least, to the point at which she had come down through the clouds, and had seen that it was not water but earth over which she flew, and that the earth had been very near. But after that she could remember nothing at all.

"I must have done some fool thing," she thought, "and smashed the plane and myself too."

She lifted a neck that was stiff with cold a few inches from the ground, and saw enough to confirm her guess. The plane lay some distance ahead.

"I must have been thrown clear," she thought, "before that."

She saw that she lay in a field, large and bare. One on which it should have been simple to land in a better light. Ten yards on her left hand there was a brick wall. It was long and high, so that she could see nothing over it or beyond. There was a tall hedge on the other side of the field, much farther away.

On the field lay a deep snow. Most of it must have fallen before, but some since she fell, for it covered her, even to her face, except that her breath had thawed it from round her mouth.

"It must," she thought, "have softened that fall. Perhaps I must thank it that I am still alive."

But how much was she alive? How much of thanks would be due? She found herself in no haste to know, having too much fear. But she was quick to think that the snow had another use. Her right arm was stiff with cold, but otherwise seemed unhurt. She fed herself with the snow.

After that, her mind wandered again, to be recalled by the noise of many engines that filled the air. She looked up and saw a squadron of bombers crossing the sky.

They were so directly overhead that she could count them without moving her eves. There were twenty-one. She thought: "They are dropping bombs. Was I not dead enough, without that?"

Then she made a good guess that their objective was the other side of the wall. A munitions works, more likely than not. But she remembered that bombs will miss, that even a large objective, she had been told, will often suffer less than its immediate environment from a concerted attack. There was no comfort in that. Yet she was not greatly alarmed, taking it all in a passive way, as being killed in a dream.

The bombers came very low. She could not now see those that had spiralled down, beyond two or three, one of which passed directly above her head trailing a vulture-shadow across the field. Something struck the ground with a heavy thud not more than two yards away, scattering the snow.

With a sudden energy, she raised herself on one hand to look, and fell sharply back. She had seen something that might have been no more than a large tin of salmon or fruit, but at one end a fuse hissed. She supposed that it might burst in the next moment, blowing her apart.

Could she escape if she lay flat? Hardly, she supposed, being so near. Could she have a moment to crawl farther away? It was an added risk to raise herself up, inviting a death which, she supposed, she would never know. Yet she did raise herself enough to learn that one leg was hurt, how badly she could not tell, but, for the moment, its use was done.

It had bled much, for an artery had been torn, from which it is likely that all the life she had would have drained away, but that the snow had been twice her friend, freezing the wound.

She lay back. She could do no more. Let the end come, as, in the next moment, no doubt it would. Or perhaps the bomb was one of those that were charged with the freezing gas?

It seemed a likely guess when, a moment later, it burst in a mild way, doing her no harm. Cautiously, she raised her head again, and saw something that the talk of the last three days enabled her to understand.

From the bomb there flowed out a stream of molten metal, a mixture of aluminium oxide and iron which the fuse had fired, and which was now of a heat of 5,000° F., a heat for which "white-hot" is an inadequate word. The snow shrank before it in instant steam: the earth below blackened and hissed.

"Well," she said aloud, with a hysterical laugh, of which she was unaware, "if it thinks it can set fire to the snow! It seems I am to live—if I can."

From the farther side of the wall a smoke rose, yellow and dense. With an effort, ignoring pain, she turned over, and began to drag herself through the snow.

CHAPTER XLIV.

THE expediency of von Teufel's stubborn refusal to modify or delay the orders he had issued, in deference to the adverse weather conditions which must be faced by the invading air-fleets, may be reasonably doubted, and may even be held to have indicated an arrogance of spirit which would break itself in the end, brittle as thin-blown glass, against the stupendous powers to which it refused to bend.

But against this conclusion it is necessary to weigh the importance of the time-factor in the gigantic operations which he controlled and drove with so ruthless a will; and it is also fair to observe the paradoxical fact that, in locating their objectives, and, to a less extent, in the damage which they inflicted, the three raids were actually successful in inverse proportion to the climatic difficulties against which they had to contend.

The fleet which was directed to the destruction of the Midlothian district may have had some assistance in the fact that the waters of the Firth of Forth showed darkly beneath the wind-torn gaps of the sleet-squalls through which it drove, in contrast to the snow-covered land; and the fact that the majority of the inhabitants of the Haddington district on which it spread its cargoes of death had been evacuated before it arrived had no relation to the weather conditions, but solely to the action of No. 973 in obtaining and conveying information of the intended raids.

The deaths in this area did not exceed thirty-three thousand persons, and as a large proportion of these consisted of children and sick and elderly people, such as are a burden in time of war, its military effect cannot be considered serious, except as it may have daunted the courage of those who found themselves exposed to bombardments of such a nature, or hardened the resolution of more distant nations to cleanse the world of those from whose experiments such devilries came.

In addition to human victims, there were, of course, very heavy casualties among wild and domestic animals, of which none escaped, and a few birds. The trees also perished. But it appeared that the intense cold of the gas was less able to penetrate downward through the protecting cloak of the kindlier snow, and when it melted during the following week, there were wide green patches where grass survived between black, shrivelled hedges and lifeless trees.

The second raid, which was directed upon northern Worcestershire, was also successful in locating its objective, which, in this instance, must be attributed to the accuracy of the directional instruments carried, and to the fact that, flying blind as it did, its commander gave them a complete reliance, uncomplicated by any real or mistaken reading of landscapes hidden beneath a blanket of cloud, through which he did not attempt descent until his objective was gained.

Here, perhaps because a preponderance of precaution was directed upon the more densely populated districts of Birmingham and southern Staffordshire, or because the limits of the threatened area were less sharply defined, or because the people of the East Midlands were harder than the Lowland Scottish to be moved to a prudent flight (the inconveniences and doubtful safeties of which they had experienced on the previous Sunday evening)—from whatever cause, it remains a fact that the migration officially ordered was only partially and reluctantly carried out, and a large number of special constables are believed to have sacrificed their own lives while persuading others to more rapid or further flight.

The human fatalities in this area were never accurately ascertained, and have been variously placed at anything from 50,000 to 100,000 (the claim made in the Berlin broadcast was twice that figure), but the truth probably lay about midway between, and was certainly not less than 80,000 people, quaintly described as "souls" by a press which had previously reserved that word for those who perish in a large fire or are drowned at sea.

The third raid—that to the south of London—before reaching its destination had crossed and left behind the main course of the storm, and when the dawn came there was a degree of visibility which, though it could not be called good, was sufficient in theory to have rendered important help to the attacking fleet, and did in fact influence its operations in a decisive manner.

The fleet had been ordered to keep to the south of Croydon, the German High Command having been accurately informed that its aerodromes were not in military occupation, and believing that its ground defences were very strong, and it may be supposed that such instructions would be willingly followed by airmen conscious that, if they should be shot down, they would crash amidst the escape of a deadly gas which would make their ends sure, even though they should come clear of the fall.

The Air Defence unit of the Territorial Army to which the defence of Surrey had been entrusted, had been at some pains to encourage this natural prudence, by spreading an elaborate smoke-screen, which had been long prepared for such an emergency, over the land, which simulated by cunning devices of colouring, varying density, and rising columns, the aspect of the more northern districts, as it would appear from above to an airman's eye.

The Air-Admiral who commanded the raiding fleet, having explicit instructions to keep well to southward of Croydon, and seeing what appeared to be its aerodromes and landing-grounds before him, had no inclination to adventure his fleet above them with no better excuse to offer, should it be destroyed, than that he had preferred the testimony of his instruments to that of his own eyes, and that he had adopted the only method of testing their accuracy in a conclusive manner.

He preferred to lead his bombers a few points farther southward before turning them due west, and commenced to spread the freezing death, not over the more thickly populated suburban area, but upon the scattered hamlets and high open commons that border Sussex and spread southward into that county, which had already been evacuated, as far as time and circumstance had allowed, in anticipation of the blunder he had been invited to make; and those more lethargic or sceptical portions of the population—probably no more than 7,000 in all—who did not commence to flee until the angels of death were visible in the sky, may be said to have served a better purpose than they designed, by giving encouragement to their assailants to persevere in the mistake they had made.

It followed that this was the least destructive of the three raids, although it is true that it left the country from East Grinstead to Godalming and from Redhill to beyond Horsham an even more absolute desolation than Midlothian under its mantle of deeper snow; and it is evident that its real objective was saved not by weather conditions adverse to the attacking fleet, but by the clearer atmosphere of the dawn, which had enabled its elaborate camouflage to become visible from above.

CHAPTER XLV.

PERDITA commenced breakfast in some uncertainty of mind. Mrs. Rowntree said nothing to encourage her to remain, her actual words falling rather into the other scale, but her serene placidity, and the fact that she herself felt no disposition to face the discomforts of flight, supported the quiet atmosphere of the room, and thrust the idea of widespread death from the air into the remoteness of fantasy, which men imagine and dream in their darker hours, but which become unreal in the cheerful, familiar day.

She saw another practical difficulty when she thought of leaving, in the fact that there was no conveyance available. This was an evident disadvantage, as the pace at which she could move might be insufficient to take her clear of danger before the bombers should come, but it cannot be said that she made calculation of this.

She was young, vigorous, athletic, and would have used her legs without thought of hardship in the swimming-pool or on the tennis-court for a morning's length, but she had been trained to obliviousness of the fact that they could also be employed as a means of transit from one place to another, to an extent which would have been incredible to the previous generation, and is not easily understood by that which has followed.

It was a period when women might be observed to stay on the pavement edge, waiting ten minutes for a bus to take them a distance which they could have walked in five, and honestly believing that they were inevitably delayed. She thought of Mrs. Rowntree's car derelict in a distant field, as she had heard in the conversation of the previous evening, and of herself as one imprisoned in a place which she was powerless to leave.

Her hostess followed her thought. "I could ring Mrs. Heal," she said. "She might lend me her car, if you wouldn't mind fetching it from over the road. She wouldn't go out herself in this weather."

Mrs. Heal was a stout, short-winded widow, very reluctant to be convinced of the acuteness of the danger into which her country had fallen by the neglect of those to whom its security had been entrusted, and very indignant against the partial truth which had penetrated her mind. She had telephoned her lawyers (a most reputable and reliable firm, as they were likely to be) to enquire who, as a regular ratepayer, she could hold responsible for any disaster to life or property which these unrestrained commotions might cause. Her sense of fundamental proprieties did not allow her to visualize any violence to her own person, but suppose her staff.... "If Ada," she asked, "were to get hurt...?"

The lawyer's reply, though provokingly difficult to follow, had not been entirely unsatisfactory, and beyond that it was clearly a matter for the military authorities, and that excellent body, the

Worcestershire Constabulary. Possibly, if a policeman should appear in person to lead her forth…. But not certainly in such weather as this.

"It sounds," Perdita said, "as though there's a car at the door now."

"It wouldn't be likely that that's hers."

"It's a dark saloon. Rather a—I mean, not a very new car."

Mrs. Rowntree, who was seated with her back to the window, and knew her ears to be less reliable than her eyes, even in the half-light of the dawn, got up to look; but as she did so the door opened, and Eustace Ashfield was announced.

"I remembered," he said, "that your car was crocked, and I've got hold of the best I could."

Mrs. Rowntree rang for another place to be laid.

"You'll have some breakfast," Perdita said. "You'll have time for that."

She spoke equably, and the whole scene may have been typical of the stolidity of the English character, for which an alien might consider stupidity to be a more accurate word, yet it showed that her values shook, for would she have given such an invitation a week ago in a house in which she was no more than a recent guest?

"Thank you," he said, "I shall be glad if I can. They tell me that the sirens at the Austin works will be sounded half-an-hour before the fleet can arrive. So 'unless or until,' as the lawyers say, we ought to be right enough. I've left the engine running, so that it won't take us any time to start, and we can get over a lot of ground in half an hour. But, if you've finished, it might be wise to get ready."

"Mrs. Rowntree was saying she'd rather stay here," Perdita replied, "but I hope now you've brought a car—"

"We only ran into danger last time when we tried running away," the old lady said doubtfully, and with a natural thought of regret for her own car, which might have been safe in the garage now. The one outside did not look as though it would hold more than four at a squeeze, and the cook was a large woman. Yet she hesitated, and as she did so, a siren screamed.

One long blast and three short. Then a pause, and again the long blast and the three short. So it went on, the warning that all had been told to heed, the signal that German bombers were in the air.

The sound had a penetrating quality, which Mrs. Rowntree was able to hear, and it appeared to have more effect than arguments of more logical kinds.

"Yes," she said. "I expect you're right. It may be wiser to go."

A rough voice called in the road: "Tumble in. There's no time to lose."

Eustace moved quickly to the window, in time to see a group of men—road-repairers by their appearance—crowding into the car he had brought.

He ran out in time to see it already twenty yards away, and disappearing at a pace which made any thought of pursuit absurd. Men who had been unable to crowd into it were clinging to either side. As he looked, one was pushed off or fell, and rose unsteadily, feeling an injured knee.

Well, it was no use upbraiding him. Useless, even, to blame himself, though that was beyond his power to avoid.

"I'm sorry," he said, "that I was such a damned fool. In fact, there wasn't any means of locking the car, but I needn't have left the engine running to help them off."

"I don't think," Mrs. Rowntree said justly, "you could have expected that to happen. There's scarcely been anything of the sort. Anyway, not about here." She added: "I think they were a gang who've been mending a shell-hole down the road."

"Yes," Perdita said absently, "they looked something like that." Their appearance had given her an idea—but how far off was it? Would there be possible time?

The sirens, terribly reminiscent of those she had heard in a burning Prague only a few nights before, had roused her to a livelier sense of the danger approaching now, and the desire to escape, thwarted as it had assumed the guise of a settled thing, became keener from its defeat.

She looked at her hostess in a questioning way, and was answered as though she had spoken aloud: "No, my dear. You can try for Mrs. Heal's car, if you like. It's the next house but two down the road on the other side. Sunville's the silly name on the gate. Or you might meet someone who'll pick you up. But I've made up my mind to stay where I am. And I expect you'll find that cook and Clara will feel the same."

So it proved that they did. But the house had been home to them. There was a difference in that, illogical but subtly potent to hold them within the familiar walls.

But Perdita felt no such bond. With a hurried parting words of goodwill and hope, she went out with Eustace Ashfield to seek such safety as might be found while the sirens wailed, and it was hard to guess in how few minutes the bombs would fall from the sky.

CHAPTER XLVI.

THEY were spared loss of time in inquiring for Mrs. Heal's car by the sight of an empty garage. Borrowed, stolen, or sold, it was clear that the car was no longer there.

Perdita gave it one glance, and turned sharply away.

"Quickly!" she said. "There's one chance." Her eyes lifted to the dark sky, as though seeking to pierce it to see the danger that might already be overhead. Her ears searched the sounds that the wind brought. But as yet no noise of engines came from the skies.

They had started to walk quickly up the snowy road before she explained: "It was those men who brought it back to my mind. There were a lot yesterday cutting a cave in the side of the Lickey Hills. It was quite high up. We know that the gas keeps low. I don't see how it could get there, unless a bomb were actually thrown inside, and that couldn't be done from above."

"Well," he said, with more confidence than he felt, "it's a good idea. We can try. I wonder how many others will think of that?"

"I don't see why they should. There aren't many people about now. I suppose they're gone already, or decided to stay indoors."

So it might be. But he was caught in a double doubt. Would it be crowded already by those who could not be asked to make way for them? That was question enough, but there was an even larger chance that they would not be there before the bombs would commence to fall. There would be no purpose in saying that. They were going now at a quick trot, and the road rose.

Twenty minutes later, the noise of unseen engines was overhead, a dull continuous roar seeming to fill the heavens' extent above the stretched blanket of cloud.

"I've brought you right into it," she said. "I wish you hadn't listened to me."

"We may do it yet. It's not far."

They ran on faster, more breathlessly than before. No bombs fell.

"Perhaps," she thought, "they're our own planes." but she lacked breath to say it aloud, and it was soon to be evident that it was a wrong guess. In fact, the fleet delayed only until it was completely over the area which had been chosen for destruction. Then, at a signal, every bomber was to commence to ply its release-lever at the same moment. By this method it was calculated to reduce the risk that some spots would be bombed to excess, and others escape. The gas was to be spread as an even carpet of death from the equal sky.

Now they were in sight of the goal they sought. The workmen had already tunnelled deeply into the side of the hill, toiling to make one of those aerodromes secure from aerial attack, which should have been provided in time of peace. A broad-banked causeway, timbered in places, ran up to it from the farther side.

There were a number of people who stood looking out from the tunnel-mouth, and it appeared to be crowded within, but not so that there would not be room for others to enter. Up the causeway a woman ran with a heavy child in her arms. Behind her a man came, similarly burdened, driving two older children before him. The children ran with stumbling, exhausted steps, and he kept behind them, driving them on with fierce curses, of which he may have been unaware.

It was at this moment that the bombs fell. They were lightly made, and only weighted sufficiently to bring them down in a straight line and to ensure that they would burst on striking the ground. They were of the size of a child's balloon. They fell as gently as snow.

Those who watched from the tunnel saw them descend. They shrank back at the sight, except two, woman and man, who ran boldly out to catch the hands of the stumbling children and draw them in.

Eustace and Perdita had not tried to reach the causeway. They saw the first of the falling bombs, and that it would be vain to attempt. Nearer there was a narrow, single-plank gangway, safe enough for practised workmen to wheel their barrows upon it when it was clear, but it was now covered with two inches of slippery snow.

"There's no time," Eustace said. "We must try this."

They struggled up, Perdita first, slipping at times, but with no absolute fall. Hands reached out, drawing her in. She lay for a time, breathing hard, on the tunnel floor, only learning from her exhaustion how great was the effort she must have made.

Voices spoke over her head. "They'll never do it. They've no chance in the world." "That's the best thing they can do. They ought to be safe there."

She sat up to look. Two boys who had been running across a field had found themselves surrounded with falling bombs. They had stopped at a hedgerow oak, and were now swarming up to its topmost boughs. Well, they should be safe there.

Beyond that, it seemed that nothing happened at all. The bombs, having burst, lay flattened upon the snow. They were colourless, barely visible. Otherwise there was nothing new to observe, except that a blackbird, and then another, fluttered out of a hedge; tried, it seemed, to rise on wings that had lost their power; and in the next second were stiff and still.

The people in the cavern became bolder, crowding along its brink to look down where there was so little to see.

Then came a loud crack, which was not like thunder, nor a cannon-shot, nor a bursting bomb, though it was as loud, as menacing in its sound. Those who have heard a great tree split to the heart as the lightning strikes will be nearest to understand. Perdita turned her head at the sound, and saw that the oak up which the two boys had climbed had split from the root up, as though a gigantic penknife had ripped its length. She saw its human fruit fall to the ground. They wriggled a moment and lay stiff. It could not have been ten seconds before they died.

A woman behind her broke into a nervous laugh. She spoke with a forlorn effort of courage through chattering teeth: "Well, it's a cleaner death than the filthy gas that they used in the last war."

A man's voice answered: "They don't choose it for that. They don't want people left alive that are no use, with their lungs half gone. They want us dead, or else healthy slaves."

Another said: "If I could get the man who invented that!" His fingers moved as he spoke, as though they closed round the throat of one of the scientists who, as they say themselves, are the benefactors of all mankind.

An hour passed, and the next, and the little crowd looked down from their lofty perch that showed like a huge sand-martin's nest in the side of the hollowed hill. They saw no more. What could there be further to see? The birds lay stiff and dead, and so did the boys, and the sun shone from the pale blue of a clearing sky. It shone on the fields of snow that flashed back a dazzling brilliance of diamond light, having been frozen as snow seldom is, except in the polar wastes, which was the single sign of the ruin which would blacken the land to a distant day. For the snow had lain more thinly here than on the banks of the Forth, and had been insufficient to protect the soil, in which there was left neither fertile seed nor a living worm. And a terrible silence had fallen upon the land.

Those who looked down and survived, with death beneath and on the flattened hilltop above, could not guess how long they would continue to live, for they shook with a deadly cold, which they thought at times to become worse, though in that they may have been wronged by their human fears.

Eustace spoke at times to the girl who had shared his escape, but his thoughts were seldom of her, nor were hers of him.

He thought of one with whom, so few hours before, he had exchanged the first vows of faith, the first kisses of love, and who had then gone into the perilous night on such a quest as must make her life no more than a doubtful guess. He tried, with a poor result, to take comfort from previous dread. Had he not believed her dead only two nights before, with what had seemed to be more reason than now?

There had been many wars in the world, and always there had been those who survived. Would it not be so again? Here was hope to hold, though it was not easy to do. For was this war like any other that went before? It moved at such fatal speed, and was so ruthless in what it did.

Even the last war, with its millions slain, had been a process of orderly years. There had been always leisure to count the dead. But this! In three days.... He looked down on the lifeless fields, and feared to guess what the end might be.

Perdita's mind, stunned to intermittent blankness by the horror of that white silence which had fallen across her familiar world, and the two small corpses that lay so awkwardly on the snow, made efforts at times to adjust itself to more normal moods by recollection of other emotions and other scenes. Certainly he was, he could be, nothing to her. He was not of her age, her kind. He came from another world, to which he was already returned. He would have forgotten her already, as one he had had to use, but who had been of little assistance to him—had, indeed, put him to much trouble and danger because she had proved a coward in an inexcusable way. But he had a face, a manner, a voice, which would not easily leave the mind.

Out of the east, a plane flew. It circled high in skies which were clearing of cloud, and in which the sun was now risen to its February height.

The plane circled round. It descended slowly, in a wide arc. It bore the symbols of England beneath its wings, but by its build it appeared to be one of those private planes which lacked speed and other qualifications for military use, but were now being used for various auxiliary services. When it came round for the third time, it approached so closely to the cavern entrance, and flew so low, that the two men who occupied the control-cabin could be plainly seen.

Gaining confidence, perhaps, from the sight of those who still lived in this place of death, it swooped lower yet, barely clearing the hedgerow trees, and skimming the surface of the frozen field. Then it rose and flew away in the direction from which it came.

Those who looked on, seeing that its occupants had not been overcome, ventured out, one by one, and slowly down to the lower ground. They trod a road that thawed in the sun. Their feet sank in the softened snow.

They went on through a land of silence and death, wondering less at it than at the miracle of their own lives.

CHAPTER XLVII.

WHILE Perdita gazed down on the land of death from which she had escaped by her own wit and a narrow chance, No. 973 sat in the office of Mr. William Smithson, who, since the destruction of the offices and printing plant of the London newspaper on which he had held a similar appointment, had become assistant editor of the *Bristol Advertiser*.

An editor may interview all manner of persons without suspicion being aroused: he may communicate with the headquarters of the British Intelligence Service through many channels. He may do these things without it occurring even to the most watchful of foreign spies that he is one of its controlling chiefs.

Yet such interviews should be rare for those who regard their own lives, and the value of what they do. William Smithson and Richard Steele had not met for eleven years, and now that it had become necessary to do so, they had wasted no words either in idle personal talk, or in discussion of that which had just occurred, and with which Steele had no more concern.

Mr. Smithson asked some questions concerning conditions of German life, and of occurrences of which he was glad to learn, or to confirm information he already had. Then he asked, in his usual casual manner: "You are expected to return to Berlin?"

"Yes."

"You would not object?"

"There are forms of suicide which I might prefer."

"You were expected to discover a secret aerodrome?"

"Yes. They have a report that there is one, probably in Wales, which is not on their maps, of which they are anxious to know."

"It is in the Brecknock Mountains, four miles south of Llan Gorse."

"Am I to betray that?"

"It might be less trouble to us than they suppose, and less gain to them; and it is a secret which could not be kept for a day if we should bring it into active use, as we are likely to do. There is another matter of more concern."

"Very well. I will go. What do you want me to do?"

"For the past two years we have been receiving wireless messages from a correspondent in Leipzig, which have been transmitted on microwaves of a length which is not otherwise used. Since midday yesterday these transmissions have ceased."

"It is a short time. There may be a hundred explanations of that."

"A message was broken off when a sentence was half complete."

"So that you judge that the German police must have got your man?"

"Probably so. But we think that they have the man only, and have not discovered what he had been doing. Otherwise they would have used it to fool us with lying news, and to draw information from us. It is the man, not the secret, that they have got."

"What do you want me to do?"

"To save the man, if you can, who has been of much service to us. But I would not ask you for that alone, which would be too great a risk of a double loss. We wish to have the service in operation again."

"How can I get back in the quickest way?"

"The Germans have established a strong post at Bridgenorth, from which they will be hard to dislodge. They have a landing-stage there on the higher ground, to which they are bringing troops and supplies. If you join them there, I suppose they would take you back in an empty plane."

"I should prefer to enter their lines during the night, for it must appear to be done in a secret way. That will give me time. You must let me have a fast car, and a driver from Brecknock who will be ready to think me a German spy and who will be no loss to you if he be captured by them."

"From Brecknock? Can you not take my word without going there?"

"I could take your word. I was thinking of other things. I have to deal with those whom I must convince, and whose suspicions are already awake. I must do it my way, or none."

Mr. Smithson smiled. "So you always would." He went into details concerning the man whose voice had abruptly failed.

When he had finished, Steele rose up to go. He said: "I will do what I can. What do you suppose will be happening here?"

The question did not appear to disturb Mr. Smithson's mind. "Oh, I suppose," he said, "we shall muddle through. I wonder who said that first?" He smiled without disturbing the gravity of his visitor's face.

"It is in the air," Steele said, "that we appear likely to fail."

Mr. Smithson took a more serious tone. "Should you say that? You may say that we have failed there already. We have a few planes that are left, and I call our airmen the best in the world. The pity is that so many are dead. We are turning out new fighting machines at the rate of about twenty a day, which will become more if the factories stand, or else less. We have been joined by some Scandinavian planes, and some Belgian and Dutch. Most of the French that survive are still fighting for their own land, or are going south to Algiers. You cannot blame them for that. We must fight the air from the ground. Day by day we shall be more completely reduced to that, and it may not be easy to do so. But I do not say we shall fail."

"You may hope that a few days will be sufficient to bring relief, by which time von Teufel should be diverted to other fronts."

"So it may prove, but I am not sure that hope is the right word, if we can look at it in a broad way. Rather, it is here that we should hope that von Teufel will continue to waste his strength, to which end we must still resist, at whatever cost it may be. For every hour that he is busy with us, the Christian forces of land and air will be gathering on the North African coast.

"Even now, Cyprus may be a nut on which he will break his teeth with too hard a bite. There are three hundred planes from the Cape which were due there at today's noon, and there will be many more on the way.

"You may call us besieged by our own fault, but I should not say that the walls are down, nor that they will fall while the seas are ours, as they still are."

"Well, so we must hope it to be."

Steele left him with that word, having his plans made, and it not being a time for prolonging talk. He was conscious that he had not spoken himself in a sanguine way, but he was inclined to a sombre mood, having no liking for what he had undertaken now, and but little hope, though it had not occurred to him to refuse.

He might return to Berlin, having found out that for which he was sent, but he would still be watched and suspect. At the best, they would give him some other mission. How could he aid No. 428, or discover the secrets from which he might have been suddenly torn away? It was not reasonable to expect.

He would have liked to do other things. Among them, to ascertain beyond doubt that a girl was dead, which, from what he had heard, was one of those things that must be nearly sure, but not quite.

If he were certain of that, she would more easily leave his mind, where, at such a time, she had no business to be.

But he had not devoted his life for twenty years to this coming hour that he should turn from the service of England now

Deliberately, he directed his mind to the larger issue: the problem that faced mankind. Would it find some basis of lasting peace? Or would it be entirely destroyed by its own wars? Or would it revert to some better barbarism, such as might be within the larger purpose of God, that men might commence anew? He saw that, even if no divine intervention came, the third question was the most likely to find an affirmative reply.

For how could men hope to abolish war?

It would not be done by denouncing it as something too dreadful to come, nor by appealing to fears or greeds.

It would not be ended by force, though that might be the most plausible way: to organize a controlling tyranny to be called police, which might be just, till its rulers changed.

It would not be ended by the humourless suggestion of Mr. H. G. Wells that the human race should become the abject slaves of the scientists whose inventions had already brought them so near to a final wreck.

To abolish war, it would be necessary to change the natures and hearts of men.

Could it be done in the Name which had been rejected by those who had now broken loose to subdue the world, and in that of the three-fold Cross which was the symbol of British power?

It was hard to say. But if not, it was clear that the civilization of Europe, if not of the whole world, must go down in a red twilight of blood. Which did not alter the present urgency of that which he had undertaken to do.

ABOUT THE AUTHOR

SYDNEY FOWLER WRIGHT (1874-1965) penned over seventy volumes of science fiction, fantasy, classic mysteries, historical novels, poetry, and non-fiction, many of them being published by the Borgo Press Imprint of Wildside Press. Please visit his website at:

www.sfw.org